"This is ridiculous. We've got to try to keep each other warm."

With that, Rick rolled over into the back seat and put his arms around Liz, drawing her close. "We'll use our body heat," he said, trying to sound casual about it when he was anything but.

"Hey, it's a good thing we called a truce. Otherwise you'd have let me freeze to death."

"No, I wouldn't," Rick said gruffly. "It's late. Maybe we need to stop talking and go to sleep so the night will pass quickly."

"I used to do that, you know. As a kid, I used to lay awake half the night on Christmas Eve so Santa Claus would hurry and come. Only, it didn't work."

"That's what you get for believing in Santa Claus."

"Oh, and you didn't?" She turned her face to his.

Huskily Rick murmured, "If I did, I'd ask him to leave you in my stocking."

Dear Reader,

May marks the celebration of "Get Caught Reading," a national campaign the Association of American Publishers created to promote the sheer joy of reading. "Get Caught Reading" may be a phrase that's familiar to you, but if not, we hope you'll familiarize yourself with it by picking up the wonderful selections that Silhouette Special Edition has to offer....

Former NASA engineer Laurie Paige says that when she was young, she checked out *The Little Engine That Could* from the library fifty times. "I read it every week," Laurie recalls. "I was so astounded that the library would lend books to me for free. I've been an avid reader ever since." Though Laurie Paige hasn't checked out her favorite childhood storybook for a while, she now participates in several local literacy fund-raisers and reads to young children in her community. Laurie is also a prolific writer, with nearly forty published Silhouette titles, including this month's *Something To Talk About.*

Don't miss the fun when a once-burned rancher discovers that the vivacious amnesiac he's helping turns out to be the missing Stockwell heiress in Jackie Merritt's *The Cattleman and the Virgin Heiress.* And be sure to catch all of THE CALAMITY JANES, five friends sharing the struggles and celebrations of life, starting with *Do You Take This Rebel?* by Sherryl Woods. And what happens when Willa and Zach learn they both inherited the same ranch? Find out in *The Ties That Bind* by Ginna Gray. Be sure to see who will finish first in Patricia Hagan's *Race to the Altar.* And Judith Lyons pens a highly emotional tale with *Lt. Kent: Lone Wolf.*

So this May, make time for books. Remember how fun it is to browse a bookstore, hold a book in your hands and discover new worlds on the printed page.

Best,

Karen Taylor Richman
Senior Editor

Please address questions and book requests to:
Silhouette Reader Service
U.S.: 3010 Walden Ave., P.O. Box 1325, Buffalo, NY 14269
Canadian: P.O. Box 609, Fort Erie, Ont. L2A 5X3

Race to the Altar

PATRICIA HAGAN

Silhouette®

SPECIAL EDITION™

Published by Silhouette Books

America's Publisher of Contemporary Romance.

To Joe Kennedy,
one of the best racing PR reps
I ever had the pleasure of working with.

 SILHOUETTE BOOKS

ISBN 0-373-24397-9

RACE TO THE ALTAR

Visit Silhouette at www.eHarlequin.com

Printed in U.S.A.

Books by Patricia Hagan

Silhouette Special Edition

Bride for Hire #1127
My Child, Our Child #1277
Race to the Altar #1397

Yours Truly

Boy Re-Meets Girl
Groom on the Run

Harlequin Historicals

The Daring #84
The Desire #143

PATRICIA HAGAN

New York Times bestselling author Patricia Hagan had written and published over 2,500 short stories before selling her first book in 1971. With a background in English and journalism from the University of Alabama, Pat has won awards for radio, television, newspaper and magazine writing. Her hobbies include reading, painting and cooking. The author and her Norwegian husband, Erik, divide their time between their Florida retreat in Boca Raton and their home in Bergen, Norway.

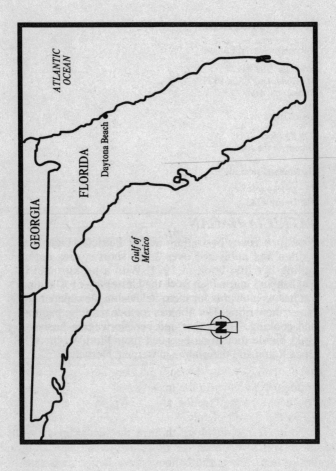

Chapter One

Liz Mallory knew high heels and a business suit were not appropriate attire for a racetrack. But she couldn't help it. On her way from New York to Daytona she had missed a connecting flight, and her luggage hadn't made it. She had planned to change into neat slacks and a blouse once she got to her hotel. Instead, there was no time to even stop by a mall and buy anything, because the plane was late, and she'd had to come directly to the track.

So here she was, feeling as out of place as a Christmas tree on the Fourth of July.

She drove the rental car through the tunnel and into the infield, which reminded her of a huge circus, sprawling in all directions. Flags and balloons were flying, thousands of people were milling about, and it wasn't even race day.

But that's how it was at Daytona in February during Speed Weeks. She had learned that much, at least, during the brief time she'd had to study up on the sport since being given her new assignment.

Never in her wildest dreams had she thought she would find herself involved in the world of stock car racing. She knew absolutely zilch about it.

When she had said as much to Jeff Strohm, her boss at Star Media Enterprises, an advertising and public relations agency, he had told her she had better learn fast. Star had obtained the contract to represent Big Boy's Pizza in their sponsorship for up-and-coming rookie driver Rick Castles, and Liz had been assigned as PR person only a week before the season opener at Daytona.

She had bought every book and magazine she could find on racing though hadn't had time to read them all. But she wasn't too worried about it. It was her job to market Rick Castles and get as much exposure as possible for his sponsor. It was PR plain and simple, and she knew how to do that.

She followed the map she had been given to the press parking lot, which had a chain link fence around it.

An attendant wearing an orange vest over his T-shirt held up a hand, and she promptly stopped and rolled down her window.

"Sorry, lady." He pointed to a sign that read Media Only.

"Well, that's me," she said cheerily, holding up the pass she had been given when she checked in at the speedway's PR department.

The man shook his head. "That gets you into the pits. A parking decal gets you in *here.*"

"Maybe I've got one. They gave me so much stuff back there." She fumbled through the big white envelope, then triumphantly held up the red-and-white decal.

"Lick it and put it on your windshield so I won't have to stop you next time."

"I sure will, and I'm sorry I didn't know to do that. This is my first time, and—"

Behind her, a horn sounded impatiently.

She wet her finger, then rubbed it over the back of the decal and affixed it to the glass.

Satisfied, the attendant motioned her in.

It had been raining earlier in the day, and there were muddy places where the grass was worn down. She stepped out of the car and into a puddle, groaning as her heel sank to her ankle. She was going to have to pick her way along carefully and opted to leave her heavy briefcase behind.

Pausing beside the car, Liz gazed up at the crystal-blue sky and marveled at what a beautiful day it was. Not a cloud in sight, and a balmy breeze was blowing in from the ocean, just a few miles to the east.

Despite her trepidation over her new assignment, she was grateful for the tropical respite from the cold chill of New York in February.

According to the schedule she had been given in her credentials packet, it was the day before trial runs, and several cars were out on the track taking practice laps. Now and then a roar from the grandstand would herald a favorite driver pulling onto the track.

Elsewhere in the infield, campers and trucks were parked. She could also see that a lot of tents had been erected.

The air was thick with the smell of food sizzling on charcoal grills, and seagulls circled overhead, drawn to the picnics going on below.

There were concrete buildings for toilets and showers. First-aid stations were dotted about. Concession booths sold souvenirs—mostly T-shirts and jackets emblazoned with different photos of drivers and their race cars.

It was, Liz thought, like a small city. Fans actually lived at the track almost the entire month of February, and the local economy welcomed them with open arms.

She found her way to the concrete retaining wall behind the area where cars made their pit stops for gas and new tires. According to the speedway map, by walking alongside it, she would eventually reach the garage area, where she hoped to find her driver.

Liz had no idea what Rick Castles looked like. There were not, as yet, any publicity photos, but she planned to take care of that right away. She was glad she had tossed the caps imprinted with the sponsor in her carry-on bag instead of packing them in her checked luggage. Otherwise, she couldn't have had the photos taken today, because Rick and all his crew needed to be wearing them to give Big Boy's exposure. And she could not afford a delay. His press kit had to be made available as soon as possible.

At the garage gate, a separate pass had to be issued. While the guard was making it out, she asked if he could tell her where she could find Rick Castles.

"Well, let's see…" He pulled a clipboard from under the counter and scanned it. "Castles is car number sixty, and he's got stall fifty-five."

She thanked him, pinned the garage pass to her badge, took a deep breath and entered her new world.

The first thing she did was trip over a lug nut someone had dropped.

She almost fell, but a man in a greasy jumpsuit grabbed her arm and brusquely warned, "Lady, you better watch it in those shoes. This is a dangerous place."

She gave a nervous little laugh. "Oh, I agree. And thank you. I'll know better next time, believe me—"

He grabbed her again, this time to keep her from being run over by a car whipping off the pit road to enter the garage area. "You're gonna get yourself killed if you aren't careful. What are you doing here, anyway?"

Liz pulled herself up to her full height of five foot four and tried to look self-confident, which wasn't easy when she had just been rescued twice. "I'm the new public relations representative for driver Rick Castles. Could you tell me where I can find stall fifty-five? That's his garage space."

He glanced about thoughtfully. "Well, let's see. Castles is a rookie, so he won't be with the hot dogs, that's for sure. Fifty-five should be back that way." He pointed, then started to walk away but paused to repeat his warning for her to be careful. "If you don't keep an eye out around this place, you won't make it. Trust me."

Liz was puzzled. She didn't see any concession stands

inside the garage and wondered what difference it made if Rick were a rookie as to whether his garage space was near them. Maybe being located near the food stands was some kind of privilege older drivers got that newer ones didn't.

Someone whistled as she continued walking.

Again she wished she could have changed. Ordinarily she would have traveled in leisure clothes, but Jeff had insisted she join him and the rest of the staff for brunch to say goodbye before going to the airport. So she'd had to dress for that.

Spotting a young man with several cameras hanging from straps around his neck, she waved and called, "Hi there. Are you a freelance photographer?"

"That I am," he said with a tip of his ball cap. "The name's Pete Barnett, and I'm the best in the business. What do you need and when?"

"Publicity shots of Rick Castles. I'm Liz Mallory, PR rep for his new sponsor—Big Boy's Pizza. And I'd like them done this afternoon and possibly delivered tomorrow." She held her breath hoping he wouldn't laugh in her face for such a quick deadline.

She was relieved when he said, "Not a problem. I'm going to do a shoot right now. Where will you be in about an hour?"

"Space fifty-five in the garage. That's where his car is."

He laughed. "Not with the hot dogs, eh? Ah, the curse of being a rookie."

Again Liz wondered about that and continued on her way.

The garage was noisy, crowded and chaotic. Race cars drove in and out on the way to and from the track for practice. Air wrenches roared and engines revved as the track loudspeakers tried to break through the din.

Spotting numbers on the concrete, she began to count. When she reached number fifty-five, she was relieved to see a car with the logo for Big Boy's Pizza on the hood, top and sides. Painted blue and yellow, the Monte Carlo had dozens of little decals around the fenders, and a big 6-0 on the doors.

No one was around, and Liz thought that odd when everywhere else crews were working like mad on their cars. Maybe Rick and his crew had gone to eat.

Then she glanced at her watch. Four o'clock. Too late for lunch and too early for supper.

So where were they the day before the all-important twin-qualifying races?

The stalls on either side were empty, cars no doubt on the track with crews watching behind the retaining wall.

Liz's annoyance was growing with each passing moment, because things had gotten off to a terrible start, and she was determined not to fail in her career...*again.*

She was not worried about failing in her *personal* life, because she did not intend to have one. After all, being deceived by not one man, but two, had sent her plunging to the bottom rung of her career ladder.

She had been on the very top and probably still would be if not for having been so naive...and, yes, stupid.

Liz had begun her career in her native California, where she had worked her way up from PR rep to account executive, making top wages. Then she made the mistake of falling in love with Craig Hatcher, who happened to be employed by a rival company.

They became engaged, and Liz believed him when he said they could keep their work separate even though their agencies were competitive. But, too late, she discovered he was only using her to further his career and had accessed her files. By the time she found out what a lying, two-timing worm he was, he had succeeded in taking her top three accounts away from her agency.

Not only had he broken her heart, but his deviousness made her lose her job, as well.

Forced to start over with a new company, Liz foolishly made the mistake of rebounding into another relationship with Mike Lowry, a co-worker. That didn't last long. There was too much job conflict between them. When it ended, she decided not only to change jobs but to move to New York and make a whole new life.

Twice burned, twice shy, she promised herself that never again would a man best her, nor would she become involved with anyone she worked with.

Depressed by her bitter musings, Liz began to circle the race car slowly, trying to get her mind on something else, like familiarizing herself with the car.

She noted there were no windows, just net coverings, and only one seat for the driver.

The inside of the car was completely gutted, and she knew the tubed frames were called roll bars, to keep the car from being crushed if, God forbid, it turned over.

Fascinated by all she was seeing and learning, Liz did not notice the feet sticking out from the under the car. She tripped, screamed and was barely able to grab a window frame to keep from tumbling to the ground.

Beneath the car, Rick Castles jerked his head up to painfully bump it. "Ouch. Damn it, who's the nitwit that can't see where they're going?"

Lying on a roller board, he angrily swung himself out from under the car, ready to lambaste the person responsible. "Why don't you look where you're going?"

He found himself gazing up a skirt framing a very shapely pair of legs.

But only for an instant.

Embarrassed and red faced, the woman connected to the legs quickly stepped back.

"I…I'm so sorry," she said. "I didn't see your feet down there. I didn't know anybody was under the car."

He stood, taking in the rest of her as he did so and, despite his annoyance, liked what he saw. Her legs weren't the only thing about her that was shapely. Long, thick lashes framed very apologetic green eyes that sparkled with little flecks of gold. Her turned-up nose gave her a saucy, playful look.

But there was nothing playful about her full, sensuous lips.

They begged to be kissed, and, with a warm rush, Rick was reminded how long it had been since he'd had a woman.

"If you can't see feet as big as mine, lady, then you need glasses."

Liz automatically looked at his feet and saw that, indeed, they were large. Then, unable to help it, she thought of a dirty joke she'd heard once about the size of a man's feet being indicative of the size of his—

She blushed, all the way to the roots of her flame-red hair, and turned away lest he be able to tell what she was thinking. "I...I'm truly sorry," she stammered. "I was just mesmerized by the car, I guess. I've never seen a race car up close."

Rick bit his lip to keep from laughing. He knew the joke about women comparing the size of a man's foot to the size of something else.

Her red hair was pulled up in a knot on the top of her head, and she looked quite dignified in her gray linen suit and matching heels. But he also did not miss how her breasts strained against the white silk blouse, nor how her skirt hugged, then cupped, her high, tight buttocks. She was a knockout, all right, but he was still irritated.

"I've got work to do," he said grouchily. "Why don't you move along? The garage is no place for women, especially wearing stupid shoes like that." He pointed accusingly at her heels. "It still amazes me how they'll give just about anybody a garage pass."

Liz felt rancor quickly rise. She could have told him she had every right to be there by introducing herself, but she wasn't about to. Whoever he was, she didn't like his attitude. After all, she hadn't stepped on his feet on purpose. Still, she couldn't help noticing how his broad shoulders and chest filled out the tight, grease-stained T-shirt, or how his jeans molded his muscular thighs so deliciously. And despite his oil-streaked face, she found him ruggedly good-looking, his sleepy, mocha-colored eyes complemented by his thick, black hair.

She had feared there might be some leftover macho types

who would resent a woman working in what was considered a man's sport. This one was obviously a member of Rick's pit crew, and she decided it best to try to make friends. After all, it was important she get along with all the guys. The fact his nearness sent her heart into overdrive had nothing to do with it.

"Actually," she said, "I'm looking for Rick Castles. I take it you are a member of his crew."

Rick wasn't about to reveal himself, instead stringing her along in hopes of getting rid of her. Cute or not, he wasn't about to take up time with another groupie. "Yeah, you might say that. What do you want with him?"

"I just want to meet him."

"So you're a fan," he said, unimpressed as he noted her media badge. "What are you doing wearing that?"

"Somebody gave it to me," she replied, which wasn't a lie. "And, yes, I'm a big fan, but I haven't been for long. Rick is my favorite driver, though," she added with a confident grin, then pointed at the logo. "New sponsor?"

He shrugged. "Yeah. Just think. We get free pizza for painting that all over the car."

Liz stiffened. Even if this guy was just a part-timer, hanging around to get into the races free, he was going to have to learn how to act around people. What he should have said in response was that yes, Big Boy's was the new sponsor, and Rick and all the guys were grateful. Not act as though it was no big deal because all they were getting out of it was free pizza, for heaven's sake. Besides, for the kind of money the sponsor was shelling out to try to make the car competitive, even a part-timer should be appreciative.

Rick was watching her out of the corner of his eye, thinking again how good-looking she was and wishing all the more she'd disappear. He had no use for females hanging around the pits. Or anywhere else around a racetrack for that matter. They were nothing but trouble and got in the way. "Look, I don't know when Rick will be back, so you might as well go on—"

"But where is he?" She had seen the schedule in the office, knew that this was the last practice session before tomorrow's race. "How come he's not here to try the car out?"

"He practiced this morning. He's at the beach this afternoon. Sunbathing. Now you really should get out of here. The garage area is a dangerous place."

"I've heard that before." She was almost petulant, fighting to hold her temper all the while. Obviously Rick Castles was not taking himself, or his career, seriously. Otherwise, he would be at the track and not the beach. And even if he weren't planning on practicing anymore he should be around to greet fans.

There was also another problem with his absence. She had the photographer lined up to take his publicity photos.

She suddenly remembered the blackboard she had seen on the wall of the booth where she'd gotten her garage pass. "There's a drivers' meeting at five o'clock. Won't he have to go to that?"

"Yeah, probably." Rick wondered if he was going to be able to get rid of her, after all.

"Then I'll wait." Before he could protest, she pointed to the smooth tires on the car and, figuring she might as well spend her time learning something, innocently asked, "How come there's no tread?"

"They're old tires. All worn-out. Can't afford new ones." He felt no guilt at the lie. He had no intention of being her racing tutor, for Pete's sake. Let her go bother somebody else.

He lowered himself to the board again. "I've got to get back to work."

"Oh, don't mind me." Her eyes went to his thighs, and a tremor ripped through her tummy. His jeans fit like they were molded to him, and she couldn't help noticing the manly bulge, and...

She told herself to get a grip. Even if she was interested

in men—which she wasn't—she would never get involved with this one, because he obviously had an attitude.

"Keep hanging around, and you're liable to get embarrassed," he warned, rolling himself out of sight. "Sometimes guys cuss around the garage."

"Don't worry. I'll ignore it."

"But you have no business here," he said again, this time with gritted teeth. "And Rick Castles has got a girlfriend," he said, adding another lie. "So you're wasting your time."

"Oh, I see," she said, her teeth also grinding. "Just because I want to meet the man, talk to him, I want to go to bed with him."

He rolled back out, barely missing her as she quickly jumped out of his way. "Now did I say anything about thinking you want to go to bed with him? Jeez, what's wrong with you? I just wanted to let you know if you had any notions about flirting with him, he's not interested."

"And I'm not interested in him that way." She was so tempted then and there to introduce herself and then say, *By the way, you're fired. The team no longer needs to swap work for race passes. They can afford to hire good help.* Instead, she reminded herself he wasn't worth getting all steamed up over.

She had not moved far enough away, and, once more, he could see up her skirt. Quite an eyeful, too, and he forced himself to roll back under, lest she see his heat show.

Just who was she, and what did she want with him? He was tempted to end the charade but was too mad—with her, but, most of all, with himself. After all, he had learned his lesson about women in racing. They either couldn't stand the stress and got hysterical every time he spun out, afterward tearfully begging him to give it up, or they found somebody else while he was traveling all over the country.

He thought of Maggie and twisted the wrench too hard. It slipped and flew back to pinch his finger, and he swore.

Liz heard and teased, "Hey, you were right. I do hear somebody cursing."

He ignored her and continued to allow memories of Maggie to wash over him, to bathe him in rationale as to why he was not about to let the cute redhead get to him. Maggie had sworn she loved him, sworn she wanted to share his racing life with him. He'd loved her, too, and so they had married.

Then a year later she left him for a guy with a steady job who came home for dinner every night.

After that, Rick promised himself that never again, while he was involved in racing, would he have a serious relationship with a woman. Those he went with just for sex knew that, but lately those times were getting further and further apart. Casual lovemaking had begun to leave him feeling empty and cheated. So instead he worked all the harder, trying to make his dream of becoming a competitive driver on the NASCAR circuit a reality.

Liz leaned in the car window on the driver's side to examine the seat. "How come there's a hole in the bottom?"

Rick did feel a teeny bit guilty when he brazenly asked, "Well, where do you think a driver goes to the bathroom when he's on the track four, maybe five, hours at a time?"

Once again Liz felt her cheeks flame. "I...I hadn't thought about that," she mumbled.

"Yeah, they say NASA is interested in using the same type of toilet for the astronauts."

"Well, that's great." She saw there was no ignition for a key to turn. "What starts the car?"

"See that button?"

"Yes."

"Well, when the signal is given for the race to start, the driver pushes the button. That signals the control room, and another button is pushed there that starts the engine."

That sounded strange, even to a novice like Liz. "Why go to all that trouble? Why not just turn a key like in regular cars?"

"Well, the officials want to make sure all cars start at exactly the same time so everybody gets a fair chance."

Liz wondered if he was jerking her around. "Are you sure?"

"Of course, I'm sure. That's what I'm under here doing now—making sure the wires to the button are hooked up like they're supposed to be."

Her stomach rumbled. She hadn't had time to eat lunch. "Where do the rookie drivers eat since they aren't given garage stalls near the concessions stands?"

Rick blinked, sure he hadn't heard her right. "Excuse me?"

"When I was asking where Rick's garage area was, someone said he wouldn't be near the hot dogs, because he's a rookie. So I was wondering where there is to eat around here? I'm awfully hungry."

He choked back a laugh. "Well, I'm afraid you'll have to walk back up front, because they told you right. Rookies don't get space near the hot dogs. That has to be earned."

Though he was silently laughing at how gullible she was, he began to feel mean. Besides, he couldn't help thinking about those long, shapely legs and where they had ended the last time he accidentally got a glance up her skirt. But he couldn't let her get to him. Not that way. The best thing to do was really get her hackles up so she'd leave. "You're stubborn, aren't you? I told you—Rick has a girlfriend. You're wasting your time."

"Well, you've got it all wrong. I'm not some bimbo groupie chasing after him."

"Then what do you want with him?"

"That's between him and me." Just then she saw the photographer she'd hired approaching and quickly ran to meet him lest he give her away. "The driver isn't here, and I don't know whether or not he will be. We may have to postpone this till tomorrow."

He looked as disappointed as Liz felt. "Can't do it then. I've got three shoots lined up before the first qualifying race.

Everybody is wanting photos the first race of the season. There's a drivers' meeting pretty soon. Maybe he'll show for that.''

She had forgotten about the meeting in her annoyance with the smart-mouthed mechanic. "Good idea. I'll see if I can find him there."

"Okay. I'll hang around outside and look for you. Good luck."

She returned to the car, planning to ask the mechanic to tell Rick Castles if he did return that she was looking for him. "Excuse me?"

From beneath, Rick saw her shoes and groaned. Whatever she wanted, he wasn't interested. Maybe she was good-looking, but after his marriage had broken up because his wife couldn't handle racing, he wasn't looking for girlfriends at race tracks.

Just then someone called, and Liz turned to see several men, all dressed alike in blue pants and red T-shirts, rolling tires along as they came toward her.

Rick had not heard them and did not know anyone else was around as he came sliding out from under the car, face cold with fury. "You're getting on my nerves, lady."

He fell silent to see his crew chief, Mack Pressley. "See if you can get rid of her," he snapped and disappeared under the car. "I'm sure as hell not having any luck."

"Hi," Mack held his hand out to Liz. "I'm the crew chief—Mack Pressley. What can I do for you?"

"Well, I—" She was about to introduce herself when she saw the tires they were rolling had no tread left, just like the ones already on the car. "What are you going to do with those?"

Mack exchanged grins with the other crew members, who, like himself, were intrigued by the pretty young woman wearing a media badge. "Well, you can be sure we aren't going to tie them to a rope and swing from a tree. We just bought them, and we're going to put them on the car."

She was stunned. "But they're no better than the ones already on there."

Mack blinked, equally bewildered. "They certainly are. The others are almost ready to blow. That's why Rick hasn't taken the car out to practice. We had to go get these. We've got a new sponsor, and we just got the money from them today to buy the right kind of tires for qualifying."

Beneath the car, Rick grimaced. If Mack kept talking to her, being nice to her, she'd never leave, damn it. And if she didn't, she'd find out he'd been putting her on.

Liz continued to stare, not understanding about the tires.

Mack set the tire down and pulled a rag from his hip pocket to wipe his hands. "Like I said, I'm Mack, the crew chief." He gestured to the others. "Bobby, Weyland and Jake. We've got to get these tires on, but if you have any questions, I'll try to answer them. We're just so pleased for this sponsorship we've got with Big Boy's Pizza, and it'd be nice if you could work their name into your article.

"Who are you with, by the way?" he asked over his shoulder as he bent down next to the car.

"Well, I'm not a reporter, I'm—"

She was drowned out by the noise of the jack lifting the car, followed by the whine of air wrenches removing the tire's lug nuts.

"Sorry," Mack said when it was quiet again. "Go ahead. What paper did you say you're with?"

"I'm not with a paper. I'm Liz Mallory, the PR representative for Big Boy's Pizza, and—"

That was all she had time to say before Rick came careening out from under the car, and this time, he did knock her down.

She fell right on top of him, her bottom landing on his stomach.

Reacting in time to grab her and keep her from cracking her head on the concrete, he cried, "The heck you say. Tell me this is a joke."

"No, *you're* the joke," Liz cried, struggling to get up, but he held her tight, her breasts brushing his cheek as he tried to sit up with her still on top of him. "And you're out of here, mister. With your attitude you're not the kind of person my agency wants identified with the Rick Castles racing team. So you can go elsewhere and wheedle your freebie race passes."

Rick and Liz locked furious eyes while the rest of the crew burst into raucous laughter.

Liz turned to glare. "I'd like to know what's so funny. You don't realize how this man behaved...how he talked to me. He even had the nerve to intimate that all the new sponsorship meant was free pizzas. You think I'm going to put up with having someone like that around this team?"

Mack, still laughing, walked over to take her arms and pull her to her feet. "Well, I'm afraid you don't have a choice."

The mechanic was greasy, and thanks to falling on him, she was, too. She yanked the rag from Mack's hands and began swiping at the black streaks on her skirt, but it only made matters worse. Then she suddenly realized what Mack had just said. "What did you mean by that?" she demanded, eyes narrowed.

"I mean," he said, grinning, "that you're going to have to put up with him, because this is our driver.

"Liz Mallory," he said with relish, obviously enjoying the moment, "meet Rick Castles."

Chapter Two

"Mack, is this one of your stupid pranks?" Mack was the team joker and always clowning around.

Still laughing, Mack said, "I'm afraid not."

The cords in Rick's neck stood out, his lips a thin, angry line. "Tell me this is a gag," he demanded of Liz. "You can't be the PR rep for Big Boy's."

"I most certainly am." She reached down to retrieve her bag. When she'd been knocked down, everything had spilled out. She had to search for her business cards, finally thrusting one at Rick. "Here. This explains me, but I'm still hoping *you* are the gag."

He let that dig pass. "How come you didn't say who you were to start with?"

"You gave the impression you weren't a regular member of the crew, so I didn't figure it was any of your business."

"Well, regardless of whether you thought I was or not, it would have been polite to introduce yourself."

"Ha! Look who's talking about being polite. Is the snotty way you acted with me the way you treat all your fans?"

"Groupies, yeah," he said, hands on his hips, all the while telling himself not to think about how cute she looked with her green eyes sparkling mad. "If I took the time to talk to every woman who wrangles a pit pass to flirt with a driver, I'd never get anything done."

"Oh, so you assume that every woman who speaks to you has romantic notions? What an ego."

"Hey—" he jabbed his finger in the air "—don't talk to me about nerve. You were the one putting on an act. All you had to do was say who you were, and it would have been a whole different ball game, sweetie."

"Yeah, right. And I'd never have known what an arrogant, conceited, self-assuming chauvinist you really are, Rick Castles. But you did keep me from wasting my time trying to make you presentable to the public...and wasting the sponsor's money, as well."

She jabbed right back, only her finger hit him right in the chest as she added, "And don't call me *sweetie.*"

"Oh, yeah, great, fine. But it's okay for you to call me names." He pushed her hand away. "And don't touch me."

"Who wants to?" She knelt down to scoop up the rest of her things and stuff them back into her purse.

She did not see the wild, pleading look that Mack and the rest of the crew were giving Rick.

And Rick was still too mad to care.

Mack said, with a nervous laugh, "Hey, you two are acting like kids. How about both of you calming down and let's talk about all this."

"What's to talk about?" Liz said as she reached under the race car to retrieve a lipstick that had rolled beneath. She snagged her stockings but didn't care. She was already a mess.

"You two have got to get along," Mack said.

Liz stood and slung her bag strap over her shoulder, turning away from Rick to respond to Mack. "I disagree, because when I tell the sponsor what a jerk your driver is, they'll rethink things and probably withdraw.''

She was bluffing, because she doubted she had that kind of clout. Besides, if she told Jeff she detested Rick Castles, he might pull her off the account and give it to someone else. She did not want that...did not want to fail at anything in her career again...especially because of a man.

Mack said to Liz, ''Hey, please don't do that.'' Then he grabbed Rick's shoulder and shook him. ''Listen, man, we need that sponsorship money, and you know it. So apologize and call a truce.''

Liz folded her arms across her chest and tapped her foot as she waited for Rick's response. So what if she was trying to pull off a bluff? It was important to establish some ground rules here, or he'd walk all over her. And she couldn't have that. He had to know who was in charge when it came to public relations, and, by golly, she would not stand for him being unfriendly to fans, regardless of whether some of them were what he so scornfully referred to as *groupies*.

Rick started picking up tools that had scattered when he came out from under the car so fast. ''I don't see where I did anything so terrible.''

''You lied,'' Liz coldly pointed out. ''And it most certainly was my business to know who you were.''

''Yeah, if you'd told me who *you* were instead of playing coy.''

''That's beside the point. You were rude, and you don't treat fans like that.''

''Okay, hold it.'' Mack got between them. ''So you two have gotten off on the wrong foot. Suppose you start over. Liz, I'm afraid Rick acts off the track like he does when he's on it—he never gives an inch.''

''That's called being stubborn,'' she said. ''And maybe it works when he's racing but not now.''

Rick ignored her as he went about his business.

Mack allowed, ''Maybe so, but that's how he is. And who's to know how it would've been if you'd introduced yourself in the beginning? I don't think he'd have jerked you around like he did.''

Liz stared at Rick's back as he bent beneath the raised hood of the car. His T-shirt was stretched tight, and she could see the ripple of his muscles as he worked.

Her mind danced back to when she had fallen in his lap and he had instinctively put his arms around her to keep her from toppling backward. In that briefest of moments, she had felt a swirl of desire sweep over her and actually wondered what it would be like if he pulled her tighter and pressed his lips against hers, and—

She gave herself a mental shake. She had just met the man, and he had acted like a clod, and here she was thinking how great it would be to have him kiss her. She had to banish such ponderings from her mind or she'd wind up right back in the situation she swore never to find herself again—helpless and made to feel like a fool because her body, her heart, had betrayed her.

"Well, Mack," she said stiffly, angry at herself and directing it at Rick, "I'm afraid he's going to have to get down off his pedestal or it's not going to work."

Rick withdrew from beneath the hood to turn on her. "Who are you talking about being on a pedestal? You're the one trying to take over the team all of a sudden."

"That's enough. This is getting ridiculous." Mack had lost patience and was getting mad himself. He motioned Liz to stand back and told the rest of the team to get to work changing the tires. Then he drew Rick to one side.

Liz couldn't hear what they were saying, but Mack was right about one thing—she and Rick had gotten off on the wrong foot, all right. And now she feared her job was going to be even harder than she'd thought.

Pete Barnett walked up just then to ask if she were ready to have the pictures taken. "We've got time before the drivers' meeting. Where's Castles, anyway? I've never met him."

Liz cocked her head to where Mack and Rick were still in close conversation. "That's him on the right."

Pete frowned at the sight of Rick in his greasy clothes and dirty face. Loudly, he said, "Well, he'd better hurry up and change. You sure don't want to shoot him looking like that."

Rick heard and coldly demanded, "What is it now?"

Liz stonily answered, "It's the photographer I've hired to take your publicity photos, but I'm not sure we're going to need them now."

At that, Mack hurried to her, waving his arms. "Oh, now wait, Liz. We can work this out." He shot a pleading glance at Rick for confirmation. "Can't we?"

Rick did not have to think about it, even though he had let Mack argue on and on as to why he should apologize and cooperate. He knew they needed the money if they were to make a serious run for the rookie title. The smaller sponsorships weren't enough. Sure, they could sell ads on the lower quarter panels for twenty-five thousand dollars, and on the front fenders for thirty. But that was a drop in the bucket. Tires alone were over three hundred and fifty apiece. Depending on conditions, they might use six to twelve sets each race, which meant they'd have to spend nearly twenty thousand. And they just didn't have it. They wouldn't have even been able to come to Daytona if not for the new sponsorship, and, waiting for the first check had been tough, because they couldn't buy tires needed just for practice.

He stared thoughtfully at the car. He and Mack were cosigners on a banknote to buy it for one hundred twenty-five thousand dollars.

He had even had to borrow against the farm his grandmother had left him in the Georgia mountains to pay some bills. So he really couldn't afford to walk away from Big Boy's Pizza just because he didn't want to work with a woman around a racetrack.

"Come on, Rick," Mack urged, sounding desperate...which he was.

Pete asked what the problem was, and that moved Rick to

do something. He well knew how motor journalists gossiped among themselves. The last thing he needed was for rumors to start flying that there was sponsorship trouble before the first race, especially over a female. It would make good copy for the sidebars that writers needed when there wasn't much to write about.

"Let's talk." He motioned to Liz. And to Pete, he said, "There's no problem. We're just discussing maybe making the logo a little bigger. Chill out, and I'll be ready before you know it."

Pete looked relieved, glad he'd be making some more money that day after all and set about getting his equipment ready. He told the crew where to roll the car for the best light and background.

Meanwhile, Rick walked to a pavilion nearby where there was a water fountain. Mack started to go with them, but Rick waved him away. No one else was around, and that's the way he wanted it.

Rick took a paper cup from the holder and filled it with water. Then he politely handed it to Liz and began. "All right, let's get something straight. We both know I need the sponsorship, but I'd rather work with a guy."

She smiled. "Of course, you would. I know your type. You feel threatened by women."

At that, he threw back his head and laughed, slapping his hand against his forehead. "Give me a break."

"So tell me what you have against working with a woman?"

"Honey, I've *raced* against women, and—"

"Don't call me *honey*."

"Okay, okay. Sorry." He held up his hands in surrender. "I just don't think women are cut out for this kind of sport."

He had positioned himself on the other side of the water fountain. He didn't like being close to her, didn't like the woman scent of her.

Her hair smelled like sunshine, and touching her was like holding a moonbeam—so fragile, yet supple and longing to be caressed. When she had fallen on top of him, he had actually had to fight the impulse to kiss her...to taste her lips, her tongue, and then trail his mouth down her throat and on to her breasts and...

Liz was irate over how he was taking up so much time when they had little to spare. The photographer was waiting, and Rick still needed to change. "Will you get to your point?"

"I just said it was a job for a guy."

"No," she corrected. "You said women weren't cut out for it. There's a difference. But it happens to be my job until my boss assigns me to another account. So you are going to have to let me do my job. Otherwise, you leave me no choice but to go back and report you won't cooperate. Then, it's up to the sponsor what to do next, and you can believe they won't be happy campers.

"PR, in case you don't realize it," she went on, trying not to think of warm mocha coffee as she fought to keep from drowning in his gaze, "stands for public relations, and what that means is having relations with the public. Good relations. And with your attitude, I'm not sure that's possible. Now I think you should know there are several other rookie drivers that were being considered." She didn't know if that was true. She was merely trying to scare him into shaping up to make her job easier. She had no intention of quitting or reporting problems.

"In case *you* don't realize it," he said with a mocking twinkle, "the team has a contract with Big Boy's. We haven't violated any of the terms of that contract at this point. Just because you don't like me—"

"No. *You* don't like *me*. And Mack's right. We did get off on the wrong foot, and it wasn't my fault, and I'm not sure we can ever get along."

"So what difference does it make if we don't?"

"What do you mean?"

"Just this." He leaned against the wall and folded his

arms across his chest. "You've got your job. I've got mine. Stay out of my way, and we'll get along."

"It's not that simple."

"Yes, it is. I'll cooperate. I'll go right now and take a shower and put on my new blue uniform with the gold stripes and the Big Boy's logo. I'll shave and comb my hair and give you a big smile for your photos. But I don't want you hovering around while I do it."

"Well, you're just going to have to get used to my hovering—as you call it—because I plan to be around most of the time. You see, part of my job is to make all travel arrangements for the team. And I go with the team and attend all the races.

"In addition," she went on, not failing to notice how his smile had abruptly disappeared, along with his cocky air, "I arrange your press parties and interviews. I do anything and everything I can to get you public exposure. I expect you to be on time and be cordial. And your first one is tonight."

He quit leaning and stood to tower over her, anger rushing back. "No one told me anything about having to make an appearance tonight. This is short notice."

"It's not an appearance. I'm taking you and the crew out to dinner."

"Mack and I always take the guys out the night before qualifying."

"Well, surely you don't mind me joining you and picking up the check. I'd like to get to know everybody. Besides, we'll be doing a lot of things together from now on, so get used to it. I'm part of the team now." She held out her hand. "What do you say we shake on it and try to start over?"

Rick knew he really had no choice.

Beyond her, he saw Mack motioning for him to take her hand.

The photographer was also watching and, worse, raised his camera and took a picture. No doubt he'd like his own sidebar to go with it to say trouble was brewing on the Castles team before the first race of the season.

Rick shook her hand. "Okay. We start over. But I still don't want you hanging around any more than necessary."

"Fine," she said, biting back a sigh of relief. She did not want him to know she had been worried he wouldn't cave. Actually, he hadn't. Rick, she could tell, was a very dogged kind of guy. But he was willing to try, and, for the time being, that's all she could hope for.

She urged him to please hurry and change for the pictures, then turned and walked back to the garage area.

Rick watched her go, her high, rounded hips swaying as she walked. He cursed himself as another heated wave rolled over him.

He had not been bragging when he'd talked about the groupies and how they came on to him. It was a known fact that some women were attracted to professional athletes, and race car drivers were included in that group. And, being single, he'd had more than his share chasing after him.

But, focused as he was on his career, he ignored all the women he came into contact with, from groupies to fans to beauty queens.

But not this one.

He wanted her.

Badly.

And he could never have her.

Therefore, she had to go.

And the way to do that, he decided as he headed for the drivers' lounge and the showers, was to find a way to make her quit.

He figured it shouldn't be too hard. After all, she didn't look like the type who could take the extreme heat at certain tracks during the year, or the dirt and noise for very long.

Besides, it was hard living like gypsies, traveling to a different track almost every week. The NASCAR schedule currently consisted of thirty-four races, and sometimes a few got rained out. That meant running the next clear day, then heading for the next track right away.

One day he hoped to be successful enough to afford his

own plane to travel the schedule like the hot dogs—a nickname given to the top drivers. Or at least a fancy motor home that could be used at the track.

If he could win the rookie-of-the-year title, good things were sure to follow. Other big sponsorships would come in, and there would be money for better engines, better parts. He could really be competitive, maybe even one day win the big one—the NASCAR championship. Then he could write his own ticket and never have to worry about money again. After all, there was not only money to be won but endorsements and his share of sales of licensed products bearing the likeness of him and the car.

For the time being, he and Mack were owners but knew— and hoped—success would bring a real team owner, or that they would be taken on by a sponsor fielding several teams. Life would be a whole lot easier. As things were, they worked on the car themselves at a rented garage just outside Charlotte, North Carolina, the acknowledged hub of the stock car racing world.

Rick had wanted to race since he was a kid. Now, with no family except a sister up north he seldom saw, he was truly on his own and really didn't mind being a kind of gypsy. Sure, one day he'd like to be married and settle down, but everything had to happen according to plan. He could not let anything get in his way, especially a beautiful redhead that made him want to kiss her till they were both breathless.

He quickened his pace toward the lounge, because right then a cold shower was what he needed more than anything else.

Later he would figure out how to make Liz Mallory quit. Because he'd be doing both of them a favor.

"I'm just real sorry things happened like they did," Mack said to Liz while they were waiting for Rick. "He's really a nice guy."

"Till it comes to women at a racetrack," Liz said. "And he has got to stop thinking that every woman who approaches him wants to go out with him. There are plenty of genuine female race fans who aren't romantically interested in the drivers, though I realize it must be hard for someone as egotistical as Rick to believe that.

"And I mean it when I say he's got to be polite to everyone," she added firmly.

"Hey, you don't have to worry about that. Maybe you were coming on too strong, because you wanted to find out as much as you could about Rick and about the team. Ever think about that?"

She hadn't, but, now that she did, allowed that perhaps Mack had a point. After all, Rick had been working, and she'd tripped over him, causing him to bump his head. No doubt, that had put him in a bad mood. Then she hadn't gone away when he told her to. "Okay." She managed a smile. "I'll agree maybe I came on too strong and let it go."

"Good. And welcome to the team. Things will be okay, and we'll all enjoy working together."

"All set?" Pete called from where he was standing with the camera ready. "The light is good, so I hope he'll hurry up."

Suddenly Liz remembered to ask Mack, "Did the new uniforms arrive?"

"Yeah. For the whole crew, too. I have to tell you, we're going to look good tomorrow. Those are sharp outfits."

Moments passed. Liz kept glancing at her watch. They were still okay for time but would not be for long.

The noise in the garage area was deafening as drivers pulled off the track. Practice was over. Soon it would be time for the meeting.

"I'm taking everyone out to dinner tonight," Liz told Mack once things quieted down so he could hear. "It will give us a chance to get to know one another."

Mack frowned. "Well, that's nice of you, Liz, but have you told Rick? I mean, he and I are partners and we've been the ones to foot most of the bills since we started the team. It's always been sort of traditional that we take the guys out for steaks the night before qualifying. I don't think they'd like to change to pizza.

"Oh, not that they don't like pizza," he added quickly, eyes worriedly searching Liz's face in hopes he hadn't said the wrong thing. "Especially Big Boy's. That's one of the reasons we were so tickled when they offered sponsorship, because it's always been our favorite, and…" He drifted into silence, obviously embarrassed for going on so.

Liz understood and cheerily assured, "Hey, I understand. And there's no rule that says every time I take the team out we go for pizza. I've got an expense account, and steaks work for me. The only thing I'll change about your tradition is paying the bill. How's that?"

Mack said it was fine, but Liz knew it wasn't, because she could tell Rick hadn't wanted her tagging along. Well, that was just too bad. He was going to have to get used to having her around, as well as her calling the shots on lots of things from now on.

Gingerly she suggested, "Mack, I think you and I should get together for a meeting, just the two of us, and go over a few things. I realize this isn't a big operation, like Hendrick Motorsports and the Pettys and a lot of others, so there's not a team manager to really run things. But I can make things a lot smoother by taking care of motel and travel arrangements, in addition to overseeing the budget for expenses connected with team operations in general."

"And you don't want Rick to sit in?"

"Not this time. Let's you and I talk first. I'd really like to go over the budget with you, too, because while I'm sure the sponsors appreciate you cutting corners to stretch the money, there are some things I'm sure they won't like you skimping on."

Liz was unaware she could be heard by the crew working on the car next to Rick's. Not that they were purposely eavesdropping. They were just enjoying a little eye candy in the garage. Like Rick, they could not help but notice and appreciate the way her suit hugged her generous curves.

Concerned over what she had just said, Mack demanded, "Like what? Show me where I've skimped on anything."

"Those tires." She pointed. "Maybe they aren't about to blow like you said the old ones were, but I still say they don't look any better. The tread is completely gone, and—"

Liz was drowned out by a sudden explosion of laughter.

For a few seconds, Mack laughed, too, then, seeing the look on Liz's face, took her arm and led her away.

"What…what was that all about?" she stammered when they were out of earshot of the others. "What did I say that was so funny?"

"Liz, I need to explain about the tires. They don't have any tread, because NASCAR doesn't race in the rain."

"You mean they never have tread?"

"No. But you couldn't be expected to know that. And don't pay any attention to those hyenas laughing about it. You're a rookie when it comes to racing. But I'll try to help you learn along the way. Just ask me anything you want to know."

"Like I asked Rick?" she countered tightly.

"What do you mean?"

"I asked him why the tires on his car didn't have any tread, and he said it was because they were worn-out."

She could tell Mack was biting back a grin, which made her all the madder.

"Damn him," she cursed between clenched teeth. "He knew I'd make a fool of myself with that."

"No. In all fairness, I doubt he planned it that way. Remember. He didn't know who you were then. He was just annoyed you were there so he was being a smart aleck."

Liz supposed that was true but still felt deeply humiliated and vowed to find a way to get him back.

"Here he comes," Mack said. "Raise hell with him later if you want to, but let's get these photos over with so he can get to the meeting."

"By all means," she said sweetly, turning in the direction of the drivers' lounge.

Her breath caught in her throat.

Rick was probably the best-looking thing she'd seen since her last Mel Gibson movie. There was only one word to describe him—hunk.

The uniform was formfitting. And what a form he had, she mused, swallowing a sigh. He had not zipped the suit all the way, and dark hairs on his superb chest were provocatively revealed. His narrow waist emphasized great buns, and his relaxed stride was like that of a jungle animal, lazy after feeding yet ready to spring at any moment.

He reached Liz and Mack, his hair still damp from the shower. Liz clenched her fists against the ache to touch it, run her fingers through it. Her gaze dropped to his partially exposed chest, and she felt a stirring of desire to explore there, as well.

"Well, are we ready?"

He spoke curtly, impatiently, which dissipated the spellbound moment for Liz. "Yes, let's get on with it."

She turned and walked toward Pete, wishing all the while the sponsor had chosen a married driver...or, at least, one who didn't heat her blood every time she got near him.

Chapter Three

The restaurant was located right on the beach. Liz tipped the maître d' to give them a window table for a sweeping view of the ocean.

"Wow, this sure beats that greasy spoon we're used to," Benny Dyson, a crew member said. "The food was good, but choice seats there looked out on the swamp and the alligators."

Rick's jaw knotted. "Buckeye Joe's has the best steaks in Daytona, and you know it, Benny." Liz was in the ladies' room, and he seized the chance to grouse. "We'll be lucky to get anything besides caviar and roast duck at a place like this."

Mack was scanning the menu. "I don't know about that. They've got a sixteen-ounce T-bone that sounds good if she doesn't mind me ordering something that costs almost thirty bucks."

"Caviar is good," Benny said innocently. "I think you

ought to lighten up on the babe, Rick. She seems nice, and footing the bill to feed us is even nicer.''

"Let me tell you something.'' Rick picked up his fork and shook it at him. "She's not the one paying. The sponsor is. And I'd rather see thirty bucks spent on the race car.''

"Rick, I agree with Benny,'' Mack said. "Lighten up. Buying us dinner is part of the package. Enjoy it.'' He turned to Benny. "And if I were you, I'd strike the word *babe* from my vocabulary. She's got a name. She expects you to use it.''

"Yeah, all right. I'll watch it. Say, Rick, how come you don't like her?''

Mack reached for a hot roll a waiter had set on the table, along with a pat of honey butter. "Ah, you know how he feels about women in racing. They get on his nerves.''

"They're bad luck,'' Rick said, not about to divulge his real feelings. "Big Boy's could just as easily have sent a man to do the PR.''

"But they didn't,'' Mack pointed out. "They sent Liz. And like I've been telling you all evening, forget how you two rubbed each other the wrong way. We've got a qualifying race to run tomorrow, and you need to focus.''

Oh, he was focusing, all right, Rick thought furiously as he watched Liz approach.

But not on the race.

Mack had told him how humiliated she had been about the tires, and he figured on embarrassing her again. Hopefully she would then have second thoughts.

Maybe, he brooded, he wouldn't be so opposed to having her around if she weren't so good-looking. She had gone to her motel from the track, meeting them at the restaurant. She'd happily shared the news her lost luggage had been found and delivered. So she had changed from her business suit into a blue and white pants outfit. The top was scooped low enough to be sexy but still in good taste, and her tiny waist emphasized the rest of her.

She was not wearing her hair in the austere bun; instead it hung softly around her face.

He was glad she had put Mack between them. That made it easier to ignore her...or try to, anyway.

Mack leaped up to pull out her chair. "We were just saying what a nice place this is, Liz. Be sure to tell the VIPs at Big Boy's we appreciate it."

She gave everyone at the table a sweeping smile, even Rick. "You can tell them yourselves next Sunday. I had a message waiting at the motel saying Gary Staley, the CEO, is flying a crowd in for the race."

"So we get to meet them in person," Mack said. "We've only talked on the phone."

"Oh, yes. I've got to make reservations somewhere special for dinner Saturday night, and—"

Benny laughingly interrupted to remark, "Well, how much nicer can it get than this?"

"You'll see," she said with a wink, then continued, "I'll also arrange garage passes for them before the race, and—"

"Hold it."

All eyes turned on Rick.

"The last thing we need right before a race is a bunch of people getting in the way and asking stupid questions."

Mack cried, "Hey, wait a minute, Rick. We're talking about the people footing the bill for you to try to win the rookie title."

"Which won't happen if I've got to worry with them," Rick argued. "PR reps for other teams handle the VIPs themselves. They don't bring them around the driver right before a race."

"Well, I don't intend to do that," Liz defended. "I don't want them to get in your way, either. So I'll remedy the situation by keeping them a good distance away, and *I* will answer their questions."

"You?" Rick scoffed.

"Sure."

"You don't know beans about racing, Liz."

Mack groaned. "Here we go again. I thought you two called a truce."

"We have," Liz said sweetly. "We're just talking, Mack. We aren't arguing."

"Well, you've got a week," Rick said smugly. "Maybe you can learn enough to carry on an intelligent conversation, or fake it, at least."

A waiter came and took their orders. Liz emphasized they should all have whatever they wanted, regardless of the cost.

After he left, she turned to Rick. "I won't have to fake it. And I don't have to take a crash course. I know enough about your car to explain it to them."

"Yeah? Well, let's hear it." Rick leaned back in his chair and folded his arms across his chest. Maybe he wouldn't have to do anything to humiliate her. He would let her do it herself.

Liz wriggled in her seat, as though eager to show off her knowledge. Then, propping her chin on coyly laced fingers, she began. "Well, I know that the toilet facilities in race cars are being studied by NASA, because they're thinking about using the same system for the astronauts."

Benny choked on a bite of roll.

Two of the other crew members, having just sipped their beers, sprayed the table.

Mack cried, "Liz, no—"

She ignored him. "I also know about that little button on the dash that sends a signal to a big computer somewhere to make it fair for everybody to start their cars at the same time."

"Oh, man." Benny reached for his water glass, still coughing and choking.

The others reached for their beer, struggling with the hilarity of it all.

Mack grabbed Liz's wrist. "Hey, you're just clowning around, right? You don't really believe all that?"

Making her eyes wide with innocence, Liz replied, "Why, of course I do. I had a very good teacher."

Mack looked accusingly at Rick, who had been listening stone-faced and silent. "Did you tell her all that crap? I heard about the tires. Jeez, Rick..."

Liz had wasted no time once she got to her motel room unpacking the books she had bought on racing. Scolding herself for not finding the time to do so earlier, she had located information on the construction of race cars and devoured every word.

She relished the astonished look that came over Rick's face with each word she spoke. "The typical Winston Cup car weighs thirty-four hundred pounds and has a seven- to seven-hundred-fifty-horsepower engine that drives the rear wheels through a four-speed transmission. Top speed is 220 miles an hour. The roll cage inside the car is made of 150 feet of steel tubing to protect the driver. There are no doors, no passenger seat, and no speedometer. The tires have an extra layer of rubber to try to guard against a flat. They're fortified by a belt network that was designed to keep their shape under extreme stress."

She paused to sip her wine, reveling in the moment, then continued. "There are two eleven-gallon rubber gas tanks encased in steel for safety, but fuel economy would be a nightmare for the ordinary street car. Race cars only get five miles to the gallon, and, of course, they use a special kind of fuel that is much more expensive than regular gas."

A hush had fallen over the table.

Rick was the first to break it, not about to let her get the best of him, merely because she'd managed to speed-read some technical stuff before dinner. "Well, now, Liz, that's real impressive. Maybe with all that information to share, you can keep the bigwigs out of my way."

"I intend to. But I'm sure they'd like to hear about the toilet facilities. I thought maybe you could explain that to them."

Mack shook his head. "What in heck did you tell her, Rick?"

The waiter appeared with stuffed shrimp appetizers for

everyone. Rick helped himself before flippantly responding. "She can't take a joke. Or maybe she doesn't know enough about what's going on to realize it's a joke. She asked about that hole in the seat. I made up a story about how it's the way drivers use the bathroom during a race."

"When actually," Liz corrected, "it's where the driver's shoulder harness connects. You were just teasing, I know." She flashed her sweetest smile at Rick, but her eyes were cold. "But enough funny stuff. From now on I would appreciate it if you would tell me the truth when I ask you a technical question, okay?"

Rick gave a curt nod of assent and bristled to think how she might have won the lap but would never finish the race.

Not if he could help it.

Mack breezed into the motel's coffee shop and went to where Liz was waiting in a booth.

"Is Rick coming?" she asked. She had scheduled a breakfast meeting to go over a few things, and, since the night before, she had arranged for Rick to be a guest on a popular local talk show for that evening.

Mack signaled the waitress for coffee. "He's taking a shower. He said he'd skip breakfast and head to the track. He wants to get started checking the car out before the races today."

"Well, I need to tell him about a radio show I've got him scheduled to be on tonight."

Mack's eyes widened. "The one called *Pit Stop?*"

She nodded.

"Oh, man, that's great. During Speed Weeks, it's broadcast from one of the hottest nightclubs on the beach. He'll get a lot of exposure."

"I know. So will you please call him on a house phone and tell him I need to meet with him now?"

Mack frowned. "Liz, he said he'd rather me deal with you, so I'll tell him about it when I get to the track. I'm sorry, but that's just how he is."

"Well, it's not how *I* am, and he's got plenty of time. It's only seven o'clock. He can be at the track by eight. Now if you don't want to call him, Mack, I will."

She started to get up, but Mack waved her to stay seated. "I'll do it. But I can't understand why you and I can't handle everything and leave him out of it."

"That's just the point. He *is* everything. He is the focus of my job. I've also arranged an interview for him with an Atlanta journalist. Big Boy's has sixteen restaurants in the Atlanta area. They'll be thrilled to see a story about Rick in the paper. I need to tell him what time to meet the writer and where.

"Your job, Mack," she politely reminded, "is to take care of the car. I plan to ease a lot of your burdens over managing the team to give you more time to do that. Now please get Rick down here so we can discuss all this and get it over with so you can do your job, and I can do mine. Okay?"

Mack made the call and returned to say Rick was on his way. "He's grumbling, but he'll be okay."

Liz couldn't care less.

About ten minutes later, Rick all but threw himself into the other side of the booth next to Mack. "All right, what's so important it can't wait?"

Liz handed him a schedule for the week that she had prepared. "I just wanted a quiet moment to go over all this with the two of you."

Mack, reading over Rick's shoulder, said, "This is all PR stuff—appearances at the mall to sign autographs, stuff like that. What has it got to do with me?"

She explained how she needed Mack to know Rick's schedule so he wouldn't have him practicing or working on the car at those times. "I've checked the track schedule, and I've made sure there won't be any conflicts as far as what he needs to do there. I want you to coordinate with me."

"Great. No problem." Mack looked up to see Benny waving from the door. "Gotta go. See you guys later."

"We'll have dinner again later in the week," Liz said.

"Afraid not. My wife's driving in from Charlotte today and bringing the kids. We've got an efficiency, so she'll be doing some cooking."

"Well, maybe she can join us," Liz said. "I'd like to meet her. In fact, I'd like to meet the families of the entire crew. I want us to be like a family, all working together to win and make Rick a star."

Mack gave her a little salute and left them.

Rick reached for the coffee Mack hadn't had time to drink. "I knew he was going to duck out and leave me with all this."

"All what?" Liz said, troubled that he continued to resent her at every turn. "I just want to make sure you understand about the show tonight, what time you need to be there, and—"

"The show," he scoffed, staring down at the schedule. "Now I know some drivers who aren't rookies that haven't been able to get on there. *Pit Stop* features the biggies, not the little guys like me. But—" he paused to give his most mocking grin "—I guess that's an advantage to having a female PR person, right?"

"Wrong." Liz was fast getting her dander up. She knew what he was implying and didn't like it.

"Then how did you arrange it? Tell me. I'd like to hear. Exactly how did you manage within twenty-four hours of arriving in Daytona to get me on that show tonight?"

"I met Jimmy Barnes, the host, at a party last night."

"A party. After you left us at the restaurant, you went to a party."

"That's right. The invitation was in my press package. I was introduced to Jimmy, and I told him about you and the new sponsorship, and he said great, he'd like to have you on his show tonight. Simple as that."

Rick knew it wasn't that simple at all. Jimmy Barnes had been turned on by Liz like any normal man would be, and he'd let her wheedle him into putting him on the show.

Maybe some drivers would consider that an advantage—having a sexy female pave the way for them—but not Rick.

Still, he knew better than to gripe about it. He did need the exposure. And he wanted it badly. That's how other sponsors became interested in a driver.

"Well, that's nice, Liz. I'll look forward to it."

Something in his voice raised suspicion that he wasn't all that pleased, but not about the show. He probably thought she had flirted with Jimmy Barnes to get him on there. But she hadn't.

One of the things Liz adhered to was her personal rule that she would not use womanly guile to open doors. Yes, she would try to dress nicely, but she would be all business. If anyone got any ideas, she set them straight. And that was how she intended to conduct herself in the racing world.

Liz ordered breakfast, even though she wasn't hungry. In fact, she never ate breakfast, just grabbed a quick cup of coffee on the run.

She told herself the only reason she was eating this morning was because it was going to be a long day. She needed her energy. She would not even remotely consider it was to prolong her time with Rick because he was being friendly. Still distant. Still reserved. But it was an improvement over his previous demeanor.

He was wearing a T-shirt again. It reminded her of Clint Eastwood in *Bridges of Madison County*. The man might be pushing seventy, but in a T-shirt he was a sex symbol nonpareil.

Liz munched on a piece of toast she didn't want and wondered what size shirt Rick wore. She seized on an excuse to ask. "I should be receiving the new T-shirts today that Big Boy's had made up to sell at the concession stands. I'll take out a few for you guys. What size do you wear?"

"Extra-large."

She should have known.

"And how big are you?"

"Thirty-four, C cup," she blurted without thinking and

wanted to die then and there. What was wrong with her? She gulped and corrected, "I meant medium."

"I can't believe you're blushing."

"Am I?" She took a big swallow of orange juice, hoping it would cool her cheeks.

"Yeah, you are. And that's kind of nice. I didn't know women blushed anymore."

"I just got too much sun yesterday." Maybe it had been a big mistake to prolong the meeting. But she had dared to think she had her emotions under control. Last night she had lain awake for hours lecturing herself that she was a fool to be even remotely attracted to him.

The waitress brought the check. Liz reached for it, but Rick got it first.

She protested, "I'm on an expense account."

He leaned across the table so those around would not hear. "Then next time make arrangements to pay the tab before it's put on the table."

"What difference does that make?"

"I don't know where you come from, Liz, or how they do things there. But I hail from a small town in Georgia, which makes me, I guess, a country boy, with old-fashioned ways, and one of them happens to be the man pays the bill when he's dining with a lady."

"I paid it last night."

"It wasn't just the two of us."

She argued, "I'm not paying for it. The sponsor is."

He countered, "Others don't know that."

"I don't see why we should care what others think."

"Hey, aren't you the one who was giving me a lecture on public relations just yesterday? Well, we're in public, and we're having relations—social, anyway. So that means I have to be aware of what others think. Am I right?"

"You're stretching it a bit," she said stiffly.

"Oh, don't worry about it. It's not a big deal. And I don't have time to debate the issue, anyway. I need to get to the track. I'll let you know tomorrow how the show went tonight. Or maybe you'll listen to it."

He rose, and so did she to quickly inform him, "Not only will I listen, I will be there. In fact, I'd like for us to drive together, if you don't mind. It will look good for you to walk in with your PR rep."

Rick did not like that picture, at all. After the dream he'd had last night, he wanted to avoid Liz like the plague. He hadn't had a dream like that since high school, for crying out loud, which only reminded him all the more how long it had been since he'd slept with a woman. And he needed one badly. But not Liz.

She fell into step beside him. "I'm going to the track, too. In case you do really well in the qualifying races, I'll need to be around to put a spin on it."

She had been up since dawn, doing more studying and now understood the twin qualifying races. At other tracks on the circuit, drivers just went out individually for time trials. The starting lineup was set according to the average speed they ran for two laps. It was different at Daytona, where two 125-mile races were held, and the way drivers finished was how they would start the race on Sunday.

Liz realized Rick had stopped walking and had come to an abrupt halt. She whirled around to see that he was staring at her as if she'd lost her mind. "What?"

"This isn't politics."

"I don't understand."

"You don't have to hang around me putting a spin on things."

She felt totally frustrated. Was everything that came out of her mouth that day going to sound all wrong? "What I meant was—I'll be around to drum up as much coverage from the media as I can. Brag about how you did and point them in your direction."

"I guess that's okay." He started walking again.

As he caught up with her, his bare arm brushed against hers, and he cursed himself for the rush. She was wearing slacks. Tight white slacks. And a pale green blouse of some kind of cool, clingy material that emphasized her nice breasts.

No doubt about it, he thought on a sigh. He had to make her want to quit…and fast.

Liz heard Rick sigh and mistook it for annoyance at the trio of girls standing in the lobby.

"Rick Castles, it's really you," one of them squealed. She was poured into her jeans, which cut below her navel. Her braless bosom was about to tumble out of her halter top as she bounced up and down on the toes of her platform slides.

"Can we have your autograph?" asked another girl, dressed almost identically, as she rushed up to Rick.

"Yeah, sure," Rick said pleasantly. He suspected Liz thought it was for her benefit that he was being so nice about it, but the truth was he didn't mind when the girls weren't at the track. "Got a pen?" he asked Liz.

"Who's she?" one of the girls asked, scowling jealously at Liz.

"My PR rep." He took the pen Liz handed him and signed the piece of paper the girl thrust at him.

He did the same for another, but the third girl, who had been hanging back, moved in and said, "I want something else autographed." She indicated her arm.

Liz held her breath to see how Rick would react.

"Sorry. No body parts."

His smile could have melted an icicle. In fact, it kept the girl from having her feelings hurt, because she was practically swooning before it. "Then…then just sign this," she stammered, overcome by his nearness, and handed him a souvenir race program.

Outside in the parking lot, Liz offered him a ride to the track. "You could come back with one of the guys."

He shook his head, not about to be cozied up with her in a car. Too intimate. "No, I've got some stuff in mine I'll need, and it'd take too long to switch."

"Well, okay." She tried not to sound disappointed. It was

for the best, anyway. She knew she didn't need to be alone with him any more than absolutely necessary. "By the way, you were really nice to those girls back there."

"Of course, I was. They weren't bugging me at the track when I'm doing something. Besides, to them I'm just another driver."

Liz watched him walk to his car, wickedly observing that he looked just as good going as he did coming.

But he was wrong about thinking he was just another driver to those girls.

Like Liz, they knew a hunk when they saw one.

Rick was in the second qualifying race, and he and Mack and the crew used the extra time till then to keep working. Still Liz managed to get the whole crew lined up beside the car for more photos.

It did not take much to get caught up in all the excitement, and she felt so proud to walk with the crew as they rolled the car onto the track to line up for the start of the race.

The grandstands were packed. Bands were playing. All around fans were cheering for their favorite driver.

Liz wondered where she should watch the race. She didn't want to be in the way in the pits but wanted to keep up with what was going on. Then she noticed some PR guys she'd met at the party last night heading for the press tower in the infield. She fell in step behind them, figuring she couldn't go wrong following her peers.

The tower was floor-to-ceiling glass on all sides, and Liz thrilled to be able to see the entire track. It was deliciously air-conditioned, and there was plenty to eat and drink.

As writers worked on laptops, other PR reps passed out freebies like caps, T-shirts and other items with their drivers' logos. Liz hoped her own supplies would come in. As soon as the race was over and she knew where Rick would be in Sunday's lineup, she was off to work on his press kit.

"There're off," somebody shouted.

Liz found a chair and sat down to watch. The cars had

taken the pace laps. The pace car had pulled in, and the green flag was waving.

Her eyes stayed on Rick's car, and, for a while, things went smoothly. Then there was a four-car pileup right in front of him. She clenched her fists and bit down on her lower lip—hard—to keep from screaming. It looked as though he was going to plow right into the middle of the melee. Instead, he went high, and then she feared he'd hit the wall.

"Hey, look at how slick car sixty got around all that," a writer yelled. "Who's the driver?"

"Rick Castles," Liz said loudly and proudly. "Sponsored by Big Boy's Pizza."

"He's a rookie," somebody else said. "Quite a feat. He's gonna bear watching this season."

"Right." Liz was beside herself. "I'll have his press kits in a few days. Meanwhile, if anybody needs to line up an interview, I'll take care of it. The name's Liz Mallory, and I'm his PR rep."

She turned back to the race, thrilling to every second as Rick kept up with the pack. When he moved into fifth place, she heard more murmurs from the press as to his driving ability.

When he passed for third, and it looked like he might give a run for victory...actually had a chance to win, Liz could contain herself no longer. She was jumping up and down and clapping her hands and so were a lot of the writers, eager to pull for an underdog.

But he never made it closer than third. Still, cheers went up for a rookie who had done so well.

Suddenly Liz found herself surrounded by journalists clamoring to set up interviews. Rick Castles's finish was worthy of a feature story.

"Say, why don't you call down on your radio and get him up here for an interview?" someone suggested. Others agreed.

Liz felt stupid not to have her own headset and radio.

She'd seen how a lot of other PR reps had them to keep in touch with the crew chief, but that was something she just hadn't thought about. Boy, did she have her homework cut out for her.

"Radio wasn't working," she said with an exaggerated shrug. "I'll just go get him." She passed the food tables, laden with sandwiches and fried chicken. "He'll probably be hungry, anyway, since his garage space is far away from the food like the rest of the rookies."

A writer helping himself to cake squares gave her a strange look. "What are you talking about?"

"The rookies. They aren't near the food. They have to earn it, you know."

Others, overhearing, turned to stare.

"The rookies," she repeated lamely, wondering what was wrong. "They aren't near the food like the top drivers."

"Would you please explain that?" the one with the heaping plate of cake squares asked, a slow grin spreading across his face. "I mean, what does being a rookie have to do with being near food?"

Stiffly, defensively, Liz said, "That's what I was told by the garage guard my first day when I asked where I'd find my driver. He said he'd be in the back, not up front with the hot dogs. I asked somebody what that meant, and they said rookies weren't near the food stands, and—"

As the room exploded with laughter, Liz slapped her forehead and groaned to remember just who that somebody was.

The mechanic under the car.

Also known as Rick Castles.

And once again he'd made her look like a fool.

Chapter Four

There were two days left before the big race. Liz was sequestered in her hotel room going over her notes to make sure she had not forgotten anything. Gary Staley's jet would arrive just before lunch, so she had plenty of time.

Jeff was coming in on a commercial flight and had said he would meet them and take them to lunch. Liz had made reservations at an upscale restaurant and planned to join them there.

The press kits had been completed by midweek. She was very proud of them, and several journalists had complimented her on a great job. She had thanked them without explaining they would be even better once she had time to write some feature articles on Rick herself. But she could not do that till she got to know him a little better, and since the humiliating incident in the press box, she had avoided him as much as possible.

A week had passed since his performance in the qualifying races had given him a little more than fifteen minutes of fame. He had been the subject of several stories the following day in newspapers all over the country. He'd also been interviewed for radio and TV.

Liz had planned to play it for all it was worth, but the next day a well-known driver had wrecked his car in practice. The car was nothing but crumpled sheet metal, and she could not believe anyone could have survived such a crash. The driver had to be airlifted from the infield medical center to a local hospital, mercifully with no life-threatening injuries, but, of course, the media focused on him.

The day after that, something else had happened, and so it went. The sportswriters were constantly looking for new subjects to write about, so no one driver stayed in the limelight for long. Still, Liz had stayed busy trying to drum up interest in Rick. She had wanted to have a big story in the Sunday paper to impress not only the sponsor but her boss, as well.

She was sprawled on the bed, wearing shorts and a T-shirt with Rick's picture on it. The tees had just gone on sale at the track concession stands the day before, and she was anxious to find out how they were selling. But first things first.

After lunch, Jeff was to drive the VIPs to the track, where Liz had arranged for them to have passes to the pit area to watch the last practice session. However, the crew was taking a day off. Their families had arrived, and they planned to relax at the beach the rest of the day.

She picked up Rick's folder and began leafing through it. She knew it by heart. He was thirty-two. Older than the other rookies in their mid-twenties. But his had been a small, cheap operation. It had taken a lot of work and time on a very small budget to finally catch the eye of a sponsor willing to back him on the NASCAR circuit.

It had also taken skill as a driver, which Rick obviously had. He and Mack were longtime friends from a small town in Georgia. They had formed the team and run the short tracks all over the Southeast. Rick had won several local championships, made a name for himself and now he had been given a chance to run with the hot dogs.

Liz made a face to recall her humiliation in the press box. Though sorely tempted, she'd not said a word to Rick and spent little time in the garage, instead focusing on the press kits and getting them distributed, as well as trying to line up publicity for him.

She had approached him only when she needed to talk to him about something specific—like the autographing he'd done earlier in the week at a nearby mall. She had been quite impressed at the crowd he'd drawn. He was obviously popular with his fans, and she hoped to make him even more so and win new ones.

She read in his bio again about his degree from Georgia Tech in automotive engineering. He had probably commanded a high salary in that field before giving it up to go into racing full-time.

She took out the color photos from the press kit. She especially liked the one of Rick beside the race car. He made wonderful pictures, his dark, rugged good looks coming through on camera.

As always, Liz found herself wondering about his personal life and what he would be doing on a day others were with their families. Someone so handsome was bound to be in a relationship, which would explain his ambivalence to the beautiful young women who flocked around him at every opportunity. If so, it was an admirable trait. She liked loyalty in a man…something she, unfortunately, had yet to experience.

But she did not envy Rick's girlfriend his archaic views toward women. Maybe she never showed up at the track because he made it clear he thought it was no place for females. Probably he kept her in what he considered her place—at home.

That would never work for Liz. But it didn't matter. She was hoping if all went well, Jeff would move her on up the ladder to bigger accounts. So it wasn't as if she would have to remain Rick's PR rep for the duration of his sponsorship with Big Boy's Pizza.

She wondered about her own schedule. The next race was in Rockingham, North Carolina, in only a week. Qualifying would begin midweek, which gave her just a few days to return to Charlotte and settle into her new apartment. She'd rented it on the Internet and hoped it would be okay. It really made no difference, though, because with a thirty-four-race schedule to follow, she'd hardly be home long enough to unpack, do her laundry, then throw everything back in her suitcase.

A glance at the clock told her she still had plenty of time to get dressed for lunch. Still, a long, soaking bath would be nice.

She was about to step into the tub when the phone rang. It was Rick, and he sounded annoyed.

"I need your help."

She went into her public relations mode, sounding cordial but all business. "Certainly. What can I do for you?"

"Meet me in the parking lot. We need to get to the track right away. I'll drive."

"But—"

He hung up before she could begin firing questions, such as how long did he need her…and for what? Maybe she should have told him earlier about her luncheon appointment with his sponsor, and then he would've known she didn't have time to ride out to the track.

She tried to call his room, but there was no answer, which meant he was on his way to his car. She had managed to get a room at the same motel as the team for convenience sake. Now she wondered if that had been a smart idea.

She yanked on her sneakers and hurried downstairs. She wasn't thrilled over anyone seeing her dressed as she was, but she was in a hurry to let Rick know he had to find some-one else.

Pushing through the doors to the outside, she saw him parked at the curb, the car's engine running.

She opened the passenger door and leaned in. "Listen, I can't go," she began. "I forgot to tell you—"

And that was all she had time to say before he reached to grab her arm and pull her in. "Sorry, but there's nobody else. The guys are at the beach."

"But I can't go. I've got an important lunch date."

He squealed tires leaving the parking lot. "Your boyfriend can wait."

"It's not with a boyfriend." Liz was having a hard time getting her seat belt fastened as he hurtled through traffic. "And I wish you'd slow down. You're going to get a ticket."

"Sorry." He eased back on the gas. "I'm just in a hurry to get to the track and get started."

"Doing what? And by the way, the lunch date is with your sponsor. The VIPs are coming in, as well as my boss from New York, and—"

"Your boss can handle it. Isn't your job to help me?"

"Yes, in PR matters, but I can't think of anything going on at the track you need me for."

"It's not PR. And I hate asking you to do it, but it's got to be done, and I can't trust anybody but you."

"Sounds real James Bond," she said, annoyed, "but I still need to make that appointment on time." If he needed help, and she could provide it, she supposed that was part of her job. After all, if he was stressed, it could not only affect his driving but the persona he presented to the public as well. "How long will it take?"

"Don't know yet. Don't even know if it's going to be necessary, but I can't risk not checking it out."

"Well, can't you tell me what it's about?"

"It's about the team maybe getting fined anywhere from twenty-five to fifty thousand dollars."

Liz nearly choked on a gasp. "You're kidding, right?"

"Afraid not. There have been a lot of violations lately, and somebody just called to tip me off that NASCAR is going to do some surprise inspections of fuel tanks late this afternoon. I need to make sure ours is okay.''

"Well...well, why wouldn't it be?''

"Everybody is supposed to run the same kind of fuel, bought at the track. But there's always somebody trying to find a way to cheat.''

Liz flashed him a look of disgust. "Like you were obviously planning to do, and now you're scared you'll get caught.''

"Not exactly. Mack was telling me somebody has come up with an oxygen enhancer. It's an improper additive. We didn't plan to use it, but Mack did say he got hold of some and thought about testing it out in practice just for the fun of it, to see if it worked. Nothing wrong there, but—'' he paused for emphasis ''—if it's still in there when NASCAR does a check, they aren't going to believe we never intended to use it for the race. So I need to make sure everything is okay.''

"By doing what?''

"By draining the fuel out and putting the right kind back in.''

"And what do you need me for?'' Liz didn't like being a part of it.

"To keep an eye out for any NASCAR officials roaming in the garage till I can get rid of it. But it may not be in there. Mack might have been running his mouth. Who knows? But I can't take any chances.''

"Well, he never should have put it in there to start with, and then you wouldn't have to worry about it.'' Though it was not in her job description, Liz knew when she saw Mack she'd say something to him about even toying with anything illegal. The sponsor would be furious if the team were caught and fined.

"Okay, so maybe we do need to check, but I'm not dressed for this,'' she grumbled.

Rick was pleased she wasn't. That would add to her misery. It was a hot day, even for Daytona in February, and the humidity was so thick you could almost slice it. "Don't worry. I've got some overalls in the truck. You can wear those."

"As hot as it is? I'll die."

"Can't be helped. They'd never let you through the garage gate wearing shorts, even if you do have a pass." He stole a look at her legs. Nice and shapely. And if he ran his hand across her thighs, her skin would probably feel like satin—

Perspiration beaded his forehead, and he knew it was not from the heat outside.

"Overalls." Liz sank down in the seat looking as if she wished she were anywhere but there. "I hope this won't take long."

He felt a twinge of guilt. She had been doing a great job. The guys liked her, but, more importantly, the press seemed to, also. He'd never dreamed of having the exposure he'd gotten in the past week. He could tell his number of fans was growing by the attendance everywhere he had gone to sign autographs.

All in all, Liz was pleasant to work with. And if she were a man, he'd be tickled to death. But she wasn't. And she didn't belong.

Not at the track.

Not in his dreams.

And she sure as heck paid him a nightly visit in those.

Turning into the speedway entrance, he glanced at her out of the corner of his eye. She was cute in her shorts and T-shirt. Her red hair was pulled back in a ponytail. And even though she wasn't wearing any makeup that he could tell, she was still gorgeous.

She hadn't told him about meeting the VIPs. If she had, Rick would probably have changed his mind. He had chosen this afternoon, because he knew the guys wouldn't be around. But maybe it would even work out better that the big kahunas were around. They'd be annoyed she didn't show up for her appointment. And they would also raise eyebrows to see her in greasy overalls. He, of course, would give the impression—when Liz wasn't around, of course—that she had insisted on getting deeply involved with the team.

"I really shouldn't be doing this," Liz protested as they walked toward the garage. "Even if we left right now, I'd never get to the restaurant on time."

He kept a tight hold on her arm. "This is more important." Actually, his conscience was really starting to bother him. He only wanted to make her ask for another assignment. Not get fired.

"I don't even have my credentials with me," she pointed out. "I didn't plan on coming with you."

"Doesn't matter. We can go to the NASCAR office and tell them you forgot. They'll issue temporaries."

When they reached the garage entrance, the guard on duty stepped out of the booth and held up his hand. "You can't go in there like that." He pointed to the open-toed sandals Liz was wearing, then raked her legs with an appreciative glance. "And you can't wear shorts, either."

Liz, not wanting the guard to think she didn't know any better, attempted to explain. "I didn't intend to come dressed like this, and—"

Rick cut her off. "I've got overalls in the truck she can wear. How about giving us a break? And I'm going to make sure she doesn't get hurt. Come on, we don't have a lot of time, and there's something I need her to do."

The guard scratched his chin. "Well, I don't know..."

"I told you I had overalls for her."

"Oh, all right." Frowning, he waved them on their way as he said to Liz, "If you're gonna work around a track, learn how to dress."

"This wasn't my idea," she called over her shoulder.

Rick gave her a tug. "Come on. We've wasted enough time."

Liz was mad all over again. He seemed to have a knack for humiliating her. The guard would probably laugh about how Rick Castles's PR rep was such a rookie she showed up wearing shorts and sandals. And, once again, she'd be the butt of jokes and snickers. All week she'd had to put up with writers making cracks about how she should bring them a *hot dog* when she went into the garage. She wondered how long it would take to live that down.

The overalls had long sleeves, was way too big for her, and Liz was sweltering before she even got it buttoned. Perspiration made her eyes sting, her ponytail hung limp, and she felt like a wilted dandelion.

She was exhausted from the hectic pace she had been keeping. Working on the press kits had taken a lot of time. Then there were all the parties she felt obligated to attend to meet everyone involved in corporate sponsorships, as well as speedway personnel. After all, racing was like one big family, everyone traveling together from track to track throughout the year. And she wanted to be a part of it, to be accepted.

She had also been busy with Rick's activities, making sure he got where he was supposed to be on time and connected with his fans.

Once she got the hang of things, Liz was sure she'd be well-organized and have plenty of time for everything. But for the time being, she could only stumble through and do the best she could.

Rick could see how her impatience and annoyance was building. He decided to make it even worse. "Listen, I think it's time you realized that PR work in racing is different. Real different. It's not a nine-to-five job."

"It never is," she snapped, "and I wish you'd quit talking and hurry."

"I am. Don't worry. And I'm trying to help you here, because I think you've got this candy-coated idea that your only function is to line up appearances for me and schmooze the press into writing about me every chance. But it's more than that, because sometimes we get into a bind—like now— and you have to go above and beyond the call of duty.

"But," he continued, "you being a woman, you naturally aren't willing to pitch in like the regular reps."

She scowled. "And by *regular* you are no doubt referring to the male reps, right?"

"Hmmm," he pretended to ponder, "I guess you might say that. I don't hear them complaining when they have to do something besides hand out press kits or go to a cocktail party."

Liz was seething. "I can do my job as well as any man."

"Okay." Rick's shrug was practiced nonchalance. "Well, I'm about through. All we have to do is refill the tank, and then we'll be ready to leave." He turned his back so she wouldn't see the grin he could not hold back. She was mad, all right, which was exactly what he wanted.

Liz blinked to see him roll a red wagon out of the back of the truck. It looked identical to one she'd had as a child. "And what is that for?"

"For you to go to the fuel shed and get two containers and bring it back. It's too heavy to carry.

"Even for a man," he added with a wink. "All the guys use wagons."

"Well, maybe you'd better go get it. I have no idea where it is."

"Follow Rusty over there." He pointed to a man with an empty wagon and called, "Hey, Rusty, take Liz with you and show her the ropes, okay?"

Rusty gave her a wave to fall in with him.

"Why can't you go?" she demanded of Rick.

"I just remembered I've got some more photos in the truck I need to sign for a Boy Scout troop coming by first thing in the morning. You go on. I'll wait for you."

After she'd gone, Rick got in the cab of the truck and leaned back to relax, feeling he had taken the first step in making Liz want to quit. She was going to have to stand in line for the gas a half hour, maybe longer, just to hear she had to have a gas card. Then she'd turn around, come back, only to have to do it all over again.

It was nearly noon. He wasn't sure what time her luncheon appointment was, but, if she was lucky, and the lines weren't long for fuel, she might get to the restaurant in time for dessert and coffee.

He grimaced to think about it. The truth was, he didn't like playing dirty tricks on her, but it was for her own good. Too many bad experiences had made him a firm believer that women did not belong in the world of racing...experiences he didn't like to think about. So he was actually doing her a favor to make her quit.

It was steaming hot. Rick rolled down the windows of the truck and leaned his head back, hoping to catch a breeze. He had almost dozed off when someone yelled, "Hey, Castles. Somebody wants to see you at the gate."

"What for?" He gave his head a brisk shake to wake himself up. One of the NASCAR officials was standing at his window.

"I dunno. Something about a special request for you to see some kid in the parking lot. I think they said he's got a cast on his leg or something."

Rick thanked him for bringing the message and promptly got down out of the truck and hurried to the gate.

A woman was waiting, scanning faces anxiously, and when she recognized Rick cried, "Oh, I'm so glad he found you. My son broke his leg last week. It's in a cast, and he can't get around very well. We'd had this trip planned for months, so we brought him on, but he's insisting we get your autograph for him.

"He's only six," she added, almost apologetically.

Rick smiled to think how race fans sure started young. It was one of the reasons the sport had grown to a thriving two billion dollar industry fifty-two years after it started as a small family business on the Daytona Beaches. Attendance in the past ten years was up sixty-four percent, and it was the second-highest-rated sport on television, trailing only pro football.

The woman shyly held out a souvenir program. "I was

really sorry to have to bother you, but Jamie adores you, and if you'd sign your picture in here, he'd be thrilled to pieces.''

"Well, I'll do more than that," Rick said. "Stay right here and wait for me."

He hurried back to the truck and found the box of T-shirts Liz had left there for the crew's families. He found one he thought would fit a six-year-old and also took a press kit.

"Okay, let's go find Jamie," Rick said when he returned to the gate.

The woman looked at him as if she'd just met an angel. "I don't believe this," she said in wonder, and began to lead the way.

Liz saw Rick walking beside the woman, heading out of the pit area, and abruptly dropped the handle to the wagon. Rusty had loaned her his card to get fuel so she wouldn't have to go all the way back to the garage, and now, hands on her hips, soaking wet with perspiration, she squinted in the glaring sun at Rick and wondered what the heck was going on.

It took only a few seconds for her to decide she would find out. She'd be darned if she was going to haul gas around while he went traipsing off with women.

Abandoning the wagon, she took off behind them, right into the crowded infield.

It was like a sprawling campground. Men sat on top of platforms built on the backs of pickup trucks. Woman lay on the hoods of cars sunbathing. Children ran and played among the picnic tables and folding chairs.

"Hey, look," someone shouted. "It's Rick Castles."

"Hey, Rick," another hollered. "You're the man. You're gonna win the rookie title, for sure. Blow 'em off the track."

A crowd began to gather, asking Rick for autographs and wanting to talk racing. Liz hung back to watch, marveling at his charisma and also his popularity with the fans. Even children were tugging at his sleeve wanting him to sign a cap or T-shirt.

He was obliging, even to the bikini-clad women who fawned over him. He was, Liz realized, certainly different from when she was around him with his fans. He was now loose, laughing, laid-back. Not stilted or coolly polite.

This was a side to him she'd not seen...and one she liked. A lot.

Eventually he moved on, and Liz followed him to where a small boy sat in a chair outside a camper. His right leg was in a cast from ankle to hip. He looked very uncomfortable, but, at the sight of Rick, he became a neon sign of joy.

"Rick Castles. Oh, Mom, wow. I can't believe you got him to come see me."

Rick gave him the press kit and T-shirt, signed the shirt, as well as the cast. Then he sat down and took the time to chat with him and ask how he'd broken his leg, where he was from and so forth.

The boy was entranced, as were his parents and all the fans gathered about to watch.

Afterward, when Rick said his goodbyes and started back toward the garage, Liz surprised him by falling in step beside him.

"Hey, what are you doing here?" He gave her a withering glare of displeasure. "You're supposed to be getting fuel."

She thought about how she'd left the wagon in the middle of pit road and hoped it hadn't been stolen. Rick's car number was painted on it, so maybe it was all right. If not, he was going to be really mad, but she would apologize and buy another. "That was really nice of you, Rick. You're going to be one of the most popular drivers on the circuit. Just wait and see."

He didn't say anything, wondering how much she had seen.

"I was also impressed over how you handled the women. You usually seem to be so averse to having them around."

He stopped walking to look down at her with scathing eyes. "Listen, you've got it all wrong. I have nothing against women race fans. They buy tickets and help make the sport what it is today. I just have a problem with them hanging around me, you got that?

"And that's what you're doing right now," he added to goad. "Hanging around me when you're supposed to be getting fuel."

Suddenly Liz had had it. With a childish stomp of her foot, hands clenched into fists, she met his blistering glare with one of her own. "No, I'm not supposed to be getting fuel. I'm not supposed to do anything that doesn't fit the job description of public relations, by damn."

She gave his chest a hard jab with her finger. "But I did it to help you, only you don't appreciate it. And *I* don't appreciate you using me to do your dirty work, either.

"Look at me," she ranted on, "I'm soaked to the bone with sweat in what has to be the worst heat and humidity I've ever seen. Added to the fact that I'm supposed to be having lunch with your sponsors at this very minute, I've broken two fingernails, all thanks to you."

She wished she had brought her cell phone and swore then and there to strap it to her ankle, if need be, to keep from ever not having it with her. "I'm leaving. I'm going back to the motel if I have to pay a taxi to take me there. Then I'm going to see if I can salvage what's left of the day."

Rick was pleased to see she was starting to break. A few more sweaty days, a couple more broken nails, and she'd decide she wasn't cut out for the job. "Okay. I'll drive you back. Just give me a few more minutes." He was hoping against hope the VIPs would come to the track when Liz didn't show.

A half hour later, Liz had enough of his dawdling. "That's it. I'm out of here."

She was about to peel out of the overalls, when she heard a familiar voice laugh and say, "Well, I think I've seen it all."

She groaned out loud at the sight of Jeff striding toward her with four very important looking suits.

"I hope you're happy," she whispered to Rick.

"Sorry," he murmured. "But there was work to be done."

"And you could've done it without me." Quickly she yanked off the overalls, then remembered she wasn't dressed much better beneath and felt even more foolish.

Jeff made the introductions, and, adding to her misery, Liz forgot to wipe her greasy fingers before shaking the hand of Gary Staley, the CEO of Big Boy's Pizza.

"I am so sorry," she cried, looking around for a rag.

"Not a problem." He took a neatly pressed handkerchief from his pocket and took care of it himself. "You are really something, Miss Mallory."

"I...I don't know what to say." She was floundering for a way to explain herself. She did not want to blame Rick. To do so would mean telling about the possibility the fuel was illegal. That could get everyone in trouble.

"No need to say anything," Gary pleasantly told her. "I think it's obvious we couldn't have asked for a better PR rep for our company."

"Excuse me?" Liz whispered, darting a look at Jeff to see he was beaming with approval.

Gary continued, "When you didn't meet us at the restaurant, and we couldn't get you on your cell phone, Jeff said evidently something was going on at the track. We wanted to see for ourselves, and, believe me, we're glad we did." He gave her a gentle pat on her back. "Good job, young lady. Obviously you needed to lend a hand to some mechanical work here, and that's wonderful of you."

Liz wasn't sure but thought something flashed across Rick's face before he became all smiles to greet the VIPs. He seemed to register annoyance that she'd come out of this smelling like a rose...instead of in hot water.

It dawned then that Rick's animosity toward her was not solely due to his dislike at having women around the track.

The truth was—he did not like her.

And, again, she felt like a fool to think how she had been losing her grip on her emotions despite resolve.

But no more.

If he wanted them to be polite enemies, so be it.

Chapter Five

"I just can't get over how well you're doing on this account, Liz. The sponsors couldn't be more pleased, and neither could I."

It was race day, and it was early. Not quite seven o'clock. Liz and Jeff were supposed to be having breakfast in the motel restaurant, but she was too excited to eat. Her very first race, and she could hardly wait.

"Liz, did you hear me?"

"What? Oh, I'm sorry. I was thinking about something." Actually she'd been imagining Rick soaring around the track at over two hundred miles an hour. She had watched him practice, but racing with forty other cars was going to be different. If he ultimately won, it would be wonderful, but at the very least she wanted him to finish ahead of all the other rookies. It was vital for the points race.

Jeff took a sip of coffee before repeating his compliment.

This time, Liz graciously thanked him, adding, "I have to say it's probably the most fun account I've had."

"Well, to be perfectly honest, I had reservations about giving it to you, but there was nobody else at the time, and you know how quickly it all came together. But later we can work it out for you to be transferred, if you like."

"Oh, no," she said quickly. Too quickly, actually, because Jeff looked at her quizzically over the rim of his coffee cup.

Quelling her enthusiasm, she quietly murmured, "It's a challenge, and I really like it."

"Tell me. What is Rick really like?"

"Well…" She floundered for a response that would not expose how she really felt, how he was drop-dead good-looking, had a cute personality—with everyone but her it seemed. He was also strong, dynamic, and somewhere beneath that rugged, almost feral, part, she sensed a tender, sensual side.

"He's a nice guy," she said finally. "Good with the fans. Gets along with his crew. A terrific driver. I think he's a serious contender for the rookie title."

"Which is what Big Boy's wants. The more exposure he gets, the more pizza they'll sell." He grinned. "At least that's how it's supposed to work."

The waitress came to take their order. Jeff gestured to Liz, but she shook her head. "Nothing. Coffee is fine."

"All right." He ordered for himself—eggs Benedict and orange juice, then said, "I guess there will be a lot of food in the press box if the fare in the VIP box yesterday was any indication. It rivaled Sunday brunch at the Plaza."

"I'm not going to be up in the press box."

"Oh, I forgot. They've got one in the infield, too."

"I'm not going to be there, either. At least not during the race. If Rick does well, I'll go, of course, to put a spin on things, but I plan to be in the pits with the team.

"They're giving me a headset," she went on, unable to contain her excitement any longer. "I'll be able to hear Mack talking to Rick."

Jeff cringed at the thought. "But it's so noisy there, and hot. Good grief, you'll melt."

"And next week at Rockingham I'll probably freeze," she said good-naturedly. "I don't mind, Jeff, really. I want to be where the action is. Not feasting on a lot of sugar and carbs with the media bunch."

"Well, do what you want. As long as the sponsors are happy, I'm happy. Oh, hey—"

He waved, and when Liz saw who it was, she felt the familiar, thrilling rush.

"Morning, Jeff," Rick said pleasantly, taking off his cap.

Liz almost missed the nod he gave in her direction, for it came and went so quickly.

Jeff beamed. "Wearing the Big Boy's cap, I see."

"Oh, yes, sir. And I've got a lot of others to remember to put on if I win the race."

"Oh, that's right," Jeff said, "I remember seeing on TV how the driver changes caps so many times in victory lane."

"That would be my job to help him, I suppose," Liz said to no one in particular. "It's considered a courtesy for the driver's PR person to help him switch hats for photo takes. Every sponsor that spends money on the car, by way of decals or whatever, wants a picture of the driver with the company logo."

"Don't worry about it, Liz," Rick said, almost mockingly. "If I do luck out and win, there will be plenty of folks around to help me with hats. Besides, it's a long way from the media tower to victory lane."

She replied equally as tongue in cheek. "True. But it's not far at all from the pits."

He looked at her then, unable to conceal the annoyance that flashed across his face. "What did you say?"

"Oh, come on and sit down," Jeff said, pulling out the chair next to him. "I've already ordered. Liz didn't want anything." He nodded to Mack, who walked up just then. "You, too."

Mack declined. "Thanks, but I just came to speak to my wife. She's over on the other side with her parents. See you all at the track."

He walked away, but Rick hung back. "Liz, what did you mean about being in the pits?"

"That's where I plan to watch the race."

"But that's ridiculous."

"Why do you say that? I know of several PR guys planning to do the same thing."

"Not that many. And the key word is *guys.*"

Jeff noticed the tension and looked from one to the other. "You have a problem with her being in the pits, Rick?"

Mack called, "Hey, Rick, do you want coffee to go? We gotta hustle, man, before the traffic gets bad."

"Yeah, fine," Rick told him, eyes on Liz the whole time. Then he forced a smile and told Jeff it was okay. "I just worry it's dangerous. See you two later."

"Nice that he's concerned about you," Jeff commented after Rick walked away. "You two get along well, do you?"

Liz could tell by Jeff's crafty smile what he was thinking and decided to nip that notion in the bud then and there. "We have a professional relationship and nothing more."

He continued to smile. "I wasn't suggesting anything else. I think it's nice he takes a personal interest in your safety and well-being, that's all."

The waitress brought his breakfast, and Liz was relieved Jeff turned his attention to that and let the subject drop.

Interest in her safety and well-being, indeed, she bitterly mused. Rick just did not want her around—period. For some strange reason he seemed to have hated her at first sight, and she would just have to deal with it…as well as her helpless, hopeless, attraction to him.

"What's with you and Liz?" Mack bluntly asked of Rick as they drove to the track. The other crew members were in different cars.

Rick gave him a sharp glance of surprise. "I don't know what you're talking about."

"How come you don't like her?"

"I never said I didn't."

"You never said you did, either."

"So?" Rick shrugged, pretending indifference. "It doesn't matter, anyway. She's got a job to do. And so have I."

"Yeah, but it's obvious you don't want her around. The crew and I were talking about it, and it's a shame. She tries really hard. And you have to admit she's got you more press exposure in a week than you've had in your whole career."

"Maybe so, but you have to remember my career, thus far, has been dinky little dirt tracks in the South. Besides, this is Daytona, and it's oversaturated with journalists looking for something to write about. She didn't have to twist their arms."

"Well, she pointed them in your direction."

Rick did not like the conversation. "Can we talk about something else—like the five hundred miles I'm about to race? I'd think that'd be foremost in your mind instead of some bimbo."

"Hey, Liz is no bimbo. And I think you ought to lighten up on her. You don't make her job any easier by being surly."

"Surly?" Rick echoed, indignant. "I'm as nice as I can be to my fans—to all the race fans—and you know it. So how come you're on my case?"

"Because it's obvious you give Liz a hard time. I mean, sure, I can understand your clowning around when you first met, but you act like you're ready to snap her head off over the least little thing."

Rick knew that was probably true but was not about to admit it. "You're imagining things."

"And you've got to remember she's not like the others."

That rankled, and Rick snapped, "I don't need this, Mack. Especially now."

"Okay. You're right. I'm sorry. You don't. But when I was walking up to the table, I saw and heard how excited she was over being in the pits during the race. But you sure busted her bubble of joy with your reaction."

"I don't like women up close and personal at the track and you know it…just like you know my reasons."

"Yeah, I remember lots of hysteria at the short tracks. Drivers' girlfriends getting in fights with other drivers' girlfriends over something that happened on the track.

"I seem to recall," he added mischievously, "that a few of yours had a catfight or two."

"We were younger then, and the short tracks were the bull rings. Anything went. It's different in NASCAR."

"Then why are you opposed to Liz being around? She's got a reason, man. She's your PR rep. She can't help it if she's a babe." He gave Rick a nudge with his elbow. "And don't tell me you haven't noticed."

Rick had noticed, all right, too many times to count. But that had nothing to do with it. He was around beautiful women all the time. Beauty queens—titled Miss Something or other—were always being escorted around the pits and garage. He didn't mind. They came and went.

Which is what he wanted Liz to do.

And the sooner the better.

Mack dared to point out, "Maybe that's the problem— you have noticed. And it bugs you. I remember what you said after you and Maggie broke up—how you'd never get involved with another woman while you were racing, but sometimes things happen to make you change your mind."

"Such as?"

"Such as a cute PR gal."

"You're crazy. And I wish you'd stay out of my business, Mack."

"In a way, I think it is my business, because me and the guys are afraid your attitude might get us in bad with the sponsor if Liz goes back and tells it."

"What's to tell? I don't like women around the tracks, that's all. But I'm polite to them, and to Liz, and more than that I don't think you or anybody else has a right to ask.

"*Now* can we talk about the race?" he asked with finality.

Mack obliged, immediately launching into strategy, how

long the tires should last, worries over making quick pit stops…all the things crew chiefs were concerned with.

Rick was glad Mack quickly got lost in himself, because he'd just been given a wake-up call.

He had to be real nice to Liz around the crew.

There was just no way he could let them ever say he gave her a hard time.

But Mack had triggered something else—thoughts of Maggie.

God, he had loved her once upon a time, but she had proved love can quickly turn to hate.

No, not hate.

Rick didn't hate her. He didn't think he was capable of hating anybody.

But she had sure destroyed any feelings of love he'd had.

One night she was in his arms, all fire and passion, saying she wanted to make sure he didn't forget her while he was off racing for the next two weeks. And he had sworn there was no way that could happen. He was only twenty years old, just getting started in racing, unsure of himself in lots of ways but not when it came to Maggie. Not then. Because she swore she loved him with every breath in her body. And he had believed her.

They had met at a short dirt track in Savannah, Georgia. Maggie was there visiting her cousin. They'd gone to the race as a lark, but she said later that when she saw him from the grandstand through binoculars, she knew she had to meet him.

And she had.

He had won the race, and, afterward, Maggie had fought her way through the crowd to introduce herself and ask for his autograph.

Only she hadn't wanted it on a souvenir program.

Nor on a piece of paper.

She had boldly whispered in his ear that she wanted it in a very personal place.

Later that night, Rick had obliged, and they were together from then on.

Maggie was a knockout. Blond hair, big brown eyes, and a body guys drooled over.

Rick was young, naive, and hadn't had much experience with women. He believed Maggie when she promised a forever kind of love. They had wed, moved into a double wide in his hometown of Dalton, and she went through the motions of settling down to married life.

Unfortunately, that hadn't lasted long.

All too soon she began nagging at him to quit racing and get a real job. She wanted to start a family, but she wanted a husband around to help. Also, the money he was making back then just didn't stretch far enough, not with Maggie's expensive tastes.

Still, he believed she loved him, and he begged her to bear with him. Give him a chance to make it big. He'd make it up to her later.

She consented...or pretended to.

And two weeks after she'd made love to him so fervently it had made him hot to think about it the whole time he was gone, he returned to find a note saying she'd moved out. She couldn't take it any longer. She was running away with a man who could be there for her all the time.

Rick heard later she had moved to Florida, marrying her new love before the ink on the divorce papers was dry.

For a long time after that, Rick blamed himself. After all, she had given him warning...told him she was miserable the way things were with him on the road all the time. She got lonely. And somebody else was around to ease her ache.

For a long time Rick tortured himself with thinking how maybe he could have stopped it...could have saved the marriage. All he would have had to do was give up racing and get a regular job. He'd make decent wages. He and Maggie could have had a good life. Kids. The whole nine yards marriage is made up of.

Only he hadn't.

And now that he was over her completely, he could see it probably would never have worked, not when she could walk out on him so easily and never look back.

As time had passed, he was confident he had done the right thing. Racing was his life, and Maggie had known that when she met him…known it when they married. She had promised to accept it but hadn't been able to. And even though his guilt over his failed marriage eventually faded, Rick vowed that only when he parked the race car for the last time would he marry again.

The years passed. His short track career took off, and he made decent money. So did Mack as co-owner of the car and crew chief. Rick started a savings account. He had a few girlfriends here and there who didn't want to get married, much less care what he did for a living. Yeah, *that kind,* but what difference did it make the way he was spinning his wheels when it came to romance?

He was glad when they reached the track, relieved to be caught up once more in the thrill of it all.

"We're gonna do good today," Mack said, pounding the steering wheel with his hands as they drove through the tunnel into the infield. "I can just feel it in my bones."

"Me, too," Rick said, although he didn't. Mack believed in positive thinking and getting all hyped up over something. Rick just believed in doing his best and whatever happened, happened.

"I think now that we've got a big-money sponsor, you're a cinch to win the rookie title. We'll have all the parts and supplies we need, you're a good driver, so the sky's the limit."

"With a little bit of luck," Rick reminded him.

"Oh, we've got plenty of that," Mack said confidently. "Like with Liz. It was just luck we got her for PR. She was telling me the other day how it all happened fast, and she was the only one available to take the account. Otherwise, they'd have sent a guy who might not have been willing to try like she does. I mean, she gives a hundred and fifty percent, you know?''

Rick did not want to hear any more about Liz. Not now. He needed to focus on the race, not think about smoldering green eyes and a soft, sweet laugh that made him feel like a teen with his first crush.

Trying to shut him up, Rick goaded, ''Does Rosie know you've got a thing about Liz?''

Mack hooted. ''Me? Why, no. I mean, she knows I'm impressed with what she's been doing…that I like her as a friend, but that's it.''

''Are you sure?''

''Yeah, I'm sure,'' Mack said, sounding a little defensive.

''Then how come you can't stop talking about her?''

They were through the tunnel, once more in the brilliant blue sky, the sun beating down as seagulls drifted in the gentle Florida breeze.

Mack slowed, despite the bumper-to-bumper traffic, to turn and look Rick straight in the eye. ''I keep talking about her, because I don't like how you can't seem to stand her, Rick. I know you've got this thing about women and racing, and I'm afraid you'll run her off…whether intentionally or not. I like her. The guys like her. So whatever you feel, or don't feel, I'd appreciate it if you'd chill out. Do your job. Let her do hers. Leave it at that if you want, but I think deep down you just might be fighting your true feelings here.''

''You're crazy.''

''No, I'm not. I think you do like her, and that's what's bugging you.''

Rick chuckled at the supposed incredulity of such an idea. ''I don't see how in the world you came up with that notion, Mack. I think you've been out in the sun too much this week. So put a sock in it, okay? And let's get busy and race.''

Like her? he silently scoffed as they drove on toward the paddock area reserved for drivers, crews and their families. She was a pain in the butt. She also had the staying power of superglue. No matter what he said to her, she came right back at him. Maybe in the beginning she had been easily intimidated, but evidently when she wasn't at some fancy corporate party she was doing her homework. He had to admit she had quickly learned enough about racing to carry on an intelligent conversation.

But she was still new to the game. A real rookie. And, being a woman, sooner or later she would cave.

Then he would be rid of her and, hopefully, the dreams about her, as well.

Liz was not feeling well. She was so keyed up and excited she hadn't been able to even finish her coffee at breakfast.

It was overwhelming, and she was loving every second of it, but she was also exhausted.

During the day, she was at the track, trying to drum up interviews and appearances for Rick, and passing out press kits and free caps to the media. And since Daytona was the first race on the schedule, there was lots of socializing. Some nights she'd felt the need to show up at several parties after being in attendance with Rick at things she'd managed to set up for him. Then, when she had finally gotten back to her room, she had studied her racing books till she couldn't hold her eyes open any longer. So she'd had very little sleep and was glad it would soon be over...for a few days, anyway.

Also she had not been eating the way she should. Finger food at cocktail parties, a bite of a hot dog at the track. Food on the go. So in addition to being worn-out, her diet had also suffered.

Jeff rode with her in her car to the track. The airport was adjacent. He'd have no trouble getting there for his flight back to New York after the race.

They went together to the VIP section where Big Boy's had rented a private booth for the bigwigs and their special guests. Arena-style seating in soft cushioned chairs before floor-to-ceiling windows allowed for a panoramic view of the two-and-a-half-mile oval speedway. In the rear, tables were laden with gourmet treats, all catered by white-jacketed

waiters. Champagne was on ice, and a bartender stood ready
to fill any drink order.

And, of course, there was plenty of pizza. Special ovens
had been brought in to make sure it was hot and fresh. Liz
suggested that trays be sent to the press box to schmooze the
sportswriters, and Jeff said it was a great idea.

Liz made sure she introduced herself to everyone, shook
their hands, urged them to let her know if they needed any
information at all about their driver. She said and did all the
right things.

"Are you sure you don't want to stay up here?" Jeff asked
as she made ready to leave.

She could see the drivers were lining up to be introduced
at the start and finish line. She had wanted to be there to see
Rick when he waved to the crowd, dressed in his colorful
new driver's suit. But she had tarried too long and would
have to hurry if she were to cross the track before NASCAR
closed the gates from the grandstands. "I really want to be
down there, Jeff. If anything should happen, good or bad, I
need to be around."

He warned, "It's going to be awful hot out there. Try to
stay in the infield press room as much as you can, where it's
air-conditioned."

"Sure, sure," she said, knowing she would take her place
behind the pit wall in the section marked for car sixty. "Talk
to you next week."

Jeff gave her a thumbs-up. "Good job, Mallory."

She hurried out, feeling a little dizzy. The smell of pizza
hadn't helped her stomach any, and she wondered if she
should have a cracker, then laughed at such a notion. Crack-
ers at a racetrack? Get real. They'd be about as available as
chicken noodle soup.

The ride to ground level in the elevator made her so woozy
she had to grip the railings to steady herself. Then she was
outside and pushing through the crowds, trying to keep from
stumbling as she walked down the steps toward the high
chain link fencing that separated the stands from the track.

"You just made it, lady," the track official said as he ushered Liz through the gate. "Hurry now."

Running across the already steaming asphalt was sheer misery. By the time she reached the pit area, she longed for a cool drink and a place to sit down.

Mack stuck a clipboard and pen in her hand and handed her a headset and a stop watch. "Try to keep up with his lap times if you can."

The cars began the parade laps. One of the crew members helped Liz climb up into a tall, wooden chair. She was grateful for the tiny umbrella perched over it that offered some respite from the relentless sun.

But there was nothing to be done about the oppressive heat, which only got worse as the race got under way. The hot roaring engines and the blistering tires on the asphalt sent temperatures soaring. Liz wondered how the drivers stood it.

When Rick came in for his first pit stop, she watched as one of the crew members handed him a big bottle of cool water. He drank some of it, then squirted the rest of it on his face.

At one point, Mack called up to her, "You doing okay?"

She was fanning herself with the clipboard. "Yes, but next time I'm going to bring one of those little battery-operated fans."

"You don't look so good. How about going over to the media room and resting a spell to cool off?"

"No. It's my first race, and as long as my driver is on that track, I'm watching."

But Mack did not hear her, having turned back to the action on the track.

There were spinouts that brought the crowds to their feet. Liz bolted upright, too, anxious to make sure Rick was not involved. Then there was a crash, and she held her breath till she saw number sixty streak right past the melee.

Now and then a crew member would remember to hand her a bottle of cool water. Twice during the afternoon she got down off the chair to go to the rest room. Splashing water on her face, she was stunned at how pale she looked.

But there would be time to rest later.

She had to get back out there and keep an eye on Rick, all the while telling herself it was just a job. Nothing more.

The roar of the crowd was deafening as the gleaming red Monte Carlo whizzed down the front stretch.

Rick was in fourth place with fifty laps to go. Phenomenal for a rookie, and he actually had a chance to win.

And then it happened.

A car spun directly in front of him, and, to keep from hitting him in the driver's door—called a T-bone—which could be fatal to the driver, Rick took the wall.

He smacked on the side, felt sheet metal crumple, then spun sideways, tires smoking. All the while he prayed with gritted teeth that nobody else would slam into him. Then, mercifully, he was on the apron and sliding to a stop.

By the time the emergency crew got to him, Rick had unsnapped the window netting and crawled out, unscathed.

He was staring mournfully at the damage that had taken him out of the race when Benny and a few other crew members came running up to ask if he was all right.

"Yeah, yeah, I'm fine, but the car's had it for the day. Damn it, we were running good, too." He glanced around. "Where's Mack?"

"He stayed with Liz, to make sure she's gonna be all right."

Rick was kneeling beside the car but quickly straightened. "What's wrong with her?"

Benny flashed a knowing grin. "I guess you're right about women at racetracks, Rick."

Rick tensed. "What are you talking about?"

"When you spun out, she fainted."

Rick shook his head in disgust and once more thought the sooner he got rid of her, the better.

Chapter Six

By midweek after Daytona, Liz was ready to go again, but Jeff phoned to advise her to take it easy.

"You gave us quite a scare," he said. "So get some rest."

She insisted she was fine. "The heat got to me, and I hadn't been eating like I should. The doctors said that's all it was."

"Still, you'll make the Big Boy's folks feel a lot better if I can tell them you're going to stay in bed for a while."

"No way," she said emphatically. "I'm not about to miss a race if I can help it. Besides, I've always heard Rockingham is a beautiful place. It's in the area known as the Sandhills of North Carolina."

Jeff warned, "It's also still February, and the weather report doesn't look good. I hear that race has been snowed out a few times."

"Think positive. Besides, it's nice and warm here in Charlotte, and it's already Wednesday."

"Have it your way, but take care of yourself."

After he hung up, Liz stared at the phone, trying to recall once again what had happened last Sunday. For the life of her, it was just a big, gray fog.

She had been perched high up on her chair, the umbrella giving some shade, but the heat and glare radiating from the concrete below was almost blinding. It also felt like steam was rising. She longed for shorts, halter top and a cool breeze.

The race had gotten tight, and Rick's crew naturally forgot about her. There were no more bottles of cold water passed up. And she was not about to climb down and get her own, her eyes glued to number sixty as it circled the track.

Then things began to blur just as a huge wave of sound erupted from not only the grandstands but the infield and pit areas as well. Something was happening on the track, and Liz shielded her eyes with her hands and tried to see what it was.

And that was when the feeling of steam rising from the concrete had become a choking fog, swirling around to make her sway as she struggled to breathe.

Through the confusing mist, Liz was able to grasp that she had to get down off her perch or she was going to fall.

One foot, then two. Turning, she grabbed the arms of the chair and continued trying to get down. She felt violently sick to her stomach, and her head was throbbing.

And then there was nothing.

She awoke in the infield hospital with unfamiliar faces staring down at her. A doctor asked what she had eaten, how much she'd had to drink. When she admitted she'd had no food and very little water, he said she was dehydrated. He had wanted her admitted to a hospital overnight and given fluids, but she had refused, insisting she'd be fine.

Mack came to see how she was doing. He said Rick had hit the wall and spun out, and he wasn't sure where he finished. He was on his way to find out and also see how badly the car was damaged.

She had planned to join them, but the doctor insisted she have one bag of IV fluids before he would allow her to leave.

Then, just as she thought she could escape and go find out about Rick, an aide to the CEO of Big Boy's came to escort her to the corporate jet. She was flown directly to Charlotte, where a car was waiting at the airport to take her to her apartment. Her luggage was picked up and delivered, as well as her rental car, which she had left parked at the airport.

"Nothing like working for the big guys," Jeff had said when he heard of her VIP treatment. "They really like you, Liz."

She was appreciative but also embarrassed to have caused such a stir.

She wondered what Rick thought about it all. The team had driven all night after the race to return to the shop in Charlotte. They had to get ready to leave for Rockingham. She had read in the paper about the wreck, how Rick spun out, and felt bad for him and the whole team.

The phone rang, startling her from her reverie.

It was Mack, saying they were about to leave and had a few questions about when checks would be received for expenses and so forth. She told him to get all receipts to her, and she'd prepare reports.

When she said she'd see him in Rockingham the next day, he was surprised.

"You really feel up to it?"

"Of course, I do. I just fainted, for heaven's sake. And I didn't even get hurt when I fell."

"Well, if I were you I'd just settle in and not plan to go. The weather report looks bad. You're probably making the trip for nothing, and so are we, but we don't have a choice."

She told him she'd be there, anyway, not about to miss anything. Besides, if the weather forecasters were wrong, as they sometimes were, she'd be miserable at home watching the race on TV.

"So the car wasn't messed up too badly from the wreck?"

He said it was mostly sheet metal damage. "We had that

banged out before we even loaded it on the truck. No problem. See you this weekend.''

"For sure. By the way, is Rick really okay? I saw it on the news, and he really slammed into that wall. Do I need to get out a press release assuring everyone he's all right to race?" She had been worried but had hesitated to call him, instead relying on Mack to let her know what was going on.

"He's fine. Now give me a call on my cell phone if you decide to stay home and keep warm this weekend. See you."

"Yeah, see you."

Liz hung up and got busy packing. Nothing was going to keep her from going to Rockingham. The sponsors thought she was doing a great job. So did her boss.

But she was just dedicated, that's all.

Wanting to see Rick again had nothing to do with it.

At least that's what she wanted to believe.

The air was crisp and cold and pungent with the sweet fragrance of pine. The sandhills of North Carolina were known for rolling plains, covered in pine needles. It was golf country, as well as horse country.

Liz had fallen in love with the area on sight.

But the air also smelled like snow, and the dark gray clouds gathering overhead were likewise ominous.

Time trials had been held without a hitch. Liz was thrilled Rick made the top fifteen in the lineup for Sunday's race…if there were to be a race. It was now Saturday, and everyone was holed up in their motel rooms as the temperatures plunged and snow flurries began whipping through the air.

Liz had taken the team out for an early steak dinner at a restaurant across the highway from the motel. Rick had sat at the opposite end of the table, ignoring her as much as possible but polite when it was necessary for them to talk to each other.

If the race were snowed out, it would be run on Monday—weather permitting. If not, it would be worked into the schedule later.

Next up was Las Vegas, and she had waited till the whole team was gathered for dinner to announce the good news she'd received via e-mail on her laptop computer only a few hours earlier. The sponsor was having delivered to the Charlotte shop on Monday a brand-new hauler for the race car. There was even sleeping space for the crew, but, she said, they would be flown out so they wouldn't be tired from the long drive.

The team cheered, but Liz noticed Rick didn't seem to share their enthusiasm and wondered why. If something was bothering him she figured it was part of her job to find out. After all, if he was feeling down, it could affect how he was perceived by not only his fans but also by the media. Rumors would start flying. She'd heard how that happened often in racing. Crew chiefs were hired away. Drivers switched around. She did not want that sort of gossip circulating about *her* team.

After dinner, everyone had retired to their rooms. There was not much hope the race would be run, but they had to be rested and ready in case it was. That was why Liz did not call Rick later that night to try to find out what was going on with him, if anything. After the race, she'd make it a point to hang around for a one-on-one chat. So what if he didn't like her? She was his PR person and was there to help if he'd let her. If he didn't, well, at least she'd know she had tried.

The next morning Liz opened her drapes to a winter wonderland. The snow was already up to the hubcaps of the cars in the motel parking lot and still coming down heavy. There was no way the race would be run.

The phone rang. It was Mack, confirming it. "But the good news is that according to the latest weather bulletin, this is a fast-moving front. It should be out of here by midday and then it's supposed to warm up. Things should be melted by morning, and the race is set to run then."

"And meanwhile we stay over and play in the snow," she said, looking forward to it. "See you at breakfast."

Liz was not prepared for such weather. She had jeans and a heavy jacket but no gloves or boots. As she made her way along the sidewalk to the motel restaurant in the front, she decided she had spoken too soon about snow games.

And that was when a huge snowball hit her right on the side of her head.

It was Benny, and before he could roll another, Liz had scooped up a handful of snow and made one of her own. She threw and hit him dead center in his face.

"Hey, you'll pay for that."

He took off after her as she tried to run down the snow-covered walkway.

"In here," someone shouted, yanking her into a room as she ran by.

"It's us against them," a bevy of sportswriters chorused. "Get ready, we're going to hit 'em hard."

Liz was amazed to see ice buckets filled with snowballs. "What have you guys done? Stayed up all night getting ready?"

"That's right," cried a writer she recognized from Atlanta as he opened the door to throw a snowball at another driver.

Quickly it became an all-out war. The media against the drivers. Liz joined in the fun and got in her share of dead hits. But she took a few herself, and it wasn't long before she was soaking wet, her hair stringing down.

Anxious for a hot bath and dry clothes, she rolled one last, huge snowball and threw it without really looking.

It hit Rick square in the back of his head, breaking apart to run down the collar of his brand-new leather racing jacket emblazoned with their sponsor logo. Liz had just passed the jackets out to the team the day before.

He whirled about to identify his assailant and locked eyes with Liz.

Her hand flew to her mouth to stifle the giggle she was trying to hold back. "Oops."

"Oops, indeed," he roared, and started toward her.

Liz was right in front of her room and turned around to try to fit her key in the lock. Her hands were cold and shaking, and she did not make it in time.

Rick was upon her.

"Now you're going to pay. Ruin my jacket, will you?"

"Hey, it's not ruined," she protested as he grabbed her and pulled her out into the snow-covered parking lot. "And if it were, I'd get you another one, and—"

That was all she had time to say before they reached a snowdrift and he put his hand on the back of her neck and bent her over to wash her face in snow.

He stood back, hands on his hips, looking quite proud of himself. "There. We're even."

"Not yet," Liz cried, scooping up snow and flinging it wildly.

He grabbed her, laughing all the while, and they rolled, over and over.

Mack walked by, heading for the restaurant, and paused to shake his head and tell them they were both crazy and would probably catch pneumonia and die. Then he continued on, dismissing them as pesky children.

Rick was on top of Liz, holding her wrists with one hand while he used his other to throw snow on her. Suddenly, abruptly, he stopped. "He...he might be right," he said slowly, then got to his feet, pulling her up along with him. "I guess we got a little carried away."

"The hidden child within us," Liz said, no longer cold. How could she be with him standing so close? "I can't remember the last time I had a snowball fight."

The others who had engaged in the playful combat had drifted away, wanting dry clothes and warmth.

"I guess so," Rick murmured, dusting off his jacket.

"It isn't ruined, is it? It's leather, and—"

"It's fine. Just wet. I'll go back to my room and hang it up to dry."

She looked down and laughed at herself. "I look like a snowman getting ready to melt. What a mess."

"That makes two of us."

He walked away, and Liz resisted the temptation to stand out in the cold and watch him. It made her feel so wicked to lust after his retreating butt. He had a nice one, all right.

But so had Mike and Craig, and they'd done their best to ruin her life. She was not going to let it happen again.

Besides, Rick couldn't stand her, so that made him easier to resist.

She hoped.

Still, as she stood in the shower, the hot water streaming down, her heart began a heavy, strong beat as heat began to creep through her. A restless feeling, aching and throbbing, stirred inside. She felt her breasts tighten as she soaped them, remembering how it had felt when Rick had been lying on top of her. Had he felt them, too? Her jacket had come open. Her sweater had been wet and plastered against her. She hadn't been wearing a bra.

What if he had suddenly caressed them and begun to knead her flesh beneath his palms? Could she have pushed him away? Feeling a tingling between her legs, she knew she could not have. He had, in those few moments of frolic in the snow, awakened instincts and needs she had tried to quell and bury within to focus instead on her career. Now she found it frightening that he had so easily been able to make her body aware of such strong emotions.

She suddenly realized she was breathing heavily, bosom heaving, and scolded herself. This was lust, pure and simple, as well as betrayal by her own body.

She could not let it happen.

Turning off the water, she wrapped a towel around her and dug her hair dryer out of her bag.

This was silly. To allow herself to become aroused in a ridiculous snowball fight was absurd. Here she was actually imagining how it would have felt for him to touch her intimately, while he was probably thinking how immature she was.

"Okay, okay," she said out loud to the mirror and her flushed reflection. "Get a grip here. The guy hates you. He enjoyed wiping your face in the snow, and he couldn't wait to get away afterward."

She dried her hair, put on makeup and found a clean pair of jeans and a sweater she'd thought to pack just in case.

Her stomach gave a hungry rumble, and she went into high gear to finish dressing. No way was she going to let herself get in the same shape as she had in Daytona.

When Liz reached the restaurant, she met Mack coming out the door with two paper sacks. "Hey, you're too late. They just shut down and won't open back up till five. But you're in luck. I was picking up the order Rick phoned in, and if you want to take it to him you might be able to make him share. I happen to know there are two hot chocolates in there and an extra doughnut."

He thrust the bags into her arms.

"And where are you going? Why can't you deliver it?"

He winked. "The boys just got a little card game together in Benny's room, and I think they've actually found a pizza delivery place with four-wheel drive. But don't tell our sponsor," he added conspiratorially. "It's a rival company. See you."

Liz was too hungry to be shy about asking Rick for handouts. She went straight to his door, knocked and, when he answered, promptly said, "I've been elected delivery boy, and for my tip I'll take the extra hot chocolate and doughnut. The restaurant was closing when I got there."

He almost smiled...but didn't. "What happened to Mack?"

"Card game in Benny's room."

"It figures. Come on in. I'll dig out your share."

Stepping inside, she closed the door after her to shutout

the bitter cold wind. If a warming trend was coming, it sure had a long way to get there.

Rick took the sacks to the dresser and opened them. He took out two drink containers and a cardboard box that smelled of bacon, eggs and hot buttered biscuits. "Want any of this?" he asked tonelessly. "There's plenty."

"No. Just the chocolate and doughnut."

Glancing about, she felt like an intruder. It was so intimate. His suitcase was opened on the second bed, which was still made, shaving stuff on the bathroom sink.

Her gaze went to the other bed. The covers were mussed, but it looked cozy, and she had a brief, scalding image of lying there with him, her head on his shoulder, his arms tight about her....

"Here."

She jumped, almost spilling the white foam container of hot chocolate he handed her.

"Sit down and drink it. You look like you could use it, and it'll be cold by the time you get to your room."

She could not tell if he was merely being polite but decided it didn't matter. It was nice to sip the chocolate then and there, while it was warm. She also noticed he was using a plastic fork to scoop eggs and bacon onto one of the biscuits and prayed it was for her.

It was.

And she all but wolfed it down. "I'm sorry. I don't mean to look like a glutton." She laughed self-consciously. "But we went to dinner so early last night, and it's almost lunchtime."

"It's okay." He took his food and sat down on the side of the bed and began to eat. "If we hadn't gotten into that silly fight, you'd have made it to the restaurant before it closed."

"Well, normally they're open for lunch, but it seems they had such a crowd because of the snow they're running out of food and have to try to find a way to get more."

He picked up the remote control, clicked it and began to

channel-surf. Liz figured it was a hint he didn't want to make conversation and supposed she should take her food and leave. But she didn't want to, instead seizing the opportunity to try to get to know him better and perhaps figure out why he didn't like her. "So what do you do with yourself when you aren't racing?"

He gave a sarcastic sniff. "And when would that be? We've got a thirty-four-race schedule, and they plan to open two more tracks in the future. With makeup dates, there's precious little time left."

"So what do you do with it when you have it?" she persisted. "You don't have any family, do you?"

He gave her a sharp glance, then turned back to the TV. "Why do you ask?"

"It's my job. I do your press releases, remember? I need to know everything about you."

"There's nothing to know. I race. I work on the race car. I read about racing. It's my life. That's it."

"But surely you've got some hobbies."

He shrugged. "Nope. But when I have time I like to be outdoors—hunting, fishing, hiking. Whatever. I just like being in the open air."

"What about girlfriends?"

This time the sharp glance lingered to become one of annoyed challenge. "Now don't tell me you need to put anything like that in a press release."

She could have kicked herself for going there. "Sorry. I was just curious. Sometimes it helps to know a little bit about a person's private life, so you can understand them better."

"Well, don't worry about my personal life." Then he surprised her by asking, "What about yours?"

"What…what about mine?" she stammered.

"You got a boyfriend? Engaged? Married? Kids? See, Liz, I don't know anything about you, but you're asking about me all the time. Fair's fair." His grin was slow and lazy. He set the paper plates aside and leaned back against the pillows. "So tell me all about you."

Liz took several sips of her chocolate and then said, "No boyfriend. Engaged once upon a time. No children. I'm afraid that's all there is to know about me."

"No, it isn't. I've been wanting to ask you why on earth you'd want to work in a man's sport."

"That—" she struggled to keep from choking on a burst of laughter "—is so sixties, Rick. There are no men's sports, or women's, either, for that matter. Even in football, there are women coaches now. So I hardly think stock-car racing could be considered for men only. Do you have any idea how many women producers there are working in NASCAR TV productions? Women actually behind the cameras?" She shook her head at his absurd notion. "You're really behind the times."

Thin, tight lines about his mouth were the only hint of annoyance over her ridicule. "Well, I haven't seen one get down and dirty in a garage yet like you did, so I guess that's to your credit."

"That was a one-time-only performance, thank you," she said with a perky nod. "But if need be, I'd do it again.

"Now it's my turn to ask questions," she rushed on, not giving him a chance to say anything. "I think it's really weird how you've got such a thing against women around racing."

He came right back at her. "Not all women. You see, I don't give a damn how many women are around at a track, just so they aren't around me. They're a nuisance."

Liz felt the familiar wave of anger starting to flow over her. Rick really knew how to push her buttons and get her riled, but she was going to hold her temper if it killed her. "And you consider me a nuisance?" she asked sweetly. "I should think you'd be grateful I'm doing such a good job. Everyone else on the team seems to be."

"I didn't say you weren't."

He was still channel-surfing, not looking at her when he spoke, which she found quite annoying. "But you're saying I'm a nuisance."

"Sometimes, yes."

"Even though I've got you more press coverage than you've ever had before?"

"I've never had a sponsor before that could afford to hire PR. So how do I know someone else couldn't have done the same?"

"You," she said, drawing a deep breath and letting it out in an exasperated rush, "are the most ungrateful person I think I have ever met. But I'll bet if you had a man doing your PR, you wouldn't consider him a nuisance."

"I would if he'd fainted when I spun out."

Liz did not, at first, grasp his meaning and was stunned when she did. "That...that is not why I passed out," she said tightly, angrily, her vow to hold her temper tossed aside. "I was dehydrated. The heat got to me. Plus I hadn't been eating like I should. I was also exhausted."

She stared at him in wonder. "But you actually think it was because I was so upset over you wrecking? I didn't even know you had. Besides, I've seen a few drivers wreck, and I didn't faint over them, so what makes you think you're so darn special?"

She got to her feet, throwing her empty chocolate cup into a wastebasket with a vengeance. "I swear, Rick, I don't know why I even bother trying to get along with you. You are absolutely the most pigheaded—"

Rick was off the bed in a shot to grab her arm and keep her from rushing out the door. Already her hand was on the knob, and he was not about to risk anyone seeing her upset. Especially coming out of his room. He didn't care that she was mad. He just didn't want speculation as to why. "Listen. I'm sorry. I didn't know."

"Well, now you do." She looked up at him with green eyes shooting red daggers of fury.

"Maybe I thought you were taking things too personal, getting too close to the team, to me. I apologize, Liz."

"Fine. But you still don't think I can handle the pressure, do you?"

He continued to hold her tightly. "Well, I guess we're all going to find out, because things can only get rougher. Racing is not a gentle sport, Liz."

"Don't worry about me. I promise I won't get in your way."

He let her go and ran irritated fingers through his hair.

"Sorry I ruffled your feathers again," she said. "But quite frankly, I doubt you could work with any woman, so I'm not going to take any of this personally."

It was all he could do to keep from taking her in his arms and kissing her till they were both breathless. To fight the notion…the temptation, he coolly suggested, "Maybe I should talk to the folks at Big Boy's and see if they could assign somebody else. You and I just seem to rub each other the wrong way."

"Not a chance," she mustered the bravado to say. "They love me. They won't replace me unless I ask.

"And if I were you," she paused after opening the door, "I wouldn't hold my breath waiting for that to happen."

After she was gone, Rick felt like smashing something. But he didn't. Instead he threw himself across the bed to stare up at the ceiling and wonder, not for the first time, why, every time they were together, they sparred. Evidently, she was the type to carry a grudge and would never get over his prank when they first met, which was probably for the best.

No, he corrected himself.

There was no *probably* to it.

It *was* best, because if they did get along, he might be tempted to yield to the feelings he was fighting so hard against. This way was better. If he couldn't get rid of her, as he'd hoped and planned to do, then let them be mortal enemies. He'd do his job, cooperate with any public appearances…anything that was asked of him.

Other than that, he'd avoid her like the plague.

He continued to stare up at the ceiling. He'd had races postponed when he was running the short track circuit, and he'd always found something—*someone*—to keep from getting bored.

He reached for the phone.

It had been a long time, and he was more than ready.

Chapter Seven

Rick's idea to call an old girlfriend to try to get his mind off Liz did not work.

Dina Fox lived in Rockingham, and when he had phoned her and asked her out that night, she had driven right over to the motel, since the roads had been cleared of snow.

They had gone to dinner, and Rick found himself wondering what he'd ever seen in her in the first place. She drank too much, giggled too much, and kept whispering how she couldn't wait to get back to the motel and get him in bed.

He did not share her enthusiasm. Maybe once upon a time, he'd have been just as eager. But not now. No more wild nights and waking up the next morning feeling like hell. Sure, after his marriage breakup, he'd been a little reckless trying to get over it, but things were different now.

Then, as he and Dina were leaving the restaurant and he was trying to think of a way to keep from taking her to his room once they got back to the motel, Liz walked in with a bunch of reporters.

She did not, at first, notice Dina, instead registering surprise to see Rick. "I thought you were playing cards with the guys or I'd have called and asked you to join us."

He doubted that. She might be smiling, but her eyes were cold as ice, no doubt because of the words they'd had earlier in his room.

"I'm not a gambler, remember?" He then spoke to those with her that he knew and introduced himself to the ones he didn't. It was important to make himself known to the media as much as possible.

Liz waited till he'd finished, then, having noticed Dina, said, "Hello. I'm Liz Mallory, Rick's PR rep."

Dina, wearing tight jeans and a scoop-necked sweater, hooked her arm possessively through Rick's and gave her long, platinum hair a toss. "Well, aren't you the lucky one? I'd love to have an excuse to be around him all the time."

Some of the writers chuckled, and Rick, strangely feeling the need to explain Dina, said, "She's an old friend…lives here in Rockingham. We just had dinner."

"And now we're going back to the motel for dessert." Dina's purple-shaded eyes narrowed as she looked Liz up and down, as though sizing her up as competition.

Liz managed a smile, though she felt sick inside. Was this the kind of woman Rick was attracted to? Someone who reeked of perfume, wore too much makeup and didn't mind announcing to strangers she was about to go to bed with somebody? Sweetly, lightly, Liz said, "Well, remember he's got a race tomorrow."

"Oh, we go way back, honey. I know all about how he likes to get to bed early the night before. Don't worry. I plan to get him there just as quick as I can." She tugged at Rick's arm. "Come on, sweetie."

The guys exchanged knowing glances. One winked approval at Rick, but Rick was amused neither by the wink nor his possessive hand on Liz's back as he steered her into the restaurant.

It was none of his business who she went out with. Still,

she was a rookie of a different sort, and he just hoped she didn't get involved with the wrong crowd. He had heard about some of the single sportswriters getting a bit wild now and then. Sometimes the married ones, too.

He wondered if he should warn her but decided against it. She might wonder why and even start thinking he had a personal reason. He couldn't risk that. Besides, she was no teenager. She could take care of herself.

At least he hoped so.

Back at the motel, he tried to get away from Dina without making her mad or hurting her feelings. "I really have got to turn in early," he said, easing out of the car. They had driven hers, because he hadn't brought his. Bobby Holmes, driver of the team's hauler, wasn't feeling good, and he'd asked Rick to ride with him to Rockingham in case he needed relief. Rick was only too glad. Actually, he liked riding in the new hauler. It had a sleeper behind the seats and was roomy and comfortable.

Dina giggled. "So we'll make it a quickie."

She got out of the car and threw her arms around him and kissed him. But all he could think of was saucy green eyes and hair the color of a Georgia sunrise.

He untwined her arms from around his neck. "Sorry, Dina. I've got to get plenty of sleep tonight. Maybe next trip."

She jerked away from him. "Well, how do you think it makes me feel that you'd rather sleep than make it with me? Why'd you even bother to call me?"

He looked about, worried someone might have heard them since she'd raised her voice. Then he attempted to soothe. "Listen, I wanted to see you, take you to dinner, see how you're doing. I didn't intend to ask you to spend the night with me."

"Fine." She got back in the car. "But don't bother calling me next time you're in town unless you want to make a real night of it."

He watched her tear out of the parking lot, tires squealing, and shook his head in disgust—but at himself, not her. He never should have called her, never should have tried to get one woman off his mind with another.

What he should have done was kick his rear end all the way around the speedway for letting Liz get to him the way she had. He wanted her like no other woman he'd ever known…and not just to take to bed. The plain truth was that he enjoyed being around her. Not only did she have a cute personality, but she was also fun to talk to.

Thinking back, it was hard to recall having a conversation in the past few years with any woman that held his interest.

Until Liz.

True, he spent as little time with her as possible, but they still had to get together to discuss the press releases she sent out on a regular basis. She would come up with a topic and want to discuss it and ask him questions.

Like the one she had written about the upcoming race in Las Vegas.

Her idea had been to offer his views on gambling, like whether he had any tips on how to win. When he'd said he didn't gamble, instead wishing he had time to go backpacking or hiking in the beautiful desert surrounding Vegas, Liz had focused on that. The result had been a press release writers latched on to as something totally different from the run-of-the mill stories about slot machines and showgirls.

But besides being a press release that could be used verbatim—something all reps strove to provide—Rick had thoroughly enjoyed everything they had talked about that night. She had phoned him at the condo he called home in Charlotte and they had talked for hours. Afterward, he wished they hadn't, because he fell asleep thinking about her, dreamed about her again, then woke up to renew his pledge to be rid of her before he did something stupid—like fall in love.

He would not let himself think he already had.

He was just attracted to her, that's all, and it was one-sided, because she couldn't stand him. So even if he hadn't sworn off romance for many years to come, involvement with Liz could only be a one-way ticket to heartache.

After another restless night, Rick met Mack for breakfast. They were almost through eating when Rick caught sight of Liz across the room with the sportswriter he now thought of as The Winker.

"Find a way to tell her not to hang around the pits so much," Rick said dryly.

Mack glanced up from the stack of pancakes he was devouring. "Huh? Tell who not to hang what where?"

"I don't want Liz hanging around us so much. She gets in the way. She's going to get hurt."

Before responding, Mack took a big swallow of orange juice, eyes riveted on Rick, obviously surprised at his edict. "No, she isn't. She's careful. And she doesn't get in the way. And none of the other crew members have complained, so how come you are?"

"How about Daytona?"

"What about it? She was sick from the heat. Could've happened to anybody. Probably won't ever happen again."

"She's distracting. You know I don't like women hanging around."

"She's not just any woman, Rick. She's your PR rep. She works for your sponsor." Mack shook his head, disgusted. "What's with you? How come you keep giving her a hard time? She's only trying to do her job."

"She doesn't have to hang around the car. She doesn't have to hang around me. She doesn't even have to go to every race. You and I both know I won't be doing autographings and radio and TV stuff at every track we go to. Just like there won't be a pizza party thrown by Big Boy's every week for the media."

"True," Mack allowed, "but it's not up to us to say where she can and can't go. That's between her and the sponsor. I say we stay out of it."

Rick had ordered scrambled eggs but didn't feel like eating. Darn it, he had a five-hundred-mile race to run, and here he was, all knotted up inside because he'd let himself get strung out on a woman.

And it had to stop.

Then an idea struck when Mack remarked that Bobby wasn't feeling any better. "I think he's coming down with the flu. His wife's driving down here to pick him up."

"Then how do we get the cars to Vegas? We've got to leave from here." Thanks to sponsorship money, they were able to have two race cars, one to run and one for a spare, which they used for a show car. Some of the bigger teams hauled more, but he was grateful for the two.

"I guess Benny will have to do it. The rest of the crew had to get back to the shop and work on the new engine. We can fly it out there with us when we leave Wednesday."

Rick looked at Liz from the corner of his eye. She was laughing with The Winker, obviously enjoying herself. Then The Winker saw Rick watching and winked again.

Rick felt like slugging him.

But an idea was also forming.

A very wicked idea.

Benny was a good old boy from the backwoods of Georgia and had about as much savoir-faire as a pig at a cocktail party. He chewed tobacco and spat four-letter words as easy as stones skipping on water. He tried to watch what he said around Liz but, more often than not, forgot.

"Anybody going with Benny?" Rick asked.

"Who'd want to? He only listens to country music turned up loud enough to wake the dead, smokes like a chimney, and you have to be dying to make him stop for anything. He gets behind the wheel and drives till the gas tank is empty."

Rick shot another glance at Liz. It would be a terrible thing to do to her or anybody else, but if that's what it took to get rid of her, so be it.

When they were through eating, Mack said they'd best get to the track. It wasn't quite seven o'clock, but there was a lot to be done.

Rick said he would meet him at the car. "I want another cup of coffee. Just bring my bag down when you come."

Liz did exactly what Rick thought she'd do when she saw Mack leaving. She got up to follow, wanting to be at the track when the team arrived. She did not see Rick until he followed her into the lobby. "Hey, how's it going?" he said, trying to sound bright and cheerful. "All set for the big day?"

"Uh, yeah, sure," she said, a bit flustered. She had worried about how to react when she ran into him, because the image of him with Dina Fox had kept her awake most of the night.

"So are you ready to race?" She managed to ask, then dared to add, though she didn't really want to know, "Did you get to bed early last night?"

"Sure did." He walked over to a newspaper vending machine, fished in his pocket for two quarters and dropped them into the slot. "There's always good race coverage in the Charlotte paper."

"Oh, that's who Mark writes for."

"Who's that?"

"Yes. Mark Higgins. He just started with the paper. You met him last night, remember? He was standing next to me outside the restaurant.

The Winker.

"He's got a nice story about you in there," she said, pleased. "We just had breakfast, and he showed it to me. It's all about how well you did in Daytona even though you didn't finish the race. He agrees with me you're a heavy contender to win the rookie title."

"But not if I don't start finishing races."

"Well, that's not going to happen. I have a good feeling about today."

"Yeah, me, too." He paused, wanting to make sure he had his act together so she would fall right into his trap. "But you know, Liz, it might be nice if you could do something on the crew once in a while."

"I don't think anybody is interested in the crew. It's the driver people want to read about."

"Oh, I'm not talking about for a press release to the newspapers. I'm thinking something for the press kit. You know, a feature-type story. Sometimes the tracks use stories they lift out of the kits in their souvenir programs. It makes for a lot of nice exposure, and the guys appreciate it, too.

"You know a driver is only as good as his crew," he added.

"True, true," she said, fumbling in the big leather bag she always carried. She found the pad and pen she was looking for. "I'll make a note to do a bio on each of them."

"Not just a bio." He tried to keep his eyes glued to the paper and not drift to appreciate her outfit—navy-blue skirt to her knees, pale blue turtleneck sweater and, of course, her leather jacket like the rest of the team wore. Only her jacket had fallen open, and the way the sweater clung to her breasts made him want to pant.

She looked at him expectantly. "So what do you suggest?"

"Oh, different stories about what each guy does. Take Bobby Holmes, for instance. He drives the new hauler, and he could tell you some real interesting road tales from our short track days. He's a hoot. He'll be leaving right after the race for Vegas, because it's a couple days' drive. If I could, I'd ride with him just for the fun of it."

Liz liked the idea. She could get a lot of mileage out of a story like that. The souvenir programs might pick it up, but there were also other racing publications. It was certainly different. After all, how many PR reps climbed into the cab of the team hauler to ride across the country just to see what it was like?

"I'll do it," she said excitedly.

"Do what?" Rick played innocent as he leafed through the newspaper.

"Ride to Las Vegas with Bobby."

Rick fought to keep his face from splitting wide-open with a huge grin of triumph. She had taken the bait.

Very nonchalantly he asked, "Why do you want to do that?"

"To write a story about it. You said you'd love to do it for the fun of it. Well, I want to do it because I think it will make good copy."

"Oh, I'm not so sure that's a good idea."

She was stunned. "Would you mind explaining that?"

"The two of you traveling alone could get awkward."

"Oh, for heaven's sake," she cried, exasperated. "That doesn't matter when I'm doing my job."

"I'm afraid I have to disagree."

"Oh, I forgot, Rick," she said, struggling to keep her temper in check. "You resent women working in what you consider a man's world."

"In some instances, yes. And say, I'll bet if you worked in pro football instead of racing, you'd be like some of those women writers who go right into the locker room with the players."

"That issue was resolved several years ago," she pointed out. "It was established that a woman sportswriter had every right to go in with her male peers to get her story. Ballplayers were still keyed up from the game and gave their best quotes right then. Otherwise, by the time they'd showered and dressed and came out, the men writers already had the better story.

"But yes," she continued without hesitation, "if I had to in order to do my job, I'd go in there, too."

They looked around as Mack opened the door leading to the parking lot and called, "Hey, let's go."

"See you at the track," Rick said, giving her a little salute. "And if I were you, I'd forget that story. You won't be able to stand such a trip."

"Oh, yeah? We'll see about that."

Rick was whistling as he crossed the lobby.

Like Liz, he had a feeling it was going to be a good day…and also a good week.

There were ten laps to go, and Rick's heart was well into overdrive. He was running sixth, and every time he passed the main grandstand, he could hear the crowd screaming over the roaring of the cars.

Jack Blevins, in fifth place, and a driver also favored to win the rookie title, was dueling it out right beside him. They were so close, tires rubbing against sheet metal sent up smoke like a blown engine.

Sweat rolled from Rick's brow, trickling behind his goggles and into his eyes to smart and burn, but he didn't dare lift a hand from the steering wheel to give them a swipe. Let them sting. A few more minutes, and it would all be over, anyway.

Mack's voice came through the headphones. "Watch him, Rick. He's gonna block you when you try to pass him. Don't let him spin you out, 'cause you need those points for finishing."

"I know, I know," Rick said, adrenaline pouring. "I can't believe we're both rookies and racing for fifth position. I've got to take him, Mack."

"Be careful. You're going to be coming up on some slow cars soon."

"Don't worry. I'll wait for the right time. Till then, I'm hanging on to position and watching traffic."

Finally, with three laps remaining, Rick saw Jack dipping low.

Anticipating that Rick was about to try to pass, Jack was getting ready to block as they charged into the fourth turn and down the straightaway.

Rick bit down on his lower lip, gripped the wheel even tighter and sucked in his breath so hard it felt as if his ribs were shoved back into the seat.

In order to get around Jack, he had to take the high side— the *suicide side*, it was called—because it was an extremely dangerous maneuver. If his car so much as feather-kissed the concrete retaining wall, if control was lost for even the blink of a second, he could spin out.

But Rick had to chance it.

They were side-by-side as they went into turn two of the next-to-the-last lap. No one cared who was going to win the race. All the attention was focused on the two rookies who had the crowd on their feet and cheering like mad.

Rick hoped the cheers were for him.

And then it was time for him to make his move. With only the slightest flick of his wrists, he swung to Jack's right and mashed down so hard on the gas it was a wonder his foot didn't go right through the floorboard. There was slower traffic ahead, but the drivers knew to hang down toward the apron—the lower part of the track—and stay out of the way of the leaders.

He was able to pass Jack, but then a slower car veered slightly upward. Jack swerved, and with only one tiny tap to Rick's right rear, both cars began spinning in a shower of sparks as fenders ground together.

Cars behind frantically tried to get out of the way, but one didn't make it and plowed right into Rick's rear.

After what seemed forever, the Monte Carlo finally came to a stop.

Rick smelled smoke and broke free of his harness, unfastened the safety net at the window, and quickly climbed out.

A small fire had erupted under the hood, but a track safety worker was ready with an extinguisher to end any danger of it spreading.

Within seconds, Mack and the rest of the crew were all over Rick, wanting to know if he was all right.

"Yeah, I'm fine," he assured with a lopsided smile of disappointment. "Nothing a steak and cold beer and a good night's sleep won't cure."

And then Liz was there, having followed the crew as they ran down pit road to Rick's car. She caught up just in time to hear the tail end of Rick's remarks, the part about needing a good night's sleep.

Fury steamed within like the smoke still coming from Rick's wounded car.

He felt her burning, accusing glare and turned to see how livid she appeared. "What?" He said, spreading his hands in a helpless gesture.

Mack was already busy checking for any damage under the hood, while the rest of the crew inspected the extent of sheet metal damage.

Liz continued to stare at him, struck with wonder that he could practically admit the wreck was his fault because he hadn't slept the night before.

He did not like the way she was looking at him and pushed through the gathering crowd. Placing a firm hand on her arm, he steered her toward the fence separating the apron from the infield. "What is wrong with you? How come you're shooting daggers at me? That doesn't look too good. Some writers are always around after a crash, and they might take it to mean you blame me."

"I do," she said quietly, coldly.

He let go of her arm, towering over her with eyes narrowed. "What did you just say?"

"I said I *do* blame you. Why does that surprise you? You just admitted it in front of all those people. Now I've got to try to put a spin on things before it hits the papers and your sponsor calls me and asks what the heck is going on here."

Rick took off his helmet and threw it, he was so mad. "This is not the time or place for this, lady," he said between clenched teeth. "But damn it, you're crazy if you think I caused that wreck."

"But you said you did."

He shook his head in wonder. "You are crazy. And what are you doing here, anyway? You've got no business here."

She lowered her voice to a barely audible hiss. "I have business being anywhere you are on this track, mister. In case you forgot, I work for people who have a heck of a lot of money invested in your career. And they won't be happy to hear that you wrecked because you were up all night with some woman.''

''Wh...what?'' He nearly choked on a gasp, then laughed at the incredulity of such a remark. ''Liz, have you totally lost your mind?''

''No, but you have if you've already forgotten what you just said—how you needed a good night's sleep to be all right. Well, you might have had one if you hadn't had a roommate last night, Rick.''

She pointed a finger. ''Get something straight. I don't give a damn about your personal life. You can stay up all night with twenty women if you want to. Just don't do it the night before a race. Because if I ever hear of you doing it again, so help me, I'll go to the sponsor, and—''

''And what?'' He caught her finger and squeezed. ''Don't threaten me, Liz. Especially when you don't know what you're talking about. The guys asked if I was all right, and what I said was that nothing was wrong that a steak and a beer and a good night's sleep wouldn't cure. That had nothing to do with last night. As a matter of fact, I slept quite well...and alone, too. Not that it's any of your business.

''So get off my back.'' He released her finger with a gentle shove that caused her to take a step backward. ''And never, ever, let me catch you anywhere near me or my car when I wreck, understand? Because when I spin out I've got enough to worry about without you running up all hysterical to misinterpret everything you hear.''

Liz swallowed against a rising knot of embarrassment and shame. The truth was she had been upset, worried sick something might have happened to someone she had grown quite fond of.

She was also forced to admit that yes, she had been jealous of Dina Fox, and that was why she had so easily lost control.

She drew a deep breath and said, ''Rick, listen, I'm sorry. I shouldn't have jumped to conclusions. I was just upset, worried you might be hurt, and—''

He cut her off, still boiling with rage. "That's why you have no business here. You can't handle it, Liz. And I want you to quit hanging around in the pits. It's not safe. Get a seat in the press box like the other PR reps. Enjoy the food and all the perks that go with it. But stay away from me during a race, and stay out of my personal life."

Contrite as she was over her misconception of his remarks, and despite her feelings for him, he was not going to stop her from doing her job as she saw fit. "You cannot keep me away from the pits, and if you try, I'll go to your sponsor and tell them how you're being uncooperative. Maybe some other driver would appreciate having me and Big Boy's around."

With that, she turned and walked straight over to the car and Mack. "Will you be able to have the car ready to run at Las Vegas? The sponsor will be calling me to ask."

"Yeah," Mack answered with a weary sigh, "but we're going to have to stay up all night to get the sheet metal damage hammered out. Then it's got to be painted. What this means is that the hauler can't go from here to Vegas. We've got to get everything back to the shop and go to work."

"So when will the hauler leave?"

He thought a minute, then walked around the car again before saying, "Tuesday morning. Maybe Monday night. I'm not sure. But the second it's ready, it's leaving."

She knew Rick was standing nearby and could hear every word.

"You have my number at home, and my cell," she told Mack. "Call me when the cars are ready to go, because I'm going with them."

"Are you serious?"

"Oh, yes," she said, turning her head slightly to give Rick a defiant glance. "I wouldn't miss it for the world."

Rick watched Liz walk away. Anybody could tell she was mad from how she moved—head high, shoulders squared, a *don't-get-in-my-way* look on her face.

"Boy, you two are like trying to mix oil and water," Mack grumbled as he brushed by Rick to get at the car.

That was probably true, Rick silently conceded, but he didn't want it that way. Not really. All he did want was for her to just go away. She had his insides revving like a high-tuned engine, and he didn't need that...didn't want it. Not now.

But neither did he want her for a mortal enemy, and he'd probably come down too hard on her just now. After all, maybe she felt justified in blaming him for the wreck, but he could have set her straight in a gentler way. And setting her up to ride to Vegas with Benny was probably meaner than necessary.

He started after her, not exactly sure what he would say or do but knowing he had to smooth things over a little bit, anyway.

And then he saw it—the car sliding through the pit road opening into the garage area. He knew at once what was going on. The brakes were slipping, and the driver was gearing down to slow the car. But Liz didn't realize what was happening. She continued walking straight ahead, her anger making her oblivious to anything unusual going on around her.

Rick broke into a run. He reached Liz just as the car swerved to keep from hitting her. Scooping her up and into his arms, he stepped out of the way as the car swerved to the side, the driver shaking his fist at Liz's carelessness.

Held tightly against Rick's broad chest, Liz suddenly felt very foolish, as well as frightened by what had almost happened. "I...I'm sorry," she stammered. "I guess I wasn't watching where I was going."

Rick felt his heat rising and fought the impulse to kiss her then and there. "And that's probably my fault for coming down so hard on you back there. I shouldn't have been so rough."

Their eyes met and held, and Liz softly apologized again,

"No, it's my fault. I know I'm supposed to be alert in the garage area.

"And thank you," she continued. "I could have been really hurt."

"He'd have missed you," Rick said, voice husky. "But you might have been scared into tripping and falling. Just be careful next time.

"And about what happened back there," he rushed to add, "I guess I worry you'll get hurt hanging around the pits. I don't mean to be so brusque."

"It's okay." Liz saw a couple of crew members walk by and grin at how Rick was still holding her. "I think you can put me down now," she said, feeling awkward…and also intensely stirred by the intimate moment.

"Oh, sure, sure." Rick set her on her feet. "Are you okay?"

"I'm fine, really. Thanks again."

"Another thing…"

She looked up at him expectantly.

"About that trip to Vegas, maybe it's not such a good idea."

"Nonsense." She gave him her perkiest smile to lighten the moment, because being so close was taking a toll on her nerves. "It's going to be great. Don't worry about it or me, Rick."

She gave him a little salute and turned on her heel, anxious to get away from him lest he sense what she was feeling right then…how she longed to throw herself in his arms and feel his strength once more.

He watched her go and this time did not follow, because he, too, was fighting emotions that threatened to spin out of control. Maybe the ride with Benny would make her want to get as far from the world of racing as possible.

And that, Rick forced himself to believe, would be a good thing.

Chapter Eight

It was Wednesday evening and since leaving Charlotte at midnight Tuesday, Benny had stopped only for gas and when she begged to go to the rest room...which he called a *pit stop*. The radio blared constantly with country-western music, Benny singing along at the top of his lungs.

Still, all things considered, she was not sorry to have made the trip. She liked Benny, and he had provided lots of interesting things to incorporate into her article. It had been a surprise to learn he was driving instead of Bobby, who was sick, but she figured it didn't make any difference since she was writing about the trip, not the driver.

They passed a sign that read Las Vegas—150 miles.

"Hey, we're right on schedule," Benny said triumphantly. "We'll be there by daylight."

"The way we've been traveling, you should be on schedule," Liz commented dryly.

He darted an apologetic glance. "You'd have had a better time with Bobby. He takes his time."

"Well, if I'd found out sooner he was sick I'd probably have passed on this trip."

"How'd you miss hearing? His wife had to go get him in Rockingham. I had to drive the rig back from there."

Something clicked. "When did all this happen?" she asked, suspicion needling.

"Oh, he was feeling poorly before he ever left Charlotte, 'cause he asked Rick to ride with him in case he had to take over. His wife came and picked him up Saturday evening. Good thing she did, 'cause she missed the snow, and he didn't have any business being out in that kind of weather."

"So he left Saturday night," she said tightly, angrily. That meant when Rick had suggested Monday morning that she do a story about riding to Las Vegas with Bobby, he already knew Bobby wouldn't be making the trip. He wanted her to go with Benny, no doubt aware of all his annoying habits. So it was just another of Rick's ploys to get rid of her.

Despite being so annoyed, Liz dozed off, only to be awakened by Benny's excited cry, "Look at all them lights. Right smack dab in the middle of nowhere. Las Vegas, Nevada. Yahoo!" He let go of the steering wheel to wave his arms.

Liz was spellbound by the glittering lights sprawling before them. It was beautiful. No, more than that. It was positively awesome.

"Where'd you say we got reservations?" Benny asked.

"The Mirage. But that's not where you're taking this truck, is it?"

"Oh, no ma'am. I'm going to the track. But I can drop you off in front of the hotel."

He did so, and Liz practically floated into the luxurious lobby.

"Ah, yes, Miss Mallory," a desk clerk greeted her when she went to register. "You've got quite a box full of messages waiting."

She took them with her to her room, intending to have the bath she'd been dying for, then order room service—a huge breakfast.

But she made the mistake of glancing over the messages and one leaped out at her. It was from Jeff, sent the day before, saying she needed to get in touch with him right away. He had been unable to reach her on her cell phone. She wasn't surprised. There hadn't been a cell tower in the desert, for heaven's sakes, and on the rare occasions when Benny had stopped anywhere, it had been an ungodly hour to call anyone back East.

When she went to the phone, she saw the message light blinking. Dialing the appropriate number, she retrieved Jeff's voice mail: "Hey, Liz. I wish I could get in touch with you, because if you don't receive this right away, you're going to freak out when you do. Gary decided at the last minute he wants to throw a huge cocktail and dinner party out there. Seems there are several Big Boy's Pizza shops in the area, and he wants to invite all the managers and employees. He wants a lot of glitz, and he also wants the race car parked outside. So get it together. I know you can do it. Ciao."

Liz hung up the phone and pressed her fingertips to her temples in frustration.

A glitzy party. But when? Oh, heck, it didn't matter when, because it was going to take some doing to throw it together regardless.

She grabbed the phone and called Jeff at home. She woke him up, realized it was only three o'clock in New York but couldn't care less. "So, is there anything else I need to know about this party before I lose my mind over it?"

His laugh was sleepy and lazy. "What day is it out there?"

"Same day as where you are," she said, unimpressed by his humor. "Thursday morning."

"He wants to have the party tomorrow night."

"Oh, that's just great. And how many people are we talking about?"

"I don't know. You'll need to call Big Boy's offices and find out.

"But don't worry, Liz," he added cheerfully. "Gary said to spare no expense. He really wants to put on the dog this time. He's bringing some investors with him, so we're talking real lavish, okay?''

Liz sank down on the bed, wishing she could stretch out and sleep for a couple of days but forget that. Forget everything but putting together a huge party in two days. "I don't know where to begin."

He laughed again, and this time it grated.

"Walk your fingers through the yellow pages, Liz. You can do it. Ciao."

He hung up, and she felt like throwing the phone across the room. Instead, she picked it up once again, this time to order coffee—strong and black, and a quick breakfast.

By the time room service arrived, she was showered and changed and ready to go to work.

Within an hour, she had a ballroom at the Mirage reserved for Friday night.

In two more hours, she had obtained the number of people to invite—forty. She then phoned the food and beverage manager of the hotel and told him she needed to see him in her room right away.

Two hours later she had arranged a sit-down dinner of lobster and steak, an open bar, and a band for dancing later.

Next she unpacked her laptop, made out an invitation, then sent it by messenger to a print shop. Forty names and addresses were a bit much for her to do herself, but she was able to find a calligrapher through the print shop to take care of it and get them delivered by courier. Thank goodness everyone invited was local.

By noon, all the preparations were made for the party. She had even called the local newspaper and made sure a reporter and photographer would cover the event.

As an added touch, she did walk her fingers through the yellow pages to find a store specializing in gifts and party favors. If she could have Rick's photo to them by that afternoon, they would be able to etch it on crystal wineglasses for every guest to take home as a souvenir.

Late in the day, she called Jeff again.

"I hope you aren't having problems putting all this together," he said warily when he heard her voice. "Gary Staley is the kind of man who doesn't like excuses."

"Rest easy. It's a done deal. All I have to do is make arrangements for Rick and the car, which won't be a problem."

"Better not be," Jeff said, a bit gruffly. "By the way, are you two getting along any better?"

"Let's put it this way—we aren't getting along any worse. He still doesn't like having me around, but it's no big deal."

"I should say not. You're doing a hell of a job, Liz. And don't worry. If the sponsor renews his contract, we'll get a male rep on the account next season and put you somewhere else. No need for you to have to put up with him acting like a jerk just because you're a woman."

Even though she was annoyed with Rick, Liz did not want Jeff to have a false impression of the situation. "Actually, he isn't being a jerk. He cooperates with me fully. He's great with the media and his fans. He's got a great personality, and everybody likes him. It's just me he has a problem with, but I'm not letting it get in the way of anything, so don't worry."

Jeff assured Liz he had the utmost confidence in her. "Every time I talk to Gary, he sings your praises. And I'll probably have to soothe his feathers when I take you off the account. But for now, just keep doing whatever you're doing, because he couldn't be happier, and neither could I."

Afterward, Liz sat for long moments brooding over how *she* could certainly be a lot happier. Still, she couldn't really complain. She had taken on the account determined to succeed, and it looked as though she had. It had not been in her plans to be attracted to anybody, much less the man she had to work with.

And, she acknowledged, it probably would be a good thing for her to transfer out of the account. But not till the end of the contract. She would not, by damn, let Rick Castles think he had made her quit.

She longed to take a nap, but it was time for the guys to return from the track. She dialed Mack's cell phone, and he was delighted to hear from her.

"I was getting worried. I just knew you'd get enough of Benny, and we'd have to go pick you up somewhere along the side of the road."

She said it hadn't been so bad. "But if I ever do it again, so help me I won't drink a drop of water for days before."

"And you'll probably take your own food and headphones to drown out that music."

"Exactly."

"I'm just sorry Bobby got sick. You'd have had a much better time with him."

She did not want to dwell on the little trick Rick had played. "Say, Mack, we need to have dinner tonight if you can make it. I have to go over a few things."

"Sure. Rick and I can meet you anytime. Right, Rick?"

She heard Rick's voice in the car with Mack. They were on their way back to the hotel. She noted he sounded less than enthused but agreed.

"Just say when and where," Mack said.

She picked up the hotel directory from the bedside table and leafed through it. There were several restaurants, but, remembering Rick did not like Mexican food, said, "The Guadalajara? Seven o'clock okay?"

"Yeah, I could use a margarita and a big platter of fried jalapeños and chalupas."

When Liz heard Rick curse, she put her hand over her mouth to smother a giggle.

Rick did not want to have dinner with Liz. All the guys were amazed she'd made the trip with Benny, and he didn't want to chance her blurting out that he'd been the one to suggest it.

But he needn't have worried. When he and Mack walked into the restaurant, Liz was already seated in a large, round booth. She had a bunch of papers spread out around her, and it was quite obvious she had more on her mind than a miserable road trip that he had instigated.

She had already ordered a pitcher of margaritas and a big platter of chips and salsa.

Rick shoved his drink in Mack's direction and ordered a beer. He also passed on the appetizer, just as he planned to skip dinner if there was nothing un-Mexican on the menu. He wondered if she'd planned it that way on purpose. He'd told her before he didn't like Mexican, and there were plenty of other restaurants around she could have chosen.

So, okay, he decided, if she was trying to annoy him to get even for the trip with Benny, he would not give her the satisfaction of letting her know she'd succeeded.

But even as he sipped his beer to wash down the rising resentment, Rick couldn't help thinking again how cute she was. Her hair was pulled back in the little-girl ponytail he liked, and she wasn't wearing much makeup. She had on sweatpants and a T-shirt. Very casual. He thought maybe she was tired from the trip and didn't want to dress up, so she'd chosen a restaurant where she didn't feel she had to. Maybe she wasn't trying to irritate him at all, and—

"What do you think, Rick?"

Mack gave him a poke in the ribs.

"Aren't you listening?"

"I guess not," he hedged. "I was thinking about the car."

"Well, Earth to Rick. That's what she was talking about—how we have to have the show car parked out front by six o'clock Friday night."

Rick gave him a blank stare. He really had been on another planet, but he got that way sometimes when he was brooding about Liz. Which was another reason for her to go away. "So what's all this about?"

Liz explained about the cocktail party and dinner she had so quickly arranged. "And Mr. Staley emphasized he wants the race car out front so all the guests can see it. He also wants you there to sign autographs. That reminds me…" She began scribbling in her notebook. "I'm going to need more publicity photos. We gave out a bunch in Rockingham. And I've got to get to the track office in the morning and try to wheedle some pit passes.''

"Sure, fine, I'll be there,'' Rick said, trying not to let it get to him how she was running her tongue across her lower lip as she wrote. He could almost taste how sweet it would be to kiss her, and…

"Great.'' She said, sitting back and capping her pen. "And I think you should wear a tux instead of your drivers' suit.''

He was quick to balk at that. "I don't think so.''

Mack held up a hand. "Rick, if she thinks it would be best…''

"Of course, it would,'' Liz assured. "This is a very formal affair. It wouldn't do for you not to be in a tux.'' She nodded to Mack. "And you, too, and anybody else on the team who wants to come.''

Actually, Rick did not mind wearing a tux. He enjoyed dressing up on occasion but wasn't about to let her know it. "Well, if I have to,'' he mumbled.

"You have to. And by the way, thanks for suggesting I make the trip out here with Benny.''

Mack, astonished, turned on Rick. "You mean that was your idea? But you knew Bobby was sick.''

"He did me a real favor,'' Liz assured, noticing the sheepish look that come over Rick's face. "It turned out great. I was able to make what I think is a nice story out of it. I ran into Larry Parks from the Atlanta Speedway in the lobby a while ago and had a chance to tell him about it. He says he'll use it for sure in the program for the November race.''

Mack interjected, "Along with a story of how Rick is leading in points and a shoo-in for the rookie title. That's the last race on the schedule, you know.''

"Yes, I know. And I plan to really have lots of things going for him then. His sponsorship will be up for renewal, and, of course, the agency will try for even more money next year.''

"Well, we'll need it, that's for sure," Mack said. "Everything goes up. Tires are the main thing besides engines. Five sets a race. But I'd like to hire another engine man."

"We'll try to make it happen."

A waitress brought menus. Rick glanced over it and didn't see anything he liked. He laid it aside and downed the rest of his beer. "I don't go for this stuff. I think I'll find a hamburger or something instead."

Liz was quick to apologize, "Oh, Rick, I'm sorry. I forgot you don't like Mexican food."

"No problem. I'm not real hungry, anyway. See you."

After he'd gone, Liz dolefully remarked, "Mack, he just doesn't like me. If I weren't so determined I swear I'd ask for a transfer."

"Hey, don't you dare. You're doing a super job. All the guys say so. And they all like you, too."

"But Rick is your driver, and if he doesn't want me around…"

Mack firmly said, "It doesn't matter. Don't worry about him. Even my wife, Rosie, thinks you're great. So don't pay any attention to Rick. He's got a lot of old baggage he carries around. Maybe he's taking it out on you. I don't know."

Liz sipped on her margarita while Mack tossed down several. And, the more he drank, the more relaxed he became.

The food was delicious and there was plenty of it. Afterward, Mack leaned back, patted his stomach and declared, "Best Mexican food I think I've ever had. Maybe the next time we run Vegas Rosie can come with us, too, and we'll eat here. She'd enjoy it."

"She doesn't go to many races, does she?" Liz observed.

"As many as she can, but with a couple of rug rats at home, it's hard for her to get away. She doesn't like leaving them with anybody, but when they're older we plan to get an RV and she'll do a lot of traveling then."

The smile on his face told Liz what she already knew— he was crazy about his kids. His wife, too.

Later, over coffee, Mack seemed so mellow and willing

to talk that Liz dared touch on Rick's private life. "I can't help wondering why he has a thing about women at the race-tracks."

"I think it has to do with his wife."

Liz had just taken a sip of her margarita and nearly choked.

Mack patted her back as she coughed. "Are you okay?"

"Yes. I'm fine." She wiped her mouth with her napkin, then swallowed a little water. "I didn't know he was married. It's not in his bio. If it were to come out, it would sure look funny that he tried to hide it."

"Oh, he's not married now. I should've said his ex-wife. He's been divorced several years."

"Are there any children?"

"Nope. No kids."

"Well, I'm sorry," she said, feeling awkward to have broached the private side of Rick, even though she longed to know more.

"Oh, don't be," Mack said airily. "It was one of those racing things, I guess."

"What did his divorce have to do with racing?"

"Everything. You see—" he leaned closer, obviously not wanting anyone around to hear "—his wife walked out on him because she hated racing."

"So he wasn't racing when they met?"

"Oh, yes. They met at a track. But she told him later she kept hoping it was just a hobby, that she didn't realize how serious he was about it. After they got married, she tried to get him to give up. Said she couldn't stand having a husband gone all the time, and she didn't like going with him. The next thing he knew, she'd run off with another man."

"I'm sorry. That must have been terrible for him."

"I don't think he was all that surprised. They weren't getting along. I know, because he'd talk to me about it and said he didn't know how much longer he could take it. And Maggie cried on Rosie's shoulder, asking how she put up with it like she did."

"And because of that he doesn't want women around the track?" It didn't make sense.

"Oh, not altogether. He's had other relationships, and the women go bananas when he spins out. Or they gripe about the heat or the groupies hanging around him. Then they fuss about the schedule, traveling all the time. The dirt. The noise. You name it. They bitch about it."

Liz continued to prod. "So he won't let his girlfriends come around the track."

"Yeah, I guess. But he's real tight-lipped about his personal life. Rosie and I always invite him to come by the house on off weekends, what few there are. You know, for dinner or cookouts. But he never brings a woman."

"Well, I guess it's lonely for him."

"Oh, I don't think so. I have an idea he has companionship whenever he wants it. Though as irritable as he's been lately, I'd be surprised if any woman would have anything to do with him on the track or off."

"So he's not always grumpy."

"Nope. He got that way after Daytona. The guys and I were talking about it on the way out here. He's not himself."

"Maybe he's just tired."

"Could be. He's under a lot of pressure, and lately he hangs out at the garage day and night, working on the car when he doesn't have to. It's like he's got something on his mind. I've tried to get him to talk about it, but he says I'm crazy. Nothing's wrong."

Liz made little circles on the tablecloth with her margarita glass. "I really hate to see him stressed-out so early in the season. Maybe there's something I can do."

"I doubt it. He'll have to work it out himself. But meanwhile, Liz, don't take the way he's acting personal."

"That's rather hard to do, when he makes no bones about the fact he doesn't want me around."

"He'll get over it. Meanwhile, just keep doing your job, because the rest of us sure as heck don't want you going anywhere."

"I'm not planning to. Not yet, anyway. But I wish Rick would unwind a little. If he just had time for a mini-vacation."

"That won't happen till the schedule gives us a break between Talladega and California for Easter. Ah, but don't worry about him. I don't know many drivers that don't get worn-out."

But Rick wasn't just any driver, Liz brooded. He was *her* driver, her account, and if he didn't perform well, then it would make it hard for her to keep getting him positive media coverage.

She would just have to keep an eye on him, that's all, yet stay out of his way so as not to annoy him. And all the while she'd be on the lookout for anything she could do to make his life a little easier…a little less stressful.

"He likes the outdoors," Mack said, cutting into her musing. "Camping. Hiking. Fishing. Anything to be out in the wilderness. Before I got married and the kids came along, he and I used to take off for days at the time. We'd just head out and commune with nature, as they say."

"I'll keep that in mind," she said thoughtfully, the wheels beginning to turn.

They were smack-dab in the middle of the desert, and if wilderness was what he wanted, Liz just might be able to arrange it.

Rick did not like himself very much.

He was giving Liz a real hard time, and she didn't deserve it. After all, she was only trying to do her job…make a living.

Just like him.

It was not her fault he had a thing against women being involved in the racing world.

Nor was it her fault she was so damned attractive he couldn't stop thinking about her…couldn't stop wanting her.

And he would not, could not, make her lose her job because of how he felt.

Neither could he draw the animosity of his crew, because he was the only one who wasn't practically doing handstands to have her around. After all, there was no denying she was doing a super job.

He had to admire her for making the best of the trick he'd pulled on her about the ride out to Vegas. He had talked to Benny about it earlier at the track, and Benny said she'd been a really good sport.

So what to do, Rick sighed to ponder as he sat in a cocktail lounge just off the hotel lobby.

And, as he fretted, he happened to look out the door and see her walking toward the bank of elevators. She was alone, and, was it his imagination or did she look miserable, as well?

He had to get off her back. That's all there was to it. From now on, he would do everything he could to get along, would not goad her or play tricks on her, or try to make her quit.

She had proved she had grit, and he admired her for it.

And wanting her like an itch that couldn't be scratched was something he just had to try to get over.

"Hey, aren't you Rick Castles?"

He glanced up and tried to see over the huge bosom in his face. "That's right."

The woman leaned over, and her breasts brushed against his cheek. "I thought so. You're fantastic," she gushed. "You're absolutely the best driver there is, and you are the only reason me and my girlfriends are going to the race Sunday. To watch you. Oh, could I have your autograph? They'll be so envious." She sat down next to him without being invited.

"Sure." He signaled to the waitress for a pen, then wrote his name on a cocktail napkin.

"Make it to Marla," she cooed, "and write something sweet."

He wrote "Best Wishes to Marla, Rick Castles," and handed the napkin to her.

She squealed with delight, folded it and put it in her purse.

"Thanks, Rick. Say, how would you like to go dancing with me? There's a lounge just down the way that plays rap music nonstop."

He gave her a polite smile as he stood. "I never could dance to rap music, and I really need to call it a day."

She likewise rose, standing very close to him as she said, "Would you like some company?"

"Not this time, but thanks."

He got out of there as fast as he could and did not look back.

He had to deal with how he felt about Liz, all right, but going to bed with another woman wasn't the answer.

It just wasn't the way to scratch that itch.

Chapter Nine

The dinner and dance was everything Liz had hoped for…and more.

The ballroom was decorated in black-and-white—colors of the coveted checkered flag in racing—with red carnations for a bright touch.

In front of each guest's setting, there was a souvenir tote bag with a T-shirt emblazoned with Rick's picture, a miniature replica of his race car, and a press kit.

Liz had stayed up all night writing the story of her trip west in the team hauler. By five that morning she had e-mailed it to all the major newspapers and racing publications.

The rest of the day passed in a blur.

Then, around three o'clock, while stuffing the tote bags, Liz remembered she hadn't brought anything really dressy enough for the evening ahead.

Hurrying downstairs to the hotel's boutiques, she found a gown of sparkling green sequins. It fit perfectly. Perhaps a bit too perfectly. But it didn't matter. The only man she wanted to impress wasn't going to give her a second glance, anyway.

At five o'clock she drove to the Las Vegas airport to meet Gary Staley's jet, then brought him and his family back to the hotel. A quick drink in a lounge to say hello and go over a few things, and Liz was off to get dressed.

There hadn't been time for the beauty salon, so she did her hair herself—a simple twist with a beaded comb to hold it in place.

The guests were due to start arriving at six, but just as Liz started to go down, the phone rang. It was the track's PR office, wanting to go over the VIP list for pit and race passes that she had faxed earlier.

Things were obviously hectic in the office, because they put her on hold for long moments. By the time everything was taken care of, it was nearly six-thirty.

Liz was late and only hoped Rick had been on time. She hadn't spoken to him since the night at the Mexican restaurant, but Mack said he'd see that he got there...and wore a tux.

As she stepped off the elevator, she knew she need not have worried.

The huge crowd in front of the hotel told the story.

She managed to make her way through, and the sight of Rick in a tux took her breath away. *James Bond, eat your heart out.*

And, of course, there was a bevy of women gathered around. From the heavy makeup they were wearing, Liz was impressed to realize some of them had to be showgirls, stopping by before show time.

"How's it going?" She stood on tiptoe to whisper in Rick's ear when she managed to reach him. Some of the women were glaring, but Liz didn't care. After all, Rick was her driver. Maybe he couldn't stand having her around, but, in a professional way, he was hers.

"Going fine," he said, scribbling his name on a glossy photo and handing it to someone, then taking another to do it again. "Where have you been? How come you get out of standing here in this heat?"

"I got tied up with track PR over VIP passes. But everything worked out all right."

"So now you can stand here and sweat."

"Actually, I can't. I have to greet the guests and make sure things are running smoothly inside."

"And how much longer do I have to stay?"

"I'd say about another half hour. See you inside."

The truth was, he loved meeting his fans. Loved meeting people, actually. And he was still flattered, even after years of being somewhat of a star on the short track circuit, that people would stand in line for his autograph.

But Liz did not need to know that. Let her think him crabby and hard to get along with, and maybe she would continue to keep her distance. He was pleased it was working so far, because she didn't hang around as much as she used to.

"Oh, I almost forgot."

She was beside him again, and this time the crowd gave a sudden surge that pressed her against him. He liked the feeling but didn't look at her. "What is it now?"

"Where did you qualify today? I asked when I called the track, but they didn't have the final lineup yet, and I haven't seen Mack or any of the others."

"Sixth," he said matter-of-factly, though he was proud to bursting.

Liz was thrilled. "That's wonderful. But what about Jack Blevins? Where does he start?"

"Somewhere behind me," Rick said curtly. "That's all I care about."

Liz was glad he spoke in a near whisper, so his fans wouldn't hear how grumpy he sounded. At least he kept a smile pasted on his face.

Mack was right. Rick was stressed-out, which was bad so early in the season. As his PR person, she felt it was part of her job to do something about it. But there was no time to think about it right then as a limo pulled up to the curb.

"Show time," she said merrily, giving Rick's shoulder a friendly pat. "See you in a little bit."

Where she had touched him felt like hot needles stabbing his flesh, and he gritted his teeth. Lord, he wished he could have turned and swept her into his arms. But he could only stand there, smiling and making small talk as he signed one autograph after another.

Liz enjoyed spreading the word about Rick's wonderful qualifying run.

Gary Staley was thrilled. "This is real good exposure, Liz. Can you put a spin on it?"

"Oh, yes," she assured. "It's the third race of the year, and the third time he's been the fastest-qualifying rookie. I'll have a sidebar e-mailed to all media by tomorrow morning."

Beside him, Gary's wife, Ida, told Liz they couldn't be happier with the publicity the team was getting. "And you've done a wonderful job here tonight. I'm just sorry Gary didn't give you more notice."

"Not a problem," Liz said, thinking how she could count on one hand the number of hours of sleep she'd had since arriving in Las Vegas.

"Rick is so handsome," Ida exuded. "Why, my teenage daughters have crushes you wouldn't believe. And he's so nice, too. He seems to really enjoy his fans. Is he fun to work with?"

Ida and Gary both stared at her expectantly.

How easy it would have been to tell the truth—that Rick was fun for everybody to work with except her and that he despised her and would like nothing better than to have her replaced.

But Liz was proud she was able to say all the right things and not give anything away.

She was also full to bursting with joy to think how, even

in the face of Rick's animosity, she had succeeded in doing a laudable job.

That meant she'd kept her promise to herself that no man would ever stand in the way of her career again.

She only wished she'd kept her vow not to fall for one, either.

The next hour she stayed busy introducing people and getting them to their seats and taking care of dozens of other little details.

Then it was time for the head table to be presented—Gary and his family, along with some city dignitaries Liz had managed to persuade to come. Like the mayor and his wife. She was especially thrilled over that. And she had invited some of the track officials, as well.

Gary, seated at the center of the head table, waved her over. She worried to see he looked annoyed.

"Where's Rick? He's supposed to sit next to me. The salads are being served. It doesn't look good that he's not here. He can't stay out there all night no matter how long the line is."

"I'll check."

And she rushed to do so, surprised to see that the crowd around Rick had grown larger, the line longer.

She began to push her way toward him again, only this time it was not so easy.

"Hey, wait your turn," a woman yelled. "Who do you think you are?"

And another chortled, "Yeah, get back in line and wait like the rest of us. I've been here twenty minutes, and you aren't getting in front of me."

Liz stood on tiptoe, craning to see above the heads in front of her. She saw Rick…saw that he was smiling and appeared to be enjoying himself and found that quite puzzling. She would have thought by now he'd look a little bit harried, at least.

She called to him.

At first he didn't hear, so she called louder, and, at last, he glanced up.

"You have to come inside now. Dinner is being served."

A groan went up from the crowd, and Liz cringed to see the angry faces turned in her direction.

"Sorry," she said in a small voice, backing away. "But we've got lots of pictures in the lobby. You can each have one…"

Rick's hand closed around her arm. "Let's go before they start throwing rocks."

Liz had to struggle to keep up with him. Her dress was very tight around her ankles, except for a slit on one side, and it was hard to match his long strides.

"Can you slow down?"

"Not yet."

He waited till they were in the lobby, then irritably accused, "You should've come out there long before now. I couldn't get away."

She was tired and not in a mood for him to light into her about anything. Other times, she could handle it, but not this night. "Listen, it's not my job to baby-sit you, Rick. You've got a watch. You knew what time it was. You could have torn yourself away. So don't blame me."

"Oh, yeah?" His hands were on his hips, feet slightly apart as he glared down at her. He was careful to keep his voice low, as the lobby was crowded. "And how would that have looked? For me to just say 'Hey, this is it. Gotta go.' I think it was your job to come get me."

"Well, this isn't the first time you've been confused about my job, is it? Now are you coming with me or do you plan to stay here and pout all night because I took you away from your moment of glory?"

"Moment…of…glory?" he echoed, stunned. "That stuff doesn't mean anything to me. I want my glory on the track, lady, not signing autographs."

"Tell it to somebody who cares," she snapped, and

walked away. He could find his own way to his seat. She'd had it.

For a moment, Rick could only stand there and look at her. Man, she filled out that dress in all the right places, and what a dress it was, too. Tight, green sequins, thin spaghetti straps, the bodice dipping low enough to show she had plenty but not enough to be overly provocative.

He liked the slit in the skirt, too, giving a nice flash of leg.

And her hair. All red and gold piled on top of her head with sassy little tendrils curling around her face.

A young man wearing a racing jacket with Rick's car number on it, saw him and cried, ''Hey, you're the man. Gimme an autograph.''

Even with him still several feet away, Rick knew he'd had one too many and wasn't about to get tied up with him. He was late enough as it was.

''Later,'' he said, waving jovially and hurrying toward the doors to the ballroom.

Glancing around, he was impressed with the decor. He was also flattered by how people, as they noticed his arrival, stood to applaud. But it kept him from seeing where he was supposed to go, and he silently cursed Liz for walking off and leaving him.

''Rick, up here.''

He turned toward the voice and saw Gary Staley waving from the head table, which was on a level higher than the rest of the room.

Rick, nodding, waving and shaking hands, worked his way there.

The applause was thundering as he mounted the steps. Liz was standing at the bottom, smiling sweetly and waving him on up. He hoped she caught the quick glance of anger he shot in her direction.

Finally seated between Gary and his wife, Rick spent the next hour or so in polite conversation, hoping he was doing and saying the right things.

Finally dinner was over. Waiters were quickly clearing away tables for dancing.

Liz walked up to the head table to ask if they needed anything.

"Yes. As a matter of fact, we do," Gary said, leaning back in his chair, eyes shining from one too many glasses of champagne. "I'd like to see my driver and my PR representative lead off the first dance."

Liz felt as if the air had suddenly been pulled from her lungs. The last thing she wanted was to dance with Rick. If he held her in his arms, he might hear the frantic pounding of her heart.

"Uh, I'm not a very good dancer," she hedged.

Rick spoke up, "I'm not, either."

"Oh, nonsense." Gary motioned them toward the floor. "Anybody can slow-dance. Come on. Get out there."

He reached for the microphone, which was still hooked up. He'd made a welcoming speech, toasted Rick and had the whole team stand from where they were seated at a table together on the floor. Now Gary used the mike to boom out the question, "Hey, does everybody here want to see your driver and your PR rep get things going?"

A roar of approval went up. Liz had endeared herself to everyone, personally greeting them, stopping by each and every table during the evening to see if there was anything they needed…anything she could do for them. A few knew her from Daytona and considered her an old friend. And, in awe over their favorite driver, nothing would please them more than to see the two dancing.

"Get us out of this," Rick whispered in her ear.

"I wish I could," she whispered back.

"Come on, come on," Gary continued, waving them on as everyone cheered and clapped. "Ida and I will break in after a few minutes and then everyone else will get up and dance."

"Let's count on that," Rick said, taking Liz's hand and leading the way.

"Hey, I don't like this any more than you do, but let's make the best of it."

He led her all the way to the center of the room in hopes no one could see the annoyance surely mirrored on his face.

He put a hand on her waist and clasped her other.

Liz raised her arm to rest her hand lightly on his shoulder.

She wondered if he had felt the involuntary shudder that jolted through her as she stepped into the circle of his embrace.

Their faces were mere inches apart. She could smell the lemony spice of his aftershave, could see the thick curl of the lashes fringing incredible coffee-colored eyes.

He was so tall, so strong, and she felt in that moment that as long as his arms were about her nothing could ever hurt her again.

Get a grip, girl, she commanded herself, forcing her face to turn from his. *If you start shaking, he's going to know it's not with annoyance, not when your heart is racing like an engine.*

"You dance real well," he said grudgingly, feeling the need to make conversation.

"Thanks. So do you." She kept her head turned so as to not look at him. Besides, it was terribly unnerving to have her lips so close to his.

"I could strangle Gary. I don't like being the center of attention."

At that, Liz couldn't help but giggle. "Oh, yeah, right. That's why you bust your butt to win a race so you can stand in front of the TV cameras in victory lane for all the world to see. Tell me another one, Castles. You love the limelight, and you know it."

"Hey, that doesn't have anything to do with it. I race to win, sure. But I don't give a damn about the glory that goes with it."

Even though he was angry, Liz noticed how he still held her with great tenderness. They were moving fluidly to the music, all eyes upon them. She wished Gary and his wife would cut in and glanced at their table as Rick turned her in that direction. They were both in animated conversation with other guests, apparently having forgotten the plan.

"I think we're stuck with each other till the music ends," Liz said, trying to sound glum while hoping all the while the band never stopped playing. He might be annoyed with her, like always, but she was secretly reveling in the moment.

"Might've known," he murmured, giving her an extra strong whirl, arm tightening.

She knew the movement came from his resentment but enjoyed it just the same. "Relax. It'll be over soon. Just keep smiling and act like you're having a good time."

"I've got too much on my mind to have a good time."

"Like what? If there's anything I can help with, tell me. That's what I'm here for."

"You can't drive the race car, Liz, and that's what I'm here to do."

Liz seized the opportunity to ask, "What's got you so stressed, Rick? I mean, it's only the third race of the season. If you're this uptight now, I hate to think what it will be like down the road."

He was not about to admit she was the cause, but before he could frame an answer, she cocked her head to one side, looked him straight in the eye and asked, "Is it me? Because if it is, I'll try to stay out of your way even more than I've been doing. But I'm not quitting, Rick. This job means everything to me right now, and I'm not going to let you ruin it for me."

He looked everywhere but at her, because he wanted so damn bad to kiss her. "Don't flatter yourself. I'm just tired, that's all. Easter isn't far off. I can take a mini-vacation then."

"Can't you take a few days off before the Atlanta race next weekend?"

"I probably could. But I won't. There's nowhere to go on short notice. I'd hoped to take some time off while we were out here and go exploring in the desert, but not a chance."

He gave himself a mental shake. He was being too chatty, telling her too much, getting close, and he couldn't let that happen. To counter, he all but snapped, "Hey, don't worry about me. I'm doing great. I plan to do even greater Sunday."

"Well, I certainly hope so."

After a few moments of silence, he could not resist teasing, "By the way, are you riding back to Charlotte with Benny?"

She squeezed his hand—hard. "Not funny."

He squeezed back—harder. "I think it is."

"You think you're so clever, don't you? Not letting me know Bobby wasn't able to go and how obnoxious Benny can be."

"Well, you have to admit it was an adventure."

They were looking at each other, about to burst into laughter.

Liz could not stay mad about the trip, despite how grueling it had been, because she got a great story out of it.

And Rick had to admit that despite how he'd tried in so many ways to annoy, she was a good sport.

But neither wanted the intimate moment of camaraderie.

"Enough of this." He took her hand and abruptly led her from the dance floor and straight over to Gary and his wife. Releasing Liz, he gave an exaggerated bow to Ida and said, "I believe you promised to cut in on me, ma'am, but since you forgot I'm not letting you get out of this dance."

Ida laughed and all but flew into his arms.

Gary, apologizing, bounded to his feet and led Liz back onto the floor. "I got lost talking racing. This is all still new to me, but I do love it."

"I'm glad," Liz said pleasantly. She liked Gary. He was very easygoing and nice to work with.

His brow furrowed as he said, "Tell me. How's he really doing? Do you think he's got a chance to win the rookie title?"

"You're asking the wrong person. I'm probably newer to racing than you are. But I'd say he's got a good shot. He's a terrific driver. Everybody says so. It's really too early in the season, though, to make any predictions.''

''My accountant has been making noises about the money we're spending. So I thought I'd send him to the Darlington race in South Carolina in a few weeks. I want you to show him around, and while you're doing it, make sure he sees how some of the bigger teams are millions of dollars ahead of us when it comes to spending money.''

''That won't be hard to do,'' she said, and laughed. ''All I have to do is take him around top drivers like Jeff Gordon and Dale Jarrett and let him see their equipment. Makes ours pale by comparison.''

Gary snorted. ''Well, if our boy wins the rookie title, I'll pull out all the stops and spend whatever it takes to put him right up there with them. This first year is a learning experience, anyway. I need to find out if the money is well-spent, whether our sales go up, and all the other figures my accountant nags about.''

''Of course. And I'm doing everything I can to see you get your money's worth.''

He grinned and gave a big whirl that almost sent them bumping into Rick and Ida, dancing next to them. ''You're doing a hell of a job, Liz. I couldn't be more pleased. And rest assured if Big Boy's does stay in racing, your agency will get the contract.''

Liz liked hearing that. ''Oh, that's great, and—''

''About the party in Darlington,'' he rushed on as the music wound down. ''Make this one for all the drivers, crew-members, as well as the media. Nothing formal. Just something fun. Ida and I will fly in for it.''

Liz said, ''Well, since it's for your accountant's benefit, I'll try to keep the cost down.''

He quickly waved away that notion. ''Don't worry about spending money till I tell you to, Liz. Now let's go mingle and make sure everyone is having a good time at *this* party.''

There was no doubt about that, and at midnight, when the

lease on the ballroom was up, Liz made quick arrangements with the hotel manager for another two hours.

She passed Mack in the hall on his way to the elevator bank.

"You're just like that battery bunny," he teased. "Still going strong."

She hadn't seen Rick in quite a while and asked Mack if had he already gone up to his room.

"Yeah, he told me he was sneaking out. I'm glad he did. We've got adjustments to make on the car first thing in the morning before practice runs." He gave her a quick hug. "You did good. It was a huge success."

The elevator doors opened. Mack stepped inside, but Liz held out her hand to keep the doors from closing. "I talked to Rick when we were dancing. He admits he's tired. I'm going to try to work out something for him to get a break. Would you have a problem with him flying home a day late?"

"Not at all. What do you have in mind?"

"I'm not sure yet. Just don't say anything to him about it. It will have to be a surprise, because feeling like he does about me he'd likely oppose any idea I came up with."

He held a finger to his lips. "Don't worry. I won't say a word."

Liz turned back toward the ballroom.

Rick had said he'd like a day in the desert. Well, she would give him one.

The only thing was—she had to be a part of the package, and he was not going to like that one little bit.

Rick stood before the floor-to-ceiling windows and gazed out at the awesome view of Las Vegas by night. Thousands, no, *millions,* of lights glittered as the city lay sprawled before him like a gigantic Christmas tree.

As always in a quiet moment, thoughts of Liz came to mind.

He wasn't tired, as he'd told her.

Neither was he irritable with the team because he needed a break.

It was Liz, and the situation was driving him crazy.

He liked her and wanted her, and, hell, he worried he might even be falling in love with her.

And no matter how hard he tried, there didn't seem to be a damn thing he could do about it.

Chapter Ten

Liz was beside herself.

It didn't matter that she had slipped in an oil spill in the pits, fallen on her bottom and had black streaks all over her slacks.

Neither did she care that her face was dirty or that her head was pounding from listening to the roar of race cars all afternoon.

What did matter was that Rick had finished the race in the top ten, and she, along with Mack and the rest of the crew were going crazy they were so happy.

Mack spun her around till she was dizzy. "This is going to put us way ahead in points. We're on our way now, for sure. Come on, let's meet him in the garage when he pulls in."

The whole team joined hands, running in a human chain and cheering at the top of their lungs.

Rick crawled out of the car and fell into Mack's arms for

a good-buddy back pounding. Then he high-fived everyone else…except Liz.

He gave her no more than a grin and a polite nod.

She made no effort to get close, instead calling out to congratulate before melting into the crowd of fans that were swarming.

Rick signed autographs for a few minutes and then begged off to go to the drivers' lounge and get a shower and change.

Liz found Benny and got him to unlock the truck so she could retrieve her laptop from where she had left it during the race. She needed to write a press release elaborating on Rick's performance. As always, there was no guarantee any of the media would use it, but she would make it available to them, anyway.

"Are you gonna be going back with me?" Benny asked, handing her the leather satchel with her computer. "I'm hittin' the road just as soon as everything's loaded."

"No," she told him, without regret, "I'm flying. But thanks, anyway."

"Well, if you change your mind let me know. I doubt you'll be able to get a flight back with the others, though."

With everything else going on the past few days she had not thought about making a reservation for the return flight home. Rushing to the infield media center, she found a quiet corner where she could use her cell phone to call the airline.

Sure enough, as Benny predicted, the late flight to Atlanta, where she'd have to change for Charlotte, was booked. Worse, there was nothing available till the next night. That meant she was stuck in Vegas. Maybe some people would not find that a bad thing, but Liz knew she wouldn't have any fun by herself.

"Would you like a window or aisle seat?" the woman on the other end of the line asked.

Liz was about to say it didn't matter when Luke Hembree, a sportswriter from a North Carolina newspaper walked in, glanced around, saw her and angrily yelled, "Hey, what's wrong with your driver? He just snapped my head off."

"I'll have to call you back," she said, and quickly hung up.

"I just asked for a few quotes," Luke said. "You know he and Blevins were rubbing fenders on those last two laps, and Blevins was already six laps down. I thought maybe it was a grudge thing, because everybody knows Blevins is the only driver who has a chance of beating out Castles for the rookie title. Well, he chewed me out and said he had enough on his mind without me trying to stir something up."

Liz tried to smooth things over. "I'm really sorry, Luke. He's just tired, that's all."

"Which is too bad, because if he's got personal problems it's not only going to affect his relationship with the media, but his driving, too. Maybe you better talk to him."

"Let me see if I can get him in here—"

Luke had started to walk away but spun around. "Don't bother. I wouldn't print his name now if he'd *won* the damn race."

Liz sank into the nearest chair, knees shaking. If Rick really was getting stressed-out, then Luke was right—eventually it would affect his racing and, ultimately, her job. Because how could she get publicity for him if no one could stand him?

She took her cell phone and hit redial. When she finally got through to reservations, she said, "Make it a window *and* aisle seat on tomorrow's flight. There'll be two of us going."

All it took was another quick call to Gary Staley on his cell phone to get everything arranged the way she wanted.

He was still in the private suite he had rented for all his guests, high above the track. There was a lot of noise in the background, and she knew they were celebrating Rick's finish.

"Didn't you say you weren't flying home till tomorrow?" she asked.

"That's right. There's a show Ida wants to see tonight. Why?"

"I was wondering if you'd like to invite Rick for a quiet little dinner tonight."

She held her breath.

"Hmm," he said slowly. "That's an idea. I really don't get a chance to talk to him much away from a crowd. But, say, isn't he going back on the late flight to Atlanta?"

"Not if you want to have dinner. I can arrange to get him home tomorrow."

"Good. Then do it. And will you be joining us, too?"

She grinned into the phone. "I wouldn't miss it for the world."

Rushing, she got together a short story on Rick's performance in the day's race, e-mailed it, then hurried back to the garage.

The crew had loaded just about everything. Only the car was left to be rolled up the ramp.

Benny teased, "I figured you'd change your mind. Just throw your stuff in. I'm about ready to pull out."

Liz merrily responded, "Well, I can't go with you unless you're leaving tomorrow."

Mack, standing nearby with Rick, heard her and said, "I thought you were flying back with us tonight."

"Can't. The big kahuna, himself, wants to do dinner."

"Staley?" Mack said, surprised. "You mean you've got to stay over to go out with him?"

"And his wife," she was quick to make clear. Then she dared look at Rick, who was quietly listening. "You, too."

"Huh?"

"You, too," she repeated. "He says he never gets a chance to talk to you when there isn't a crowd around."

"But I'll never make my flight," he protested.

"Don't worry. It's all taken care of. You're flying out tomorrow night with me." She looked to Mack. "One day won't make any difference, will it? He'll still have time to get ready for Atlanta."

Mack nodded. "Oh, heck, yeah. We won't leave for Atlanta till Wednesday. Qualifying is Thursday."

Rick looked ready to explode. "Next time, clear things with me before you go changing my reservation. Maybe I don't want to stay over."

"Well, maybe nobody cares what you want," she said frostily, not liking how he was glaring at her. "Not when it comes to pleasing the person who signs your paycheck, Castles. And you'd be wise to stow that attitude between now and seven o'clock or you might find yourself back racing hillbilly short tracks. I heard about how you snapped at Luke Hembree."

"Yeah," he admitted. "He was trying to stir something up...make it look like Blevins and I have a grudge going. I won't respond to that kind of nonsense."

"Well, I think you could have handled it a bit more tactfully. And like I said, stow that attitude."

She was almost to where she'd parked her rental car when Mack came running up.

"Listen, I'm sorry about all that. I just don't know what's eating him lately, but he's not happy about having to stay over tonight."

"That's too bad." She unlocked a rear door and put her things on the seat. "But when Luke Hembree told me how rudely he had behaved, I knew something had to be done."

"And you think making him stay over to eat with the boss is going to fix things?"

"That's not the whole plan, Mack. I just arranged having dinner with Mr. Staley to have an excuse to change Rick's reservation. I knew if I told him what I really had planned— to give him a little R and R—he'd never agree. This way, he doesn't have a choice."

"Aha." Mack leaned back against the side of the car, relaxing. "Suppose you tell me more."

"Well, we both agree Rick is uptight. He needs a break. You said he likes the outdoors, so I'm going to plan a day of sight-seeing tomorrow. Let him get out in the desert and unwind. It might not do any good, but it sure can't hurt.''

''That's a fact.'' He stepped away from the car, raised his arm, and she matched him for the familiar high-five. ''Good work. I just wish Rick appreciated you as much as the rest of us.''

So do I, she silently, soberly, agreed. *So do I.*

When the phone's shrill ringing awoke him from a sound sleep, Rick grabbed it and barked a hello. With a whole day to kill before his flight that night, he'd planned to sleep for most of it.

''Rick, hi. It's me.''

With a groan, he sank back against the pillows and threw an arm over his face. The last voice he wanted to hear was hers. ''What do you want? And how come you woke me up? If I have to waste time, at least I can try to catch up on my sleep.''

''Ah, but you aren't going to waste any time,'' she said exuberantly. ''Because I've got the day all planned, and you've got exactly thirty minutes to get ready and meet me in the lobby. And wear something casual. I think it's going to be a warm day.''

''Wait a minute.'' He bolted upright. ''What are you talking about?''

''Thirty minutes,'' she sang into the phone. ''Oh, and wear some comfortable shoes, too.''

Rick sat there listening to the dial tone buzzing in his ear as he wondered what the heck was going on. If she thought he was going to spend the day signing autographs in a parking lot in the blazing sun, she was crazy.

And he would tell her so.

He got up, opened the drapes and saw that it did look like a sizzling day ahead. But no matter. He was going to crawl right back in bed and spend it in air-conditioned comfort as soon as he set Liz straight.

He took a quick shower, put on jeans, T-shirt and sneakers, and went down to the lobby.

He was early. She'd said a half hour. It had only been twenty minutes.

His stomach growled, reminding him he hadn't eaten anything, and he went into the coffee shop.

And there she stood, right at the cash register.

He stepped up and put a hand on her arm. "Okay, what's this all about? I'm not signing autographs, because there's been no advance publicity. Nobody would show up, and it would be a waste of time."

"Who said anything about autographs?" She was signing a check, then, with a smile and a murmured "Have a nice day" to the cashier, she took the basket sitting on the counter and handed it to Rick. "You can carry this."

"Listen, I'm getting real tired of you making plans without asking me first. And whatever you've got in mind for today, you can do it alone—"

"I will not take no for an answer. Now come on. We're going to have a fun day."

"Says who? What am I carrying here, anyway?"

"We are going to the desert. You said you wished you had time when you were out here. Well, now you do."

"You're kidding."

"No, I'm not. After all, why should we waste the day? Come on. I've got it all planned. The hotel packed us a great lunch, and I've got a map that will take us to a ghost town about an hour's drive from here."

He hung back. "I'm not so sure this is a good idea."

"Well, after the way you treated Luke yesterday, I think you need to unwind. That wasn't very smart of you, by the way."

"Yeah, I know," he admitted. "I'd planned to give him a call and apologize."

"Well, you need a break, so maybe today will help."

No, Rick thought miserably as he doggedly followed her out of the hotel and to the parking lot, it was not going to help. Maybe he was stressed-out, but spending the day with the person causing it was a real no-brainer. Only she had no way of knowing that, so he could only cooperate and hope the time passed quickly.

"You drive. I'll navigate." She tossed him the keys.

He looked at her as they were getting into the car. She was wearing capris and one of his souvenir T-shirts.

With her hair pulled back in a ponytail and tied with a scarf, she was completely different from the glamorous woman he'd danced with Friday night...but still appealing...and still the one that crept into his dreams at night to make him wake up in a cold sweat.

She unfolded a map. "Do you want to see Hoover Dam?"

Her tone told him she didn't, and he wasn't particularly keen on any kind of tour. "No. Let's just go find your ghost town and then get back to the hotel."

She gave the map a loud rattle. "Now listen, buster. I told you—this is going to be a fun day. And you're going to have fun if I have to pound it into you."

They looked at each other and burst into laughter.

Rick couldn't help it. Her eyes had a mischievous gleam, and she was rattling the part of him that longed to be naughty, too. "So, okay. We'll do it even if we wind up killing each other."

She gave him a playful whack with the map she'd folded back up. "Hey, you're the one who can't stand me."

"I never said that."

"You didn't have to. You've made it clear in too many ways to count."

To change the subject, which was getting a bit uncomfortable, Rick indicated the basket he had placed between them. "What's in there? Probably silly little open-faced sandwiches, dainty little cookies, and a cooler of iced tea. *Chick* things," he added with a snicker.

"Proves how much you know." She lifted the lid to give him a peek. "Fried chicken, potato salad, ham-and-cheese sandwiches, and some fresh-baked goodies to die for.

"And—" she reached in and took one out "—ice-cold beer."

He was pleased and grudgingly allowed, "Well, maybe you are good for something besides getting in the way."

"I'll let that pass, since I don't want to let anything spoil today. So suppose we call a truce?"

She held out her hand.

He shook it without hesitation. "Deal."

With a sigh of relief, Liz leaned back and propped her feet on the dash. "Okay, let me study this map so we won't get lost once we hit the desert."

"We already are. You just can't see it for all the hotels and casinos."

And it appeared he was right. One minute they were in the glitz and glitter of Las Vegas, and the next they were surrounded by barren land as far as the eye could see.

After a while, Rick asked, "Hey, navigator. Are you sure you know how to read that map?"

"Yes. There's a road up ahead to the left. It should take us straight to it."

"And what is this place?"

"According to what the guidebook says, it was an old mining town back in the 1900s."

"Hey, you're all wet on your geography," he said gleefully. "History was my best subject. Particularly the Old West. And the days of the silver boom were the 1870s—not the 1900s."

She smirked. "Well, you need to go back and brush upon your history, because you've obviously forgotten there were new finds in all ores around the 1900s, which caused another boom."

He thought a moment, then nodded. "Okay, okay. You got me. So finish telling me about this place you're dragging me off to."

"It was rebuilt for a tourist attraction a few years ago, but it didn't stay open long. I guess people thought it was just too remote. Anyway, I thought it would be fun to visit because it's not so touristy.''

Slowing as they rounded one last clump of boulders, he said, ''Well, I'll be darned. There it is.''

It looked as if it came right out of a movie set—a long, narrow street bordered by wide-fronted buildings. Very western-looking, with tumbleweeds, caught by the warm breeze, bouncing and bobbing against the water troughs and hitching posts that ran alongside plank walkways.

Some windows were boarded up, and a few had been broken out completely. Shutters hung from rusting nails. A few roofs had caved in, and several porches had collapsed.

Liz pointed to a building in far better shape than the others. ''See the sign over the door? Silver Nugget. That must have been the saloon where they staged the Wild West shows when it was a tourist town. Let's check it out.''

He stopped the car right in the middle of the dusty street, and they got out.

''Be careful,'' he warned as Liz started down the boardwalk. ''Some of those planks might be rotten.''

He hung back to watch her and thought how she was like a kid, ponytail bobbing as she hurried along as fast as she dared, eyes shining with excitement. It was hard to envision she was the same dedicated businesswoman who could write a press release with one hand while planning a formal dinner for hundreds with her other.

She was one hell of a woman, all right, and under different circumstances he would have let nothing stand in the way of making her his own.

Think positive, he told himself as he started walking behind her. Maybe when he was ready to retire she'd still be around.

Yeah, right, he thought miserably. He had seen the way guys looked at her. Sooner or later somebody would come along and snatch her up, and he just hoped he wasn't around to see it. He ached badly enough as it was.

It was not as though he had not lent time to thinking she

might be different from other women. After all, racing was her job. She might be able to stand the pressure.

But he could not be sure.

And could take no chances.

Not with his career, his future, at stake.

Liz looked over her shoulder to see what was keeping him. He appeared to be deep in thought...brooding. She wondered why and hoped he was not angry over her practically kidnapping him to get him out there. He seemed to be enjoying himself, but she had to make sure...had to get him in the mood to relish each and every moment of the rare day off from the pressures of racing.

They entered the saloon. With the sun high overhead, there was light to see the long bar against one wall, empty shelves for glasses behind.

Everything of value had been taken. Only a few rickety tables and chairs remained.

At one end there was a stage, framed by tattered velvet drapes.

"Can you imagine?" Liz gushed as she ran to stand right in the middle of it. "What it must have been like in the old days? Women dressed in satin and feathers and layers of lace petticoats, kicking up their heels to the music of a tinny piano, while men shouted and yelled and fired their pistols in the air.

"Look." She pointed at the ceiling. "I think I can see bullet holes."

"Oh, silly, you cannot," Rick said, and laughed. "You're really getting into this, aren't you?"

"Of course. I always loved the West. When I was little, I played cowboys all the time." She wandered offstage for a moment, then cried, "Oh, look what I found," and returned carrying a cardboard box with clothes spilling out of it.

"Costumes." She set it on the floor, then dropped to her knees and began pawing through it. "Oh, Rick, just look at this. It's a treasure trove."

"For *moths*." He reached down to pull out a worn vest with a rusting star pinned on the front. "This must have been what the marshal wore in the stage show. There's a hat, too." He dusted it off. "And a holster and toy gun. I'm surprised this was left behind."

"They aren't as good at snooping as I am. It was stashed under a broken table with trash all around. No one saw it when they moved out, I guess."

She had taken out a wrinkled gown of red satin, the bodice crusted in sequins and edged with fluffy pink feathers. "This is the kind of dress I'd have worn if I'd lived back then," she said wistfully as her fingers smoothed the skirt.

"And you know what?" She looked up at him with bright, happy eyes. "I'm going to put it on and play like I did."

Rick shook his head, amused. She was having a ball, and he decided to join her.

A few moments later, when she stepped from behind what was left of the drapes, his mouth fell open.

Despite how old and worn the dress was, it was beautiful on Liz. She had found some old combs at the bottom of the box and used them to pin her hair up.

"I even found shoes," she gushed, lifting her skirt and petticoats to reveal old leather button-ups. "And this feather boa, and…" She trailed off, realizing he, too, had changed. He now wore the vest, hat and holster, and a pair of boots that were so large on him they were comical.

"I'm the marshal, ma'am," he said, tripping in the boots as he started toward her. "And I'm gonna have to arrest you for showing your ankles."

"You'll never take me alive. Besides, I've got a show to do, and I plan to show more than my ankles." She turned around, bent over and flipped her skirts at him.

"That did it," he said with a roar, and went after her.

But Liz was already doing an old tap-dance routine she had learned when she had taken lessons as a child. Rick, impressed, stood back to watch. Then she began to sing along with the steps.

She was good, and he complimented, "I think you missed your calling. You should have gone into show business instead of racing."

"I'm not in racing," she corrected with a final step and a curtsy. "I'm in public relations, and, in case you haven't noticed, that's just about the same as show business."

"Well, could be," he allowed. "I never thought of it like that." He took her hand and helped her down from the stage. "Come on. Let's take a look around town and see if there's any varmints I need to lock up."

It was nearly two o'clock when they had lunch. Returning to the saloon, Liz set one of the rickety tables with the paper plates, cups and napkins the hotel had packed.

"Okay, Marshal," she said when everything was ready. "Come eat your grub."

"That I will." He reached for a chicken leg. "All this lawman stuff makes me hungry."

Afterward, Liz put her own clothes back on, and Rick removed the vest and boots. She repacked the box and put it back where she found it, explaining, "Mack said he'd love to bring Ida out here to a race sometime. I'll tell them where this is hidden, and maybe it will still be here."

"Good idea." He motioned her to the door. "Now let's do a little sight-seeing in the desert right around here. Maybe there's an old silver mine."

There was, and Rick couldn't believe his luck in finding a tiny silver nugget in the rocks and sand. "Needs cleaning up, but I'm sure it's silver. Here." He handed it to her. "It's yours. Get it polished, and you've got yourself a genuine souvenir of the Old West."

She was touched and thanked him, and, for a moment, they stood gazing at each other in an awkward silence. Then Rick checked the time. "It's getting on close to five o'clock. We'd better be heading back before it starts getting dark. It also feels like it's getting cooler."

"I noticed," she said, wrapping her arms about her and

shivering. "I've always heard it can get real cold in the desert at night."

She gathered the picnic things, and they went to the car.

Rick turned the ignition key but nothing happened.

"I don't believe this," he said, pulling the hood release and getting out.

Liz was right behind him. "What do you think it is? Surely, you can fix it if anybody can. I mean, as much as you know about cars, it can't be a problem."

He opened the hood. "Yes, it can," he said with a resigned sigh. "Because I can't do anything about a dead battery in the middle of nowhere."

She gasped, "You're kidding."

"No. I'm not. And ordinarily it wouldn't be a problem, because we'd use jumper cables and get somebody to give us a boost. But here in the middle of nowhere?" He shook his head in complete dismay.

"But we've got a plane to catch."

"Not tonight we don't. If a car doesn't happen by, which isn't likely, we're stuck here for no telling how long."

Liz groaned as she turned around and around, fingers pressed to her temples. "This cannot be happening."

"Well, it is." He slammed the hood down. "And we'll just have to camp out here tonight, and in the morning I'll hike out to the highway. As best I remember, it's about five miles. I'd go now, but it would be dark before I got there and I might lose my way."

"You're also not leaving me here by myself, and I'm not about to strike out with you at dusk."

He motioned toward the dilapidated hotel. "We didn't explore that. Maybe they left a few beds behind."

They entered the lobby, and with the sun going down, it was difficult to see their way. Rick returned to the car and found a flashlight, then they went upstairs. Only one room had a bed still in it, an old iron four-poster with a thin, sagging mattress.

Liz saw a huge lizard scurrying in front of the flashlight's beam and promptly declared, "You can have it. I'm sleeping in the car."

She practically ran down the steps getting out of there.

Rick laughed and followed her. "We'll both sleep in the car. You take the back, and I'll fight the steering wheel in the front."

Liz bantered right back, "As if that's a hardship. Be thankful you don't have a cheap sponsor who rents economy cars. In case you haven't noticed, this is a luxury sedan."

Actually, Liz found the back seat quite comfortable, but, as darkness fell, wished for a blanket. The temperature rapidly dropped and soon she was freezing. "I wish we could run the heater."

"Sorry. Any food left?"

She found a few pieces of chicken and a stale sandwich, which they shared. There were also a couple of candy bars and some bottled water.

It was strangely quiet. Rick commented that the bugs that might have kept up a racket had probably left with the tourists.

"I think the lizards ate them all," Liz said cryptically. "Like the one in the hotel."

"Mack will wonder what happened when I don't show up tonight."

"I imagine so, but we'll call him as soon as we get near a phone. There's no way my cell will work out here in this wilderness. I've already tried, thinking we could call for help."

Neither was sleepy, and they talked on—about the coming race in Atlanta, and the one after that in Darlington. Liz told him she was going to plan a barbecue there and invite all the teams. He said he thought that was a fine idea.

Rick shared bits and pieces about his growing-up years. Liz did the same and found herself telling him about her bad marriage. He likewise confided a little concerning his own.

As the night wore on, Liz felt the wall between them tumbling down a bit at the time. They were actually starting to become friends, and if being stuck in the desert all night was what it took to do it, then she was glad the battery had conked out.

But even elation over their improving relationship did nothing to ward off the ever-increasing cold. And when her teeth started chattering, Rick said, "This is ridiculous. We're both freezing—we've got to try to keep each other warm."

With that, he rolled over into the back seat and put his arms around her, drawing her close. "We'll use our body heat," he said, trying to sound casual about it when he was anything but.

Liz turned sideways in hopes he wouldn't feel how her heart was about to leap right out of her chest. Trying to make light of what was becoming a very traumatic moment, she said, "Hey, it's a good thing we called a truce. Otherwise you'd have let me freeze to death."

"No, I wouldn't," he said gruffly, positioning himself so she would not feel the swelling of his desire that mere closeness had ignited. "It's late. Maybe we need to stop talking and go to sleep so the night will pass quickly."

She was silent for a moment, then murmured, "I used to do that, you know."

"Do what?" Lost in the battle waging within over how badly he wanted her, he had forgotten what they were talking about.

"Try to go to sleep so the night would pass quickly. I did that on Christmas Eve so Santa Claus would hurry and come. Only it didn't work. I always lay awake half the night."

"That's what you get for believing in Santa Claus."

"Oh, and you didn't?" She turned her face, trying to see him in the serene darkness.

Huskily he murmured, "If I did, I'd ask him to leave you in my stocking."

And it happened.

Her lips touched his cheek, and, with a soft moan, he turned and covered her mouth with his. Hot. Searing.

Liz's deep, delicious sigh emanated from her very soul.

She melted against him, quivering as his tongue slipped inside her mouth.

As though with a will of their own, her arms twined about his neck, her back arching to get ever closer.

The firmness of his lips, the intimacy of his tongue melding against hers, the play of his hands as they danced their way across her face, her neck, to ultimately close about her breasts, was making her mad with desire.

She felt her nipples tingling, growing hard, and was warmed by the sudden rush to her belly.

Without a word, his mouth still devouring hers, he pressed her down on the seat.

She helped him unfasten and remove her slacks, and then he was shoving her bra up.

Lowering his face to her breasts, she wriggled against him in sheer pleasure, her hands twining in his hair as he moved his lips to take each nipple in turn.

Liz had never made love in the back seat of a car before and dizzily thought how even a king-size bed could not have offered more sublime ecstasy as he positioned himself between her thighs.

She clutched his back, nails digging into the rock-hard flesh. Then his lips found hers again, his fingers closing on her breasts as he shoved himself inside her.

She gave a sharp cry that melted to raptured moans as he began moving rhythmically to and fro.

There were no questions asked, no answers given, amidst the silent acclamation of their hearts and bodies yielding at last to that which each had struggled in their own way to deny.

And when it was over, when they miraculously crested together, Rick collapsed with his face against her heaving bosom and hoarsely whispered, "I never knew it could be this good."

Liz lovingly caressed him, wishing, willing, the poignant moment would never end.

For she was afraid to face the reality of what they had done.

Chapter Eleven

Liz thought she was dreaming again. Too many times to remember, she had dreamed of Rick kissing her awake. Only that morning, it was real.

Startled, she tried to sit up, but he held her back, forcing her to succumb to the pleasure of his lips.

When at last he released her, he shook his head in wonder. "I can't believe this. I feel like I'm back in high school."

She giggled. "Well, I wouldn't know. I never made love in the back seat of a car in high school." Then, realizing how prim that sounded, she added, "I never got the chance. I was raised by a very strict aunt who didn't let me stay out after dark." And it was true. Her first real date was not until she moved out after graduation and got a place of her own.

Rick yawned and stretched. "Well, I guess we'd better get our hiking boots on."

"What hiking boots? Don't I wish. It's a long walk back to the main road." She was glad he was not dwelling on last night. After all, it probably wouldn't have happened if not for the situation they'd been in and probably never would again...much to her regret. So she supposed it was best they try to forget it.

They each went their way to tend to personal needs. Then they took bottles of water from the picnic basket and set out walking in the early morning sun.

It took well over an hour to reach the main road, where they could only sit and wait for a car to come along.

Rick said, "By now Mack has found out we weren't on the plane and called the hotel to find out we haven't checked out. He's going to be in a panic."

"I know." Liz stared at her cell phone and the flashing message denoting there was no service. "I'll call him as soon as we get near a tower."

"And what will you tell him?"

She shrugged. "That the battery went dead while we were in the middle of nowhere. What else?"

"And let him know we spent the night together?"

She tried to make light of the situation. "Well, he wouldn't think anything happened. He knows you can't stand me."

"Liz, I have never said I couldn't stand you."

"You didn't exactly go around telling people you'd like to sleep with me, either."

His eyes twinkled. "Well, you don't know that. I might have said what a cute bottom you've got."

She laughed and scooped up a handful of sand and made to throw it at him, though they both knew she wasn't about to.

He caught her wrist and kissed her closed fist. With a steady gaze, he said, "Listen, Liz. Last night was wonderful. And I'm not sorry it happened, but we both know we've got to work together, and—"

"And it can't happen again," she finished for him. She supposed she'd been expecting him to say something like that. "Right. I agree."

Mercifully, in the stilted silence that followed, a car appeared on the horizon. They leaped to their feet and began waving frantically, cheering when it stopped.

The man and woman in the car were very friendly and accommodating. They drove them back to the ghost town, gave the battery a charge, and soon they were all on their way to Las Vegas.

A few miles out of town Liz was able to use her cellphone. First, she called the airline and learned they could get a flight out in two hours if they could make it. She relayed the information to Rick, and he gave an assenting nod. Then she called Mack and said, "Car trouble," in the middle of his frenzied demand to know what had happened. She gave him their flight number, arrival time in Charlotte, then said the connection was breaking up and ended the call.

"No need to try to explain over the phone," she said in response to Rick's puzzled glance. "I think he was pretty worried. We'll try to come up with something believable as to why we didn't get in touch with him before now."

"Right, we'll talk about it on the plane."

But, as it turned out, they wound up doing very little talking on the plane. Their seats were in the very back row. And one minute they were sitting side by side, both silent and reflecting on what had transpired between them in the past few hours, and the next Rick had spread a blanket over them and they were kissing as if there was no tomorrow.

"This is crazy," he said breathlessly between kisses. "I thought you couldn't stand me…that you only put up with me because you have to."

"You're the one who's always trying to get rid of me," she said, gasping as she clung to him.

"Not anymore." His lips trailed to her neck. "You can hang around all you want to…"

"And you'll never get to race, because we'll be in the truck doing this," she teased.

"Oh, no. We're not taking any chances on anybody finding out."

"I know that," she said. "I was only teas—"

He silenced her with another kiss.

It was dark when they arrived in Charlotte, for they had encountered delays. Mack was waiting for them, and Rick immediately offered the story he and Liz had come up with—that the car had broken down on the way to the airport, and by the time they got a cab, the plane had left.

"You could've called me," he said. "I didn't know what was going on."

"Sorry." She did not look at him. "I was so tired when we got back to the hotel I fell asleep, and when I woke up it was too late to call."

Rick offered his excuse. "And I went to a show."

"Okay, okay, so now you're here safe and sound," Mack said. "Get some rest tonight. We're leaving for Atlanta at five so we can be at the track when it opens."

They reached Liz's apartment first. She avoided eye contact with Rick as she said a cheery good-night. Mack asked when she was driving to Atlanta, and she said not till Friday. "I've got a lot of paperwork to do."

Finally, in the quiet and privacy of her own place, Liz tossed her luggage aside. There would be time to unpack later. Right then all she wanted was soft music playing and a glass of chilled wine while she sat on her balcony and looked out on the lights of Charlotte.

She took a hot shower, wrapped herself in her favorite robe—a fluffy pink chenille—and poured her wine.

In the mellow darkness, tears came to Liz's eyes as she thought of the past twenty-four hours. What conversation she and Rick had shared had not been of a very serious nature. They agreed discretion was called for. It would not do for the crew, the media, and certainly not her boss, or Rick's sponsor, to find out.

Perhaps that was why neither of them had spoken of the future. After all, a one-night stand brought about by circumstances beyond their control could hardly be regarded as a relationship. She would just try to file it away under good memories to recall on a lonely night.

Her smile was bitter to think how many of those there were.

The doorbell rang, jarring her from reverie.

Warily she went to answer. It was too late for visitors, and she didn't know anyone besides the guys on the team, anyway. Probably it was a pizza delivery boy who had the wrong address.

She peered through the peephole, then gasped.

"Rick, what are you doing here?" she cried once she had the chain lock undone and the door open. "I thought—"

"I thought, too—" he grinned after a quick kiss "—about you and me and how good we are together."

He scooped her up into his arms, then smacked his lips and said, "Mmm. Kisses that taste like warm, sweet wine. It just don't get no better."

He set her on her feet but did not let her go. Instead he began to sway in time to the lilting music of the Barry White CD that was playing. "I wanted to hold you like this at the party," he murmured, pressing his lips against her forehead. "But I didn't dare."

He took her chin between his thumb and forefinger, lifting her face to his gaze. "It's okay, isn't it? Me being here, I mean? I tried to go to bed, but I couldn't sleep. I kept thinking of you…us…how good it was, how much I wanted you."

His lips covered hers to sear and possess, and then he paused to whisper, "If you don't want it, just tell me."

She was held deliciously captive in his warm embrace and completely seduced by his seeking mouth. As his hands caressed her back and slid to cup her bottom, she could only cling helplessly to him. "Yes, I do want it, Rick. I think—"

She was grateful he again silenced her, for she had been about to confess that she had wanted him ever since the first time they had met. And that would not do. He had to think last night had been spontaneous. Pride would not allow her to reveal otherwise.

He opened her robe, and it fell in a soft pool around her ankles. Holding her away from him, he raked her with feverish eyes. "Beautiful," he said softly, huskily. "Absolutely beautiful."

He leaned to take a nipple into his mouth and suckled gently, then crushed her against him to take all of her.

She threw her head back, long hair dusting her back. His hand went to her buttocks once more to thrust her against him, and she could feel his hardness.

"Not here," she said as he began to steer her toward the sofa.

Shyly she took his hand and led him into the bedroom. It was not as feminine and cozy as she would have liked. Since moving, she'd scarcely had time to do more than put sheets on the bed and throw a blanket on top. But she knew it did not matter, because he had eyes only for her as she lay back to wait while he undressed.

Liz marveled at the glorious sight of him, shivers rippling from head to toe. He had the magnificently toned body of an athlete. She knew that he, like many of the drivers, worked out to give them the strength and stamina they needed for the racetrack.

He lay down beside her. "This beats making like a pretzel last night," he said lightly, his fingers trailing up and down her side. "But I can't complain, and I'd do it again if that's all we had."

"And so would I."

She felt his erection slipping between her thighs. "I want you so bad, Liz. Here and now."

Her desire was just as fierce. Rolling onto her back, she urged him into position, then, reaching down, maneuvered him up and into her. "Then take me," she commanded.

With a low, delighted growl, he drove himself in hard and deep.

Her nails raked his back and hugged him tighter. She lifted her hips eagerly to meet his every thrust.

And then she felt it coming—the ultimate thrill of release.

And he came with her, in hard, quick jabs.

Afterward, he rolled to his side, taking her with him. He did not let her go, instead holding her tight in quiet awe of the raw desire that had captivated them so quickly.

In the velvet wake that follows tenderness and passion, Liz longed to speak, to tell him how she was helplessly falling in love with him but knew she had to remain silent.

After a while, she thought perhaps he was sleeping, because he was so still and quiet.

She started to get up.

"Where are you going?"

"I thought you were asleep. I was going to get my wine."

He grabbed her and pulled her down beside him once more. "And you thought you could sneak away from me that easily? I don't think so."

He began to rain kisses over her face, her neck, then down to her breasts and belly. "I'm going to make up for being in such a hurry. We've got the whole night, and I want to revel in every moment of it."

And revel they did.

After another wild round of torrid lovemaking, they showered together, then wound up in bed all over again. Liz knew that never had she experienced such joy and wonder in a man's arms.

Finally they slept, exhausted.

Some time later, Liz was jolted awake to hear Rick curse, "Damn it, I've overslept."

Groggy she reached for the bedside lamp and turned it on to see Rick rapidly dressing.

"It's nearly seven o'clock. Mack was supposed to pick me up at my place at six. No telling what he's thinking."

"Well, thank God for cell phones," she said. "Call him and tell him…" She trailed off uncertainly.

Rick scowled. "Yeah, right. Tell him what?"

He was buttoning his shirt as he headed for the door.

Liz got out of bed and padded after him, snatching her robe from where she'd left it on the floor the night before. "You'll think of something. Tell him you went to eat breakfast and had a flat tire or something."

"He'd wonder why I didn't call. See?" He paused at the door to grin. "Sometimes cell phones can also be a curse."

He gave her a quick kiss. "But it was worth it, Liz. See you in Atlanta. And remember—" he tweaked her chin "—go back to acting like you can't stand me."

Then he was gone, and she was once again left to her memories...which were, she smiled to think, getting better all the time.

Rick cringed to see Mack standing in the middle of the parking lot, hands on his hips, feet apart.

"So you're back tom-catting again, are you?" Mack irritably greeted. "Why didn't you tell me last night you had a late date? I could have dropped you off there and picked you up this morning to save time."

"Sorry. It was a sudden thing. And I'm only an hour behind schedule."

Mack grunted. "An hour and a half."

"Whatever. I won't be but a minute. Gotta get some stuff and shave."

He ran inside, emptied dirty clothes out of his bag and threw in some clean ones, making a mental note to do laundry his first night back. And when would that be? Sunday night. Right. It wasn't far to Atlanta. Then he'd be leaving for Darlington...when? He looked at the schedule on the refrigerator door. Tuesday. There was an annual golf tournament for drivers. Liz had said she wanted him to take part in that. Good exposure. Maybe a plug for the sponsor when he wore the special shirt with the Big Boy's logo she'd had made up for the occasion.

She was good at what she did, he thought as he took a

quart of orange juice out of the fridge to take with him. She knew her stuff when it came to PR.

And other things, as well, he acknowledged with a heated rush.

He genuinely hoped it would work out they could keep things casual. There hadn't been time for a serious conversation. It was all too new to them, that special wonder-of-it-all time between lovers. But he vowed they would eventually have an understanding. They had to, or a good thing would be ruined.

Traveling together, working together, it could be an ideal situation for both of them…as long as Liz kept things in perspective. After all, it was only sex. Certainly not romance, not the way they'd traded barbs. They each had a physical need. That's all. An itch, as Rick liked to call it. And they had scratched it and would do so again at the first opportunity.

Chances were, he reasoned, she was only using him as he was using her.

Rick was shaving and paused to stare at himself in the mirror.

He was not so sure that's how it was.

And he also wasn't so sure it was merely for sex.

He liked her. They'd had a hell of a good time that day in the desert, and she was more fun than any woman he'd ever been with. The sex part of it just came naturally. He hadn't schemed or planned to seduce her. It was just one of those things.

And now that it had happened, he liked her all the more.

Rick's cell phone rang as he and Mack neared the outskirts of Atlanta. It was Liz, telling him she had arranged an appearance for him Friday night at the grand opening of a local Big Boy's Pizza.

She apologized for the late notice but said she only found out about it that morning. "I guess they figured since you'd be in town for the race, anyway, there was no need to let us know any sooner.''

''Well, we could have had something else planned,'' he said...then wished he hadn't. It might make her think he'd been planning on asking her out. Quickly he added, ''What I mean is, you might have had a radio show lined up or something. Charlotte is a big race—six hundred miles, longest on the circuit. Lots of things go on beforehand.''

''And we'll try to make sure if there's any publicity to be had that you're right in the middle of it. By the way, were you terribly late meeting Mack?''

''Not too.'' He didn't want to talk about that...didn't want to be reminded of just why he'd been late, because it made him hot to think about it. Indeed, he felt like a teenager again, and she was the reason.

Liz did not miss the guarded way he responded. It had to be awkward for him to talk with Mack right there. ''Well, I'll see you Friday. If the team needs anything before, you know where to reach me. And don't forget to tell Mack we'll need a car there.''

''Yeah. Sure.'' He punched the button to disconnect.

''I take it that was Liz,'' Mack said. ''Anything wrong?''

''No. Why?'' He was suddenly apprehensive, wondering if his voice had given him away.

''Just wondering. She usually calls me.''

Rick bit back a curse. That was true. She would tell Mack about any appearance where the show car was needed, and then he passed along the information to him. It had been another way she had of avoiding him...till now.

''That must mean you two are getting along better,'' Mack said. ''I guess the R and R did the trick. By the way, how was your trip to the desert?''

Rick gave a careless shrug. ''Nothing special. Just an old ghost town. It was nice being in the wide-open spaces, though.''

''Well, it's good you two are hitting it off at last. Liz is quite a gal. Any guy would like to have her hanging around.''

Rick decided to nip in the bud then and there any notion Mack had of a romance between him and Liz. ''I still don't like her hanging around. Women don't belong around race-tracks. Not in a working capacity. Or as a wife or girlfriend. They get in the way, and they overreact.''

''I have to argue that point. Ida isn't like that.''

''You aren't a driver, Mack. If you were, she'd go bananas, like other wives, when you crashed.''

''Not all wives do that. Just like all wives don't mind their husbands being involved in racing. Just because you had one that did, you're judging all women, and that's not fair.

''Besides,'' he rushed on, not giving Rick a chance to say anything, ''I don't think Liz is like that. From what I've seen, she's got it all together.''

''Like when she fainted in Daytona when I crashed.''

Mack admonished, ''Don't tell me you still think that's what it was. You know she hadn't eaten all day, and she was worn-out from working and worrying over her first race.''

Rick still wasn't sure and supposed it didn't matter. What worried him now was keeping things cool where she was concerned.

His rational side told him to back away and quit while he was ahead.

But the reckless part of him could not wait to be with her again.

''Wonder if she's seeing anybody.''

Rick swung his head around to stare at Mack. ''How would I know?''

''I just thought she might have mentioned something since you two spent so much time together in Vegas.''

''We didn't get personal.'' Rick turned on the radio in hopes Mack would take the hint and shut up.

He didn't.

''I guess I worry she'll meet some guy and fall in love

and quit. It'd be a shame to lose her, too. She's done a super job. But she is good-looking, and—''

''What is it with you?'' Rick snapped. ''You got the hots for her or something?''

''No,'' Mack responded quietly, and flashed a smile in Rick's direction. ''I'm just trying to rattle your cage, old buddy, to make you see she'd be perfect for you, if you could lose that attitude.''

Rick scrunched down in the seat and pulled his cap over his face. ''Wake me when we get to the track. I'm too tired for your nonsense.''

Mack chuckled. ''That's what you get for staying out all night trying to forget how having Liz around bugs you.''

''Forget her?'' Rick raised the cap long enough to stare incredulously. ''How can I forget someone I never think about?'' Covering his face once more, he settled back down and tuned Mack out.

He had lied.

He did think about Liz.

Every day.

All day long.

And now that he knew the sweetness of making love to her it was even worse.

Arriving at the track, they went first to the credentials office to get all the passes needed for the team. Then they parked out front to wait for Bobby to arrive with the truck and the crew.

The media was also starting to come in. Several spotted Rick and waved.

''See? She's made a star out of you,'' Mack teased. ''Otherwise, you'd be just an also-ran.''

Rick didn't bother responding. He knew Mack was worried that if he and Liz didn't get along, she might just quit. And he couldn't tell him that wasn't going to happen. Not now. So he let him rave on.

''I realize you had a name before you came on the Grand

National circuit, Rick, but nothing like now. And you really do owe it all to Liz. I mean, heck, I've seen PR guys who only do what they have to. Liz goes above and beyond the call of duty.''

Rick wished Bobby would hurry up. They needed to find their assigned garage space and get unloaded so he could take the car out and shake it down. If any adjustments had to be made before qualifying runs tomorrow, there would be time to do them, and—

''Hey, Castles.''

Abruptly Rick came out of his musings.

Mark Higgins was standing next to the open window on Rick's side of the car.

''How's it going?'' He asked as if he didn't really care and, in the same breath, said, ''When's Liz getting in?''

Rick bit down on the inside of his jaw to keep from registering anger. He didn't like Higgins…didn't like his sneaky little winks. ''Friday,'' he said curtly.

''Oh, good. She'll be here in time for the big party. I'm going to see if she wants to ride with me. It's on the other side of town.''

''What party?'' Rick was fast getting rankled and knew that was dangerous.

''Oh, one of the Atlanta writers always throws a party at his house on Friday night. He has it catered, hires a band. It's for media only. She needs to go and meet some new people.''

''Well, I'm afraid she won't be able to. We've got a grand opening to do for my sponsor.''

''So?'' Mark shrugged as though it were no big deal. ''I can take her there, and then we can go to the party.''

Rick chose his words carefully, not wanting to offend Mark. After all, he was a big writer for the Charlotte paper and had done several stories on him. Neither did he want to give away his annoyance over the possibility of Liz going out with him. ''Well, suppose you call her and discuss it with her. Do you have her cell phone number?''

"No, I don't."

Rick noted that Mark drew his reporter's pad from his hip pocket in a fast draw that would have made Wyatt Earp envious.

He gave him a number, and Mark scribbled it down.

"Thanks, buddy," he said. "I appreciate this."

Rick watched him walk away, head high, arms swinging. Real happy he was.

"You don't care if Liz goes out with him?" Mack asked quietly.

Rick turned to him with mock wonder. "I don't care who she goes out with."

"Really?"

"Yeah, really."

"Then why," Mack said with a sly grin, "did you give him the wrong number?"

Chapter Twelve

Rick had qualified in the top ten for the Atlanta race and ultimately finished in fifteenth position. He was leading in rookie points and flying high.

He and Liz did not have a private moment together all weekend. She had been kept busy writing press releases and escorting VIPs around. And when they were at the same functions, there was always a crowd.

Rick had tried not to look at her when she was around, because if anyone noticed romantic sparks flying between them, then the rumors would start for sure. When it came to gossip, racing was like a small town.

At the track Saturday Mark Higgins had come up to him and said the cell phone number he'd given him for Liz was wrong.

Rick had feigned surprise. "Really? Well, you must have written it down wrong, and right now I don't remember. Check with her."

"Yeah, sure," Mark said, disappointed. "But I really wanted her to go to that party with me."

"She wouldn't have gone. Like I told you, we had to be at a grand opening for my sponsor, and she stayed the whole time."

"I'm sure she did," Mark said, sounding a bit miffed. "You know, Rick, she does more for you than other PR reps do for their drivers. She's always going to functions with you that she doesn't have to. She needs to get out and mingle more…make contacts."

Rick was checking spark plugs with a magnifying glass. "Well, you know I don't have anything to do with that, Mark. She does what she wants to, and I have nothing to do with her private life." He paused to smile. "I just drive race cars."

After the race ended, Rick and the crew had wasted no time loading up and returning to the shop. They only had three days to get ready before leaving for Darlington.

Late that night, Rick tossed and turned in his bed, unable to sleep. He wondered if Liz had made it back to Charlotte from Atlanta okay. He'd overheard her telling one of the VIPs from Big Boy's that she would be glad to take him to the airport after the race.

Several times he reached for the phone to call her but changed his mind. Maybe it would be best to let it go…let *her* go. After all, she hadn't made any effort to be with him during the weekend. They had stayed at the same hotel. She could have called him and invited him to her room but hadn't. And he could have done the same to get her to his but felt it wise to give it a rest.

He reasoned that what had happened between them actually had no substance…no meaning. They had been trapped in a predicament not of their making and fallen into each other's arms. The fact that he'd gone rushing over to her apartment right after they got home was just reaction to the tempestuous flight together. They had kissed and made out like kids, and he hadn't been able to shake being aroused.

In short, he had to scratch that itch again.

He swore at himself in disgust.

That kind of thinking made it all seem so dirty, and that's not how it had been...and not how it was. But maybe he needed to take that attitude. Otherwise, he would find himself getting in over his head.

Sometimes in a race he'd be about to pass somebody in a tricky situation. He would be right up on their bumper when instinct told him if he didn't back off he would take them both out of the race.

That's how it had to be with Liz.

Instinct was telling him to back off before they wrecked.

Liz stared glumly at the phone. It was nearly three in the morning. She had finally gotten everyone to the airport who needed to go, and then the drive back to Charlotte had taken nearly four hours. She was exhausted.

She had checked her messages the minute she walked in the door and was disappointed there was nothing from Rick. She had thought after they hadn't had a second alone together all weekend that he would have wanted to see her as soon as he got back.

She told herself she was being silly. The man had just finished a grueling six-hundred-mile race and was bound to be worn-out completely. The last thing he would feel like was making love.

But why did it have to be only for that, she wondered miserably. If he cared anything about her, he'd want to just be with her.

She was, however, forgetting that he did not care about her and never would, and they were only having a good time whenever they could with no strings.

She had no right to expect him to call and knew she should be glad he didn't. After all, feeling as she did about him, things could get out of hand before they both knew it.

Keep it casual. Keep it cool. Stop thinking about him. And

when it happens, it happens. Then forget about it till the next time.

It was the only way to keep going.

The only way to keep the promise she'd made to herself.

But as she finally drifted away to sleep, she couldn't help wishing the phone would ring.

When she arrived in Darlington midweek, Liz had given herself so many pep talks she knew her new set of rules by heart. She would not avoid Rick but neither would she seek him out. And when they were around each other, she'd be full of smiles and laughs. Nothing serious.

So the first thing she did when she got to the track was go straight to the garage to test herself. She had plenty to do, what with the big barbecue and square dance on Friday night, but she needed to know she could be around Rick and pretend it didn't matter that he hadn't called.

"Hey, Liz, glad you made it here okay," Mack greeted. "How do you like South Carolina?" He was helping Jake and Bobby install a new windshield.

"Thanks. It's a pretty state and a nice drive."

She noticed Benny working on the right rear quarter panel and walked over to him. When she saw the crumpled sheet metal and huge black stripes, fear coiled like a spring. "Oh, my God, he crashed." She glanced about wildly for Rick. "Where is he? Was he hurt?"

The whole crew laughed, and Benny said, "The only thing hurt is his feelings. He got his rookie stripes, that's all."

"And that means?" She turned to Mack, whom she could always count on for straight explanation without clowning around.

"That he hit the wall coming out of turn four." He motioned her around to the rear bumper, where she was puzzled to see yellow stripes had been painted.

"Those stripes indicate this is his first time to race here. All the rookies have them. It lets the other drivers know to be extra careful around them, because Darlington is a mean track.'' He pointed to the black asphalt, gleaming in the late March sun. ''She's called the Lady in Black and shows no mercy.

''And those—'' he pointed to the black marks on the car ''—are Rick's personal rookie stripes. You only get them when you kiss the wall at Darlington.''

''Which means,'' Benny added laughingly, ''that Rick proved what he is here—a rookie.''

''And you're sure he's all right?'' she was driven to confirm.

Mack said, ''Yeah, yeah. No problem. He was here a minute ago. I don't know where he went. Oh…'' He pointed to the chain link fence that separated the garage from a section of the infield. ''He's over there. Signing autographs.''

Satisfied all was well, Liz said, ''Well, if you guys don't need anything, I've got some things I need to do.''

She walked away but paused to look at Rick again, and that was when she saw him kneeling beside the fence talking to a little boy who looked to be around seven or eight years old. Rick signed his souvenir program, then stood to take off his cap and toss it to him over the fence.

The boy let out a loud whoop of joy and took off running, no doubt to tell everyone he knew and show off his treasure.

It was a very hot day without a cloud in the sky, but still Rick stood there talking to his fans.

Liz remembered she had a Big Boy's cap in her car, and Rick could sure use it as he stood there in the sun. She quickly went to get it, but when she returned, he was no longer signing autographs. She met him as he walked toward an infield concession stand.

He was not looking in front of him, instead watching a car out on the track. He would have bumped right into her had she not thrown up her hands. ''Whoa, there, cowboy. You're about to ride right over me there.''

He blinked in recognition. ''Oh, Liz. Sorry about that. I was watching Jack Blevins.''

Jack, Liz knew, was breathing down Rick's neck in the

rookie points chase. "So how's he doing?" she asked, eager to focus on something besides Rick's ruggedly handsome face.

"Rumor has it he's running fast enough to qualify in the top ten."

"And how about you?"

"Oh, I was doing great," he said effusively, "till I smacked the wall."

"Yeah, I know. You got your rookie stripes."

He lifted one eyebrow in surprise. "You know about that?"

"Mack told me. But he said not to worry about it. I have to admit that I…" She quickly trailed off to silence. She had been about to confide how she'd nearly freaked to think he might have been hurt. That would have been a real no-brainer. So far, she'd managed to hide the fact that every time he went out on the track she felt as if she'd swallowed butterflies.

"I was a little worried about the damage," she finally concluded.

"Well, you should have been here. When I pulled in, you'd have thought I'd won the pole. All the other pit crews jumped up on the retaining wall to yell and wave because I got my stripes. Still, it was embarrassing." He shook his head and looked toward the fourth turn wall. "See? I even left marks up there. This is some track."

She wanted to ask why it was different from any other.

She also wanted to ask why he hadn't called her or made any effort to see her—be with her—since the night they returned from Las Vegas.

She opted to say nothing except, "I've got a lot to do. Do you need anything?"

Rick knew it was her stock question whenever she walked away. She meant it as being a part of her job, but, right then he stupidly chose to interpret it as something else…and longed to say that yes, he did need something—in a big way, because she was all he could think about.

Maybe that's what he'd been doing when he hit the wall.

No, he vehemently denied. He was a professional. Maybe he did think about her most of the time, but when he was behind the steering wheel it was different. And the day he did allow personal feelings to distract him out there, he'd hang up his helmet. Regardless of the turmoil he might have going on inside him, he'd never jeopardize the lives of other drivers by losing his concentration, even for an instant.

"Rick?" she prodded, puzzled by how he just stood there staring at her and not saying anything. "I asked—"

He cut her off. "Yeah, I heard you. Just thinking about Blevins again. And no, I don't need anything."

She remembered the cap she was holding while trying very hard to keep her hands from shaking. "I brought this. I saw you give yours to that little boy a while ago. That was nice of you, Rick."

"I'm a nice guy," he said, putting the cap on and giving her a cocky salute. "When are you gonna realize that?

"Can I buy you a cola?" he added. "I was just on my way to the cafeteria."

"Oh, that's right," she teased, wanting to lighten the moment, because the tension of being with him was starting to get to her. "You aren't near the hot dogs."

He gestured as if he was about to cuff her on her chin. "You're never going to let me forget that, are you? You're going to remind me of that every chance you get."

She teased right back. "That and a lot of other things. Has NASA been around to find out about the toilet you invented in your car?"

"For that," he said, wrapping his fingers around her arm, "*you* are buying."

Laughing, they went into the cafeteria.

Liz had not eaten lunch and took a ham sandwich from the counter as they went through the line. Rick ordered a hamburger, and she said, "Hey, that's not fair. I was only supposed to get stuck with paying for your cola."

From behind, an arm reached out to snatch Liz's sandwich from her tray. "Well, I'll pay for this so you won't wreck Big Boy's budget."

It was Mark Higgins. He nodded to Rick. "Got any quotes for me about getting your rookie stripes?"

"Sure," Rick responded without hesitation. "You can say I'm glad I did it, because now I'm no longer intimidated by the infamous Lady in Black."

Mark snapped his fingers. "Good quote. I'll use that."

They reached the end of the line, and Mark took Liz's tray and walked to a table where other writers were gathered.

Rick left them to join some of the drivers, and Liz found herself wishing Mark hadn't shown up when he did, because Rick might have been leading up to asking if they could get together later.

So much for that, she thought dismally. And maybe it was for the best.

Rick was not happy over where he ultimately qualified. Two starting positions behind Jack Blevins was disappointing, even though they both made the top fifteen. Rick knew he was going to have to stay on his toes all season, or Jack would best him for the title.

Rick also wished his sponsor wasn't hosting the biggest event of the race weekend for drivers, crew and media. Everybody was talking about it and looking forward to it, because Liz had done a super job of getting out the invitations and spreading the word.

Not only was it to be catered by the best barbecue restaurant in the state of South Carolina, but she had also arranged for a popular bluegrass band to provide music.

He hadn't seen much of her since that day Mark Higgins had horned in on them. Things had been going well at that point, and Rick had dared hope while they were having lunch she might give him some indication she'd like to see him later. She'd been so standoffish since Last Vegas, and he felt she was avoiding him on purpose. He'd planned to ask her about it but never got the chance.

A time or two he had thought about ringing her room at the motel where they were all staying but decided against it. If she was trying to back off and end it, or if it had been something born of circumstance and didn't mean a hill of beans, it was best to know it now.

He had also worried that maybe he shouldn't have gone to her apartment that night. She might have thought he was being overzealous, wanting to get heavy into the relationship. After all, she had made it clear her career was first and foremost and she wasn't about to be sideswiped by anything or anybody. So she might've gotten turned off thinking he was going to get heavy on her.

No way.

He still wanted her, all right, but intended to be really careful not to let things get out of hand. The question was, however, whether or not she cared to see him again.

So it was with a lack of enthusiasm that Rick went to the barbecue. However, he made up his mind to have a good time and appear very appreciative of the fact his sponsor thought enough of him—and racing—to go to so much expense and trouble.

Liz had made arrangements with the speedway officials to have the event at the country club in nearby Florence. The evening was perfect. Not too warm, with a gentle breeze flowing in off the Santee River.

Tents had been set up, and the tables beneath were again covered in black-and-white-checkered cloths to mimic the coveted victory flag.

The air was thick with the smell of succulent ribs, pork loins and chicken cooking over a charcoal pit.

There were kegs of ice-cold beer, as well as a full bar inside the clubhouse.

Racing people, Rick pleasantly mused, knew how to have and enjoy parties.

He was amused to see the favors Liz had provided at each place setting—magnets shaped like miniature pizzas attached to coupons for free ones at Big Boy's, one of his souvenir T-shirts and, of course, a press kit.

The band was all wound up, and couples were dancing on the terrace.

The crowd was getting bigger by the minute as more and more cars drove in. Rick found himself becoming an impromptu greeter as everyone seemed to gravitate toward him. He wondered where Liz was. He had been there nearly a half hour and there was no sign of her.

He spotted Mack and asked had he seen her. "Seems she'd be here to get things organized. Everybody is just drifting around not knowing what to do."

Mack said she had been there earlier to make sure everything was set up. "But she had to leave to go to the airport. She said Gary Staley called at the last minute to say he's flying in. She wasn't sure when she'd be back, because he said they had to go somewhere once he arrived."

"That's strange. I hope she didn't have to go all the way to Columbia to meet him."

"No. There's a private airport in Florence. He was coming in on one of his smaller jets and could land there."

Rick murmured enviously, "Must be nice to have your own jet."

They were standing near the barbecue pit, and Mack had sneaked himself a rib to munch on. "Well, it could happen. Most of the big drivers have their own planes. This is just your first season. Give it some time, and you'll be hanging right in there with them. Besides, you've got to remember, till this year we were still hauling a race car hooked on a trailer behind my pickup truck. Now we've got a big rig."

"That we do. And I'm grateful. But I wish Big Boy's would spring for an RV. Just about every team's got one."

"I guess we'll be flying to Texas." Rick was glancing all around in search of Liz. There was a podium set up, with microphones. People were getting restless wanting to eat. If she wasn't back in time, was he supposed to get up and say something? He sure hoped not.

Mack confirmed Liz had said they would, indeed, fly to Texas and the other races out West, like California and Arizona. "But we'll drive to the others, like always."

"And wouldn't it be nice to do that in an RV?" Rick stared wistfully at the expensive motor home that belonged to Jack Blevins. He had a big-buck sponsor, all right—his father. Blevins Transport probably kept more eighteen-wheelers on the road than mosquitoes on the Santee River. So Jack had the best of everything, even his own plane.

Mack slapped him on the shoulder. "Listen to you. After you got your rookie stripes you don't really think you deserve an RV, do you?"

Rick shook him off but wasn't angry. Mack was just clowning around. They'd talked about it a lot, and he knew Mack wanted an RV as much as he did. It would come in real nice when Mack's kids were around.

There was a sudden stirring in the crowd as all heads turned to the patio.

Rick also looked and promptly swallowed hard and told his heart to go into low gear.

Liz was walking out of the door and onto the patio with Gary Staley beside her. But no one was looking at him. They were struck by Liz's cuteness…including Rick.

She was dressed in homespun fashion, perfect for a barbecue and square dance. Her jeans were cut just low enough to reveal her navel, and the tail of her bright plaid shirt was tied beneath her perky bosom, cleavage showing by a few buttons left undone. She also had on cowboy boots and a straw hat over beribboned pigtails.

Rick was holding a can of beer and, at the sight of her, crushed it in his hand without realizing it. Quickly, nervously, he glanced around and was relieved no one had noticed.

She stepped up to the microphone. With a big grin, she waved to the applauding crowd. "Hi y'all," she called to their delight. "I've been down South long enough that I've learned to say that instead of plain old 'hi.'"

There was a round of laughter.

She motioned Gary to come forward. "I believe you all know Gary Staley—the proud and respected CEO and founder of that great chain of pizzas known as Big Boy's."

Everyone dutifully applauded.

Searching the crowd, she found Rick and beckoned to him. "Please come up here."

Clapping with everyone else as Rick made his way forward, she stepped back, conceding the limelight to Gary.

He shook Rick's hand and slapped him on the back. "Get the rest of your crew up here, too, will you?"

When Mack and the team were lined up behind them, Gary said, "I want you to know I came here especially tonight to express my appreciation, along with everyone else at Big Boy's Pizza, for the job you've done for us. You're leading in rookie points, and we're confident when the last checkered flag of the season waves at Atlanta in November, you will be the winner of the rookie championship."

Someone from Jack Blevins's crew hollered out good-naturedly, "Hey, we might have something to say about that."

Everyone laughed, including Rick, and Liz was again impressed by the camaraderie in racing. No matter how they dueled on the track, tempers sometimes flying, when it came down to it, they were all good sports.

Gary continued, "And as a token of our appreciation and a gesture of our continued confidence, we have something for you and the team."

At his signal, a gleaming RV came driving across the parking lot, stopping at the edge of the rolling lawn.

Everyone gasped, then broke into another round of applause as Rick and the team converged on Gary to thank him.

Liz knew that an expensive motor home was no big deal

to the bigger, richer teams, but for a rookie's sponsor to provide him with one his first season was special.

She had known about it for nearly a week and had made arrangements to have a photographer take pictures. She also had the story written to go with it and ready for immediate release.

Someone announced the serving lines were open. People began moving toward the food, but Liz couldn't wait to get to Rick and the team.

"You knew about this?" he said happily when she joined them. "And you were able to keep it a secret?"

"Of course, I did. Mr. Staley insisted it be a surprise."

"And was it ever." He was walking around the outside of the RV, Liz right behind him. "This is great. We'll get a lot of use out of this, for sure."

"Didn't I tell you it would happen?" Mack cried, happily pounding Rick on his back. "I just didn't know it would be so soon. Now you've got to win that title."

"Oh, he will," Liz joined in. "And if he drops behind in points, we'll lock him out of it."

Rick grinned and playfully shook his fist. "Just try it. This baby is mine."

Liz urged, "Come on. Mr. Staley expects you to sit with him at the head table. You'll have plenty of time to check it out later."

"Right. Because I'm driving it back to the motel."

"And us, too," Mack called, falling in step behind Rick and Liz.

"Want to come along?" Rick asked her.

"Can't." She shook her head. "I've got to take Mr. Staley back to the airport. He has leave tonight."

She left them to mingle and make sure everything was running smoothly, all the while wishing she could be with Rick to share his excitement.

After everyone had eaten, including Liz, who found time to feast on the delicious barbecue, the dancing began.

She found herself the most sought after partner, because

she knew how to call a square dance. It was something she had enjoyed before she became engaged to Craig, but he had hated it, saying it was backwoods and hillbilly.

In between conducting tours of the RV after he had familiarized himself, Rick watched Liz dancing. She was so cute, so full of life, and he wished he could get right out there with her. But he didn't dare. It just wouldn't do for them to be together like that in front of everybody, because he was afraid they might give something away.

Jack Blevins came up to politely congratulate Rick and said, "You're a lucky guy, Castles. In lots of ways. You got a great sponsor, probably the hardest-working PR rep on the circuit, and a hell of a team.

"It's just a shame," he went on with a mischievous leer, "that you won't win rookie title."

Rick hooted, "Get outta here, Blevins. I'm gonna blow you away, and you know it."

They continued to exchange good-natured barbs, but all the while Rick was glancing beyond Jack at Liz. It was as though he were bewitched, unable to keep his eyes off her...unable to stop thinking about her.

Liz walked into her motel room, threw her briefcase and bag onto the bed, then collapsed in a chair.

Everything had gone extremely well...except for not being able to accept Rick's invitation to ride back in the RV. She had seen it parked in the very back of the parking lot when she drove in. Maybe she could go along when it was taken to the track tomorrow. Of course, it wouldn't be the same as being with Rick, but, too often lately their responsibilities kept them apart, it seemed.

No, that wasn't it, she thought miserably. Rick just wasn't making the time. But what could she say? They had no commitment to each other.

She jumped as someone knocked. With the chain fastened,

she peered out to see it was Rick, then quickly opened the door. "Is something wrong? It's nearly two o'clock."

"No. Everything is fine. I've been watching for you. I didn't call, because Mack has the room on the other side of me, and these walls are paper thin. Come on." He reached for her hand.

She did not hesitate to take it. "Where are we going?"

"I'm going to give you a private tour of the RV. You deserve it."

Happily they skipped across the parking lot hand in hand.

"Isn't this the greatest?" Rick said when they stepped inside. "You could live here. Fully-furnished, self-contained, fancy kitchen. It even has a computer station with a hookup for the Internet, plus a fax machine and scanner. This is really something."

Before she could respond, he kissed her, then held her away from him, and smiled and said, "Thanks, Liz. I know you're behind this."

She protested, "No, I'm not. It was Mr. Staley's idea."

"Yeah? You mean you didn't drop a hint how badly we wanted one?"

She didn't think so, then recalled when they had discussed a budget should Big Boy's continue sponsorship next season, she had mentioned how useful an RV would be to the team. She said as much to Rick, adding, "but it was totally his idea."

"Because you got him to thinking about it."

He locked the door and moved to draw her into his arms. "Boy, I've missed you," he said raggedly.

He was about to kiss her, then paused. "This thing has curtains. I think we'd better close them."

Liz was doing the ones in the bedroom, when he came up behind her to put his hands on her breasts. She yielded against him as he began rubbing her nipples, which had tightened at first touch.

The pleasure was exquisite, and she closed her eyes and reveled in it.

Then he was gently turning her about. She swayed against him as he lowered her to the bed.

She was still wearing the outfit she'd worn to the barbecue, and he swiftly unbuttoned her blouse. Her breasts spilled into his eagerly waiting hands, and he lowered his mouth. His lips closed over a nipple, sucking so strongly that she came up off the bed, back arched.

Still devouring her tender flesh, he opened the zipper to her jeans. She helped get them off, and he was out of his own clothes in seconds. "I can't wait," he said huskily. "I want you so bad, Liz."

He positioned himself on top of her, and she wrapped her legs about his hips, sighing deliciously as he guided himself inside her.

She felt a shudder from head to toe and he pushed slowly, rhythmically, within her. She felt herself squeeze against him in eagerness, waves of delight coursing throughout her body. Gasping, she held on to him tightly.

His hands cupped her buttocks, bringing her closer, giving him control of her undulations. Her flesh felt as though it were on fire as she radiated the heat of her intense desire.

She relished how his chest hair brushed against her heaving breasts. He was deep inside her, and her nerves were convulsing, wanting him to completely fill her, to consume her.

"Now," she whispered as the walls of her belly began to quiver. "Come with me, Rick...come with me now...."

And he did so, driving hard, plunging deeper and deeper until their bodies seemed to meld together.

For long, tender moments in the sweet afterglow, they held on to each other, their breathing harsh, labored, and hearts beating wildly.

"It just gets better and better, sweetheart," he whispered against her ear.

"I know," she whispered tremulously, frightened and worried to know she had broken her own vow.

Because there was no denying she loved him.

Chapter Thirteen

Like the band of gypsies Rick likened to drivers and crew, the schedule moved them onward into the season.

He was running well. He had finished every race through the spring and into the summer. Then, his luck changed in California, when they raced in Sonoma in June. The engine blew, but he was able to get off the track without hitting or being hit, which he always considered a blessing.

Things went a bit downhill from there, and he failed to finish the next few races. Still, he and Jack Blevins were running neck and neck in rookie points, because Jack wasn't doing any better.

Rick and the crew were flying back from California to Charlotte, anxious to get ready for the race the next week in Daytona. Liz was sitting directly across the aisle. She was sleeping, and he wished she was right next to him, her head on his shoulder, his arm around her.

They hadn't had any time alone together in California. Hotel rooms were at a premium in Sonoma that week, and he'd had to bunk with Mack. And he hadn't dared sneak out to go to her room during the night, afraid Mack would awaken to find him gone and ask questions he didn't want to try to answer.

He watched her as she slept and cursed himself once more over how he'd stupidly let himself fall in love with her. She didn't know it, of course, and he wasn't about to let her find out.

He was also worried over how she reacted to things that happened on or around the track concerning him...just as he had feared she would do once they became involved. For instance when one of the writers misquoted him about a spin-out, in which he made it appear Rick was blaming it all on another driver, Liz went straight to the writer and chewed him out. No one thought anything about it except Rick, who knew she'd reacted because of personal involvement.

She was making things subjective instead of objective, and that really bothered him. Next she'd be freaking when he wrecked, and he couldn't have that. And, yes, sooner or later, he was afraid she'd start making noises about how nice it would be if he could find another line of work.

He told himself he was the one overreacting now. She wouldn't go that far as long as their relationship was casual.

But that was the problem.

He hadn't wanted a relationship, but it looked as though they had one, whether he liked it or not.

He also worried that maybe he was getting in so deep that his own emotions were apt to get carried away where she was concerned. And he couldn't let it happen.

Bored, wanting to stretch, Rick unbuckled his seat belt and wandered to the rear of the plane. The very last row was empty, and he sat down to stare glumly out the window.

There was nothing to see, just a blanket of white and gray clouds stretching forever.

He continued to stew over Liz, because something had to give. The more he was with her, the more he longed to be.

As far as they knew, no one suspected anything was going

on between them. If it got out they were sleeping together, it could be bad for Liz, working as she did primarily with men. It was best to keep professional life separate from personal.

But Rick had his own reasons for wanting to keep things secret, figuring Liz would come nearer to keeping her emotions in check if she couldn't let on she had a personal interest. But he didn't like thinking like that. It made him feel he was being conceited to assume she would go all to pieces should he wreck, or that she'd go ballistic if she saw him with another woman.

He recalled a race at a half-mile asphalt track in Savannah, Georgia, one summer. He had been dating a girl named Wanda Guthrie from Atlanta. She made it to all the races she could. On that particular night one of the trophy queens came on to him after the race in the shadows of the infield. He wasn't interested and was trying to disentangle himself from her arms, which she'd thrown around him, when Wanda came out of nowhere, screaming and yelling that he was "hers."

It got nasty before it got better, with the girls exchanging blows. Rick had been embarrassed, and, of course, never went out with Wanda again.

Now he hated even remotely thinking Liz was capable of doing anything like that. Wanda had been a good-time girl. Liz had class. Still, they were women, and experience had shown him over and over that women were basically the same when it came to emotions.

And, man, he wished it didn't have to be that way.

"Can I get you something to drink, sir?"

He glanced up at the flight attendant. "No, thanks."

"Are you sure? We'll be landing in about a half hour and we're ready to put all the carts away."

"No, I'm fine."

He settled back down, happy where he was rather than up front where he was supposed to be. It bothered him to be so close to Liz. At the track or when the whole team was out together, it was different. But to be only a few feet away with nothing to do but think about how much he wanted her was unbearable.

Closing his eyes, he let the seat back, grateful for the solitude.

Daytona was going to be rough. It was July and scorching hot. Liz wouldn't be able to stand that kind of heat and would probably hang out in the air-conditioned media room instead of the garage. Though he acted as if he didn't know she was anywhere around, he was very much aware of her presence…and would miss it.

But he pacified himself with the knowledge of how things would be cozy otherwise. She'd told the team at breakfast before leaving California that she'd made reservations at an oceanfront hotel. Since it was over the Fourth of July holiday, Gary Staley had told her to make sure each room was a large efficiency so the crew could bring their families if they wanted. They all planned to, which meant nobody would be interested in what he was doing at night.

And he planned to spend every single one with Liz.

He had almost dozed off when his eyes flashed open to something covering his face.

A wool blanket.

He jerked it off. "What th—?"

Liz was sliding into the seat next to him. "I seem to recall having fun under a blanket the last time we flew back from California."

Laughing, he was about to reach for her when he remembered the crew and sobered. "This is not a good idea, Liz. They'll be coming back here to make a pit stop before landing, and if they see us together—especially snuggled under a blanket—they're going to start wondering."

"Oh, I know that," she said, snatching the blanket from him and folding it. "I was only teasing to see what you'd say. I guess I thought you'd missed me enough you'd be willing to take chances."

He knew she was still teasing. "I did, but I'm not doing anything stupid, either."

She pretended to pout. "I think I'll see if there are any other single drivers on the circuit."

He played along with her. "I think you already know there are. So what are you going to do about it?"

"Oh, see if I can find one who wouldn't be ashamed to have people know we're going together."

"Hmm. And I thought you were the one who was so dedicated to your career."

She sat up to look at him in surprise. "I certainly am."

"But now you're wanting everyone to know you have a relationship." He took the blanket from her and slowly unfolded it to spread across their laps.

"Not really," she said, her fingers dancing across his thigh beneath the blanket. "I just thought it might be nice to have somebody who thought more of me than his old race car."

"It's not the race car." He caught her hand and squeezed. "It's the race. Remember? I told you, Liz. Racing comes first with me."

"And the same with my job."

"Then why are we having this conversation? We agreed no strings. We share nothing besides a bed."

"That's just it." She jerked her hand from his and squeezed his leg so hard he jumped. "I can't get you into mine, and you haven't invited me to yours. That's the whole problem here."

Grinning, he caught her wrist and held it, because her fingers were tiptoeing upward to a very private place. "So that's what this is all about. It's your way of wanting to set something up."

"Exactly," she whispered.

"Hussy."

She laughed softly as his hand slipped beneath her skirt. "So what time can I expect you tonight?"

"Just as quick as I can get there."

He continued to caress her as they sat there gazing at each

other. And then he couldn't take it anymore. He wanted her too badly. "You'd better get back to your seat before somebody notices you're missing."

Liz started to get up, then hesitated to remark, "You know, I hate sneaking around like we're doing something to be ashamed of."

He started to respond, but she did not give him a chance, as she continued. "But I know the reason for it. Gary and Jeff might worry that I would let personal feelings get in the way of my job. I can't let that happen. My career is too important to me."

"And so is mine," Rick said as he began folding the blanket so he wouldn't have to look at her. "It would just cause problems we don't need right now."

"I suppose so, and I can't let that happen in my job again."

"You know you never told me much about your past, Liz. Just that a boyfriend caused you to lose your job."

"He was my fiancé. He used me to steal my accounts. When my boss found out, I was fired. He said I should have been smarter. Then history repeated itself. I did the same thing again. After that, I swore nothing was ever going to come between me and my job. And it hasn't...till now."

The minute the words were out of her mouth she frantically wished she could take them back. She hadn't meant to be so candid. It had just slipped out.

She glanced at Rick from the corner of her eye. He was still concentrating on the blanket. She could not read his expression.

"What I meant," she rushed to amend, attempting to smooth things over, "was that till now there hasn't been anybody to get in the way. Not that you do, of course. I just haven't been in a relationship of any kind. I swore I wouldn't, that I'd never get serious about anybody until I was at the top of my career and so secure in it that nothing could hurt it."

She was talking too fast, saying too much, because now

she'd gone and given him the idea she was serious about him. Oh, why hadn't she quit while she was ahead? That was much more information than he needed.

She was about to try to put a spin on it all for damage control when the announcement came over the speakers that the plane was making its approach to the Charlotte, North Carolina, airport.

"We'd better get back to our seats," Rick said.

"Oh, that's right," Liz said breezily. "Everybody will wonder where we are."

She hurried up the aisle, already trying to think of what she could say and do when Rick came over later to get herself out of the mess she'd gotten herself into with her big mouth. She could not have him thinking she was serious. They had an understanding, and she had blown it, and if she didn't do something to smooth things over he might back away.

And what then? The miserable thought needled as she sat down and buckled her seat belt. Even if she found a way to explain away everything she had said, the situation was still the same—Rick wanted nothing serious. And if she allowed herself to feel any differently she was courting heartache.

"There you are," Mack said from across the aisle where he sat next to the window. "I was wondering where you'd gotten to."

"Long line at the pit stop," she managed to say lightly.

"And where's the driver?"

"I think he's in line, too."

"No, he's not," Rick said cheerfully as he took his seat next to Mack.

"The boys and I were talking while you were gone," Mack said. "They're antsy to get on the road to Daytona. So they want to start work on that new engine tonight since Bobby won't be in with the hauler till sometime tomorrow afternoon. We're going straight to the garage from the airport, but if you're tired, we can get by without you."

Rick looked over at Liz. She was talking to Benny and

not paying any attention to him and Mack. He wanted more than anything to make love to her that night, but it was like an addiction. He needed a fix but knew it would only keep him hooked. And some of the things she'd just said really bothered him. Maybe she had an addiction, too, but didn't realize it. So to keep them both from getting hurt, maybe he should be the one to make the decision to go cold turkey.

"No, I feel fine," he finally told Mack. "I'll ride with you and sleep in the RV tonight."

"Good." Mack settled back for the landing.

Liz turned just then, saw Rick watching her and smiled. He did not smile back.

He felt too damn guilty over knowing how disappointed she was going to be when he didn't show and didn't call. But it was time to ease back on the throttle and cruise, and she'd realize in time it was all for the best.

Liz was putting on a front that nothing was out of the ordinary as she spoke to Rick about his appearances at Daytona. They were in the paddock area, standing outside the motor home. She had made it a point to approach him there, rather than at the hotel, once more putting everything between them on a strictly business level.

Since he had not shown up at her apartment the night they arrived from California nor called to say why, she had gone to the garage the next day. She had hoped he would catch her alone and explain, but, as it turned out, he all but ignored her as the team worked feverishly getting ready to leave.

She had not gone with them, instead flying when she could have gone in the motor home. That would have been too awkward when she wasn't sure what was wrong with him, whether he ever wanted to see her again or had gone back to wishing she'd just disappear.

She had said too much on the plane. That's all it could be. And if she ever got the chance she would tell him she had not meant for him to get the idea she was becoming serious. For that matter, she brooded miserably, she already was, and it was too late for her to do anything about it. Only she had to make him believe otherwise or she'd never be with him again.

She intended to stay with the account and had dared to hope that somewhere down the road, maybe in a few years, Rick would be so successful in his career that he would not be leery of having that relationship they both denied wanting. Perhaps things might still work out between them. After all, there had certainly been plenty of times when she thought he was starting to care. The way he kissed her and made love to her, surely that was not lust alone. Surely it meant something to him…as it did to her.

Only now she was beginning to think otherwise.

And it bothered her deeply.

"Well, Thursday night will be okay," Rick said as he looked over the sheet Liz had given him. "You want me to do the Big Boy's on the north end of the beach at five and then one on the south at eight. I think I can handle that."

She noted he was very careful not to make eye contact. He handed the list back and asked if that was all.

"I'm not sure," she said. "Mr. Staley left a message at the hotel that he may be flying in Friday. If he does, he'll want you to have dinner with him and his wife."

"Make it early, Liz. You know I don't want to be out the night before a race. It's a shame this one is run on Saturday, but that's the way it is."

"Thank goodness, it's in the morning when it's cooler. Well, I'll see you at Big Boy's." She did not offer to take him in her car as she had been doing whenever he made an appearance. It gave them some intimate moments together, only now she did not dare.

Neither did she mention riding with him.

Mack walked by, heading for the RV. "Hey, Liz, Ida made some of her famous potato salad, and I'm going to grill some hot dogs. Want to join us?"

"Thanks, but I'm not hungry right now," she said, putting her papers back in her briefcase and closing it.

"Well, remember there's always food in here. Man, this thing is nice to have around the track."

"I'll tell Mr. Staley again how much you're all enjoying it."

She started to walk away but just then spotted a young woman climbing over the fence into the restricted area for drivers, crew and their families. She had parked her car smack-dab against the fence and then crawled up on the hood to make it easier to hoist herself up.

Liz didn't say anything. It wasn't her job to stop her if the security guards weren't watching as they were supposed to.

She saw the woman head straight for Rick. "I've got to have your autograph," she cried. "You don't know how much I love you, Rick. I'm your number-one fan."

"Fine, fine," Rick said crisply, "but you aren't supposed to be in here."

"I don't care. I had to see you."

Liz looked her up and down. She was wearing shorts cut off high enough to reveal most of her rear. Her nipples were obvious in her clinging tank top, her breasts threatening to pop right out any second.

She had a picture for him to sign. "I took this of you with my own little camera," she cooed. "And I want you to sign it to 'Dearest Marcie, my sexiest fan.'"

"All right," Rick said with a long, drawn-out sigh. "But then you've got to get out of here." He scrawled his name and the inscription she asked for.

"Not till after you show me the inside of your RV."

"Sorry," he said pleasantly. "No can do."

He went inside and closed the door. The girl sighed and turned away, but, instead of returning to her car, she began walking toward the entrance to pit road. Liz figured she was going to sneak in that way, but it wasn't her business so she didn't say anything.

Then she saw the dog. He was inside the girl's car, the windows rolled up, panting and clawing at the window.

"Excuse me," Liz called, running after the girl. "Wait a minute."

She whirled about, visibly annoyed, no doubt thinking someone was going to stop her. "Yeah, what is it?"

"You need to do something about your dog quick. He's dying in that car."

"He's fine. I left a window cracked."

"That's not enough," Liz argued. "On a day like today, when it's boiling hot, the temperature inside a car can climb to as high as a hundred and two degrees in just ten minutes and a hundred and twenty in thirty. Maybe even higher. A dog can't take that heat long. If he doesn't die, he can suffer irreparable brain damage."

The girl put her hands on her hips. "So you're a vet? You know all about dogs, right? Let me tell you something." She got right in Liz's face to warn her. "You can keep your nose out of my business if you know what's good for you. That's my dog, and I know how to take care of him."

Liz was right back at her. "Obviously, you don't. And, no, I'm not a vet, but I have worked with the Humane Society, and I know what I'm talking about. Now if you don't go back to that car immediately and get the air conditioner started, I'm going to—"

"What?" The girl doubled up a fist. "You're going to do what?"

"Call the cops," Liz said, taking her cell phone from her pocket and furiously waving it at her. If there was one thing she could not abide it was animal cruelty. "There happens to be a law in the state of Florida against leaving a dog locked in a car like that. You can go to jail."

The girl took a few steps backward. "I didn't know that."

"People like you shouldn't even have a dog. Now go do something about the poor thing right now. You ought to be ashamed of yourself. Take that dog home and leave him and then come back to the track."

"Yeah, okay." She turned toward her car, mumbling to herself.

Liz continued on her way.

Rick turned from the window and slumped into a chair.

It was Savannah happening all over again with two women about to get in a catfight.

Liz had chewed the girl out for flirting and even waved her hand as if she was about to hit her. Sure, the girl had gotten right in her face, but he never dreamed Liz would be the type to threaten to hit anybody.

He was sure he had made the right decision to back off, regardless of how much he loved her.

Because she could not cope with the pressures of his career.

And he was not about to give it up.

Chapter Fourteen

The weeks became a blur of different cities, different states, as the NASCAR schedule moved through the blistering hot summer.

There were times when Liz had to stop and think where she was. A week after Daytona she had flown to New Hampshire, and from there to Pennsylvania, Indiana, New York, and on to Michigan. She was glad to finally be returning south, to Richmond, Virginia, for the September race there.

The weather was hot and humid, but she tried to stay busy to keep her mind off Rick, which was not easy.

In the nearly two months since everything between them had come to a screeching halt—thanks to her big mouth that day on the plane—it was as though they had never been intimate. Rick was polite and friendly, and that was it. He avoided one-on-one situations but did so in a way she could not take offense to. And the times when they were alone together, Liz's pride kept her completely professional. When it came to broaching anything even slightly personal between them, she refused to go there.

Likewise, Rick was all business.

But she dared steal glances at him when he wasn't looking, always feeling a glow to recall the thrill of being in his arms.

And the times she caught him watching her made it worse as she dared think he might be experiencing the same emotions.

She blamed herself for losing him. After all, she had broken the rules by making him fear she might be taking things way too seriously.

Time and again, Liz tried to think of what she could do, or say, to bring it all out in the open so she could try to explain. But what could she say? She had been told she had a knack for spinning—for twisting negative into positive to an advantage. In this instance, however, it would take an out-and-out lie, and she did not know how to go about resolving anything, anyway. It wasn't as though she could blurt out and say, *By the way, when we were on the plane I might have let it slip that I've fallen in love with you, but that's not so. What I was trying to say was—* And that's when she always drew a blank and couldn't figure where to go from that point. It would probably be just yaddah, yaddah, yaddah, and she'd wind up making things worse.

At least now Rick was tolerating her presence. He no longer made things difficult for her. And, on the surface, they were friends. So what had turned out to be no more than a dalliance between them had brought about some good changes, at least.

The team had been invited to a cookout at the home of one of Big Boy's franchisers before the race in Martinsville, Virginia. Liz almost didn't go, knowing it would be one of those evenings where she'd be thrown with Rick at every turn. It was as though people expected them to be joined at the hip when they were at social functions. If a question were asked of Rick, she was called into the conversation, and vice versa. But she couldn't think of a polite way to avoid being there.

As it turned out, just as she had feared, Liz found herself seated at a picnic table with Rick and their host.

They made the usual small talk, with Liz remarking how she loved the cool green mountains of Virginia and marveling over the friendliness of the people. Rick added to the conversation by saying he was reminded of his home state, Georgia.

Harold Barton was the franchiser host, and he asked if Big Boy's had anything special planned for Rick for the Talladega, Alabama, race in mid-October, only a few weeks away.

Liz told him she didn't know of anything, her mind slipping back to the race there in April, when, on one of the days preceding, it had rained continuously. She had pretended to drive into Birmingham for something. Rick had said he was going to lock himself in the motor home at the track and catch up on his sleep. He told the crew not to dare bother him. Liz had later sneaked in, and they had spent the entire day with all the curtains drawn making mad, passionate love.

The next morning it was like playing house together when they cooked breakfast. Then Liz had to hurry and leave before the guys came around looking for something to eat.

"Well, that's great nothing is going on," Harold was saying. "Because, Rick, I'd like for you to do something special for me. One of my pet charities is the Sheriffs' Boys Ranch organizations. We've got one in Tennessee, and I've been asked to see if I could get you to do something for the one in Alabama during race weekend."

Liz entered her PR mode eagerly to escape the web of nostalgia that had her in its grips. "What did you have in mind? Rick is always glad to help with charities." She turned to him for confirmation. "Aren't you?"

He gave a quick nod. "Of course."

"But it's kind of late to set up any kind of benefit," Liz pointed out. "I mean, for that kind of thing you need a lot of advance publicity to sell tickets."

"That's not what I had in mind," Harold said. "I was thinking if there was an evening Rick had free, he could go out to the ranch and visit the boys. They're all orphans, you see, and being in race country, they keep up with what's going on."

Harold chuckled and went on to say Rick would probably find there were a lot of fans for other drivers among the boys. "But don't be offended. After all, you're a rookie, and they don't know much about you, and I thought it'd be nice for them to see a new face, somebody besides the hot dogs."

Liz instinctively looked at Rick, and they both couldn't help smiling to hear that term again.

Harold, unaware of the joke, asked, "Did I say the wrong thing?"

"No, no," Liz assured. "Now tell us, when do you want him to visit? I'll check the schedule." She reached for the book she carried with her everywhere she went.

"Thursday would be good," he said.

She checked, then said, "That's fine. He's got qualifying, but that should be over by four. How about if he goes directly to the ranch from the track? I'll be doing a press release, and you won't need me, anyway." She was not about to go with him if she could get out of it.

But, as it turned out, she would not be so lucky.

Harold explained, "I'd like to have both of you, if you can make it, Liz. All the other drivers took PR people, and, believe me, it's a help when it comes to lining up the kids for autographs, passing out souvenirs and so forth. And we'll make a little party out of it. I'll have the local Big Boy's deliver pizza."

"Fine," Liz said thinly, thinking all the while how the last thing she needed was to attend a party with Rick...or attend anything with him, for that matter.

Rick was leading in rookie points going into Talladega only by a very small margin. But when he won the coveted pole position, he found himself the center of media attention.

Liz was thrilled, along with the crew, but as the reporters kept hovering around Rick after time trials ended, she glanced at her watch and began to worry about getting to the party at the Boys Ranch on time.

First there were the interviews in the garage, and then she went with him to the big press box on the other side of the track. As part of her job, she repeated into a microphone questions that Rick was asked so everyone present would know exactly what he was addressing when he spoke. Finally she had to end it, much to the groans of the press.

"Sorry," she apologized. "But Rick and I have a date, and—"

She was drowned out by a burst of laughter, and someone shouted, "Hey, we've been wondering when you two would get around to it."

That started a lot of good-natured teasing, and Liz tried to go along with it, all the while feeling terrible. She knew it had to annoy Rick, and he might blame her for not having made the announcement in a different way. Covering racing was a hard, tense job, and the guys leaped at any chance to kid around and have a good time.

"It's not like you think," she said when the teasing died down. Then she explained where they were going, and soon they were able to leave.

"Sorry about that," she said as she and Rick hurried to her car, which she'd left parked in the infield lot. "But those guys are a bunch of clowns. I hope you aren't mad."

"Why would I be mad?" he said quietly, calmly.

"Because I said it the way I did."

"So? We do have a date, and if they want to take it another way, who cares?"

She waited till they were on their way, following the map Harold had given them down a dusty dirt road, before mustering the nerve to comment. "Well, I think it bothered you the last time I said something the wrong way."

He was driving and gave her a quick glance. "I have no idea what you're talking about, Liz."

"Forget it," she said, pointing to the crossroads just ahead. "Turn to the right."

He could empathize with her misery, because he was trying to cope with his own. And he knew what she was talking about—how she'd said too much on the plane. But he didn't want to discuss it, afraid he'd give his true feelings away.

And, Lord, he did love her.

The past weeks had been a special kind of hell.

So many times he had wanted to pick up the phone and call her or show up on her doorstep. But he hadn't dared. It had to be this way.

They drove on to the ranch in silence. Several times he thought she was about to say something but didn't. He was just going to have to make sure that in the future they did not wind up in a car alone together for any reason. In fact, he was going to try all the harder to keep his distance, fearing that sooner or later he might yield to temptation, crush her in his arms and kiss her till they were both breathless.

Then there would be no turning back.

If that happened, he would ask her to marry him, and should she say yes, he would want to do everything in his power to make it work...which meant returning to a normal job, a normal life.

And he just didn't think he could do it.

The kids were great and very appreciative Rick had come to visit. They were even more impressed when they learned he had won the pole for Sunday's race.

Liz passed out special children's press kits she'd had made up, along with caps and T-shirts with the team logo. She also gave them miniatures of Rick's number sixty race car.

Harold was there, and, as promised, they enjoyed a big pizza party and even had ice cream and cake afterward.

On the ride back to Anniston, where their motel was located, Rick used his cell phone to call Mack. He kept him on the line, talking about things that might sound important to Liz but were foolishness to Mack.

"Listen, why are you blabbing on and on about nothing?" Mack complained sleepily. "Just because you won the pole today doesn't mean you don't have to be up early in the morning like the rest of us."

Still Rick kept him on the phone till the motel was in sight. There was no chance for conversation with Liz, which was what he had intended.

But, as she started to get out of the car, she yielded to her own temptation and bluntly asked, "What happened between us, Rick?"

"Uh...I don't know," he hedged. He had opened his door and was about to step out. "I guess it just wasn't working."

"I guess not," she said quietly. She knew she probably should have kept her mouth shut but couldn't help it any longer. "It's just that we seemed to be having a great time together, and all of a sudden there was nothing."

"Things started getting too heavy, Liz," he murmured, not sure what to say. He damn well wasn't about to admit he'd backed off because he had stupidly gone and fallen in love with her.

"They weren't getting heavy on my part," she was quick to lie. "And it's okay that you ended it. I just don't want you thinking I expected more than you were willing to give."

Rick was feeling very uncomfortable. "Why, no, it wasn't anything like that. We were just having a good time, and, besides, we never should have gotten involved to start with. But at least we're adults about it, right?" He forced a smile.

"Sure," she replied edgily. "I just thought—"

He cut her off. "Liz, wait...there's something you need to know." He was floundering for words, floundering for an answer out of the mess he'd allowed himself to get into.

The lights around the parking lot filled the car with a mellow glow. She looked at him, bewildered. "I'm listening."

He swallowed hard and glanced everywhere but at her. "I'm seeing somebody else."

She nodded, not trusting her voice to speak as a lump came in her throat.

"We'd sort of lost touch, but then we ran into each other again." His words were coming fast as the lie came to him. "Actually, it was at the airport in Charlotte that night we flew in from California. We got to talking and, well—" he shrugged "—we got together again, and that's how it's been."

Liz squeezed her nails into her palms to keep from bursting into tears. "Well...well, I'm happy for you," she managed to say. "But why haven't I met her?"

"She hasn't been to any of the races."

"I see. Because of your thing against women hanging around the track, of course." Her tiny laugh was edged with bitterness, and she swung back around, unable to look at him any longer.

"Uh, it's not that." He had to think fast, could not let her believe it wasn't serious enough to warrant him breaking his own rule. "She's a flight attendant. That's why she was at the airport. Wendy is her name," he added, thinking fast.

"Well, you be sure to introduce her to me sometime, okay?" Liz was proud of how she could sound so nonchalant when her heart had just exploded like an overheated engine in the middle of a five-hundred-mile race.

She got out and closed the door. Rick did the same, and as they came around the car, she said, "Well, I wish you well, both on the track and off. See you tomorrow."

He watched her go.

She was wearing tight white slacks and a pale pink blouse, her hair gleaming like spun gold in the street lamps above.

It was all he could do to keep from calling her back, to admit he'd lied and confess how he wanted her, loved her, and that somehow they would find a way to work things out.

But he couldn't.

Her shoulders were slumped, her head down, and he felt like the world's biggest heel.

His room was at the opposite end of the motel from hers. He turned in that direction, only to hear her call to him.

With a soft groan, he turned around, praying all the while she wasn't going to say something to make him tell her how he really felt. She was just disappointed, that's all, her feelings hurt because he'd dumped her. He didn't mean anything to her and never had except for a good time. Plus, once they went to bed together the friction between them had ceased. She felt as strongly about her career as he did his own. And even if she had started caring more about him than she should have, she was glad things were under control.

That's the way it had to be; otherwise, he was in big trouble. Because if she told him it was anything else...

"I want you to know I really don't care," she said when she was standing right in front of him. "The fact is, I'm not the kind to sleep around with just anybody, and I'm not ready for a serious romance. If we'd kept on like we were going, though, who knows? I'd probably have fallen head over heels in love with you. You're a nice guy, Rick. But I'm just not ready.

"And that," she said in finality, "is what I've been trying to tell you all along."

With that, she turned and walked away.

And this time, her shoulders did not slump, and she held her head high.

Rick quickly went to his room and, for a long time, sat in the dark, telling himself over and over he had done the right thing. Because now he knew she didn't really care for him, so he was wise to have acted as he did.

But it didn't ease the pain over losing her.

Liz slept little and had cried so much during the night that her eyes were terribly swollen. She was glad it was a sunny day so she could wear sunglasses without anyone wondering why.

She went to the track but stayed in the infield media room

where it was cool, and where she could also avoid being around Rick.

But she still couldn't get him off her mind. And now she knew why he hadn't shown up that night…why he had totally dropped her.

He had someone else.

A writer from Virginia came up to Liz and told her he needed to talk to Rick for a sidebar in Sunday's paper. "It's a big deal, him winning the pole. But even with that, it looks like it's going to go down to the wire with Blevins for the title at Atlanta. That's only three races away after this one, and I wanted to get Rick's thoughts."

Liz knew the schedule by heart—Rockingham, where she and Rick had made love in the RV the night Gary Staley presented it to the team, then back to Arizona before heading to south Florida for the race at the Miami-Homestead Speedway.

"I guess you'll be chewing your nails for the next few weeks, huh?"

Liz, lost in her musings, had to stop and think what he was talking about, then responded, "Yes, I guess I will."

"Maybe I should do a story on the two of you—how you're both finishing up your rookie season. You probably have a lot to say about what it's like to be a woman PR rep on the racing circuit. What do you say? Good press for Rick and even more so for the sponsor."

Liz was not about to allow herself to be exploited in such a way but let him down gently so as not to offend. "I would much rather Rick get all the publicity, if you don't mind. And I'll be glad to set something up. When did you want to talk to him?"

He glanced at his watch. "Well, they aren't doing anything but practicing today, so any time will be fine. I'll just hang here."

She tried to call Rick on his cell but couldn't get through. To save time so she could go on back to the motel, she went to find him herself to tell him about the interview.

As she walked along, she felt the familiar charge of excitement to be a part of the racing world. Crew members and NASCAR officials waved, a reminder she no longer felt out of place. She, too, had become a member of the gypsies and loved it...till now.

She had set her cell phone to a vibration for an incoming call rather than a ring she might not hear due to the deafening noise when the cars were on the track. She felt it jiggling in her pocket and went into the café so she could talk.

It was Jeff, saying he'd tried to get in touch with Rick to congratulate him but hadn't been able to. He also wanted to know what the point spread was between him and Jack Blevins.

"Only a few. I'm afraid it's going to be real close. He's going to have to qualify and finish well every race the rest of the season."

"You think he can do it?"

"Jeff, who knows? Anything can happen. And don't ask me. Ask Rick or Mack." She knew she sounded irritable, but she was tired of being chirpy and optimistic all the time. She had swallowed misery and complaints throughout the season. And, feeling so crushed over Rick, her tolerance level was at an all-time low.

Jeff was silent for a moment, then asked, "Are you all right?"

"Sure, sure." She was sitting at a table in the corner and hating the smell of hot grease and cigarette smoke. "I guess I'm just tired of it all."

There. She had said it. She had opened the door to doing what her heart told her she must—ask for a transfer to another account.

"You just need a vacation, and I'll see you get one after the season is over. After all, there won't be much going on till Daytona in February. But you'll probably want to go to the awards banquet in New York, won't you? Especially if Rick wins. Isn't that the first week of December?"

She drew a ragged breath and let it out in an impatient rush. "I don't know, Jeff. I don't have my calendar in front of me, but the fact is I want more than a vacation."

She heard his soft gasp of surprise. "Please don't tell me you want to be transferred to another account."

"That's exactly what I want."

There. She had said it. The words that had been teasing her mind since Rick told her he had someone. She wanted out so she would not have to bear being around him knowing he loved another.

"But, Liz, you told me not long ago you like your job," Jeff argued. "Has something happened?"

"Oh, yes," she said, almost harshly. "I finally realized I can't stand living out of suitcases. Neither can I stand the heat, the noise, and having to put a sit-down dinner together for hundreds with only a few days' notice."

"Now wait a minute," he said tightly. "That only happened once."

That was true, but she didn't care. She was on a roll of whining and complaining. "And once was enough. But everything else is on a daily basis, and I've had it. I really want out of here, Jeff."

"Gary Staley isn't going to like this. He's very happy with you."

"Well, I'm not happy with racing. I gave it a shot. I did my best. Now I want that transfer, Jeff."

He was quiet for a moment, then said, "Let me see what I can do. Meanwhile, I don't want you saying anything to anybody about wanting to quit. We don't need any stress or problems these last few weeks. Gary is talking about spending even bigger bucks next season, and I want this agency to be the one to get those bucks. Do you understand me, Liz?"

"Of course. But will you agree to take me off the account?"

"I told you way back I would if you didn't like it. It just

comes as a surprise that you're asking right as the season is winding down.''

"It's a good time for someone else to come in. They can familiarize themselves with things instead of being thrown right in the middle of everything at the first race in Daytona like I was.''

"So you're saying you won't stick it out till Atlanta? That's going to really upset Staley. Give me a break here. And what's the real reason behind all this, anyway? Are you having problems with somebody?''

"No,'' she said quickly. "I can make it through Atlanta. Just go ahead and find me a replacement and a new account, okay?''

"Okay,'' he said on a sigh. "You've done such a fantastic job I'm afraid I'll lose you if I don't. You've made so many contacts in racing you'd have no trouble at all moving on, I guess.''

"I guess,'' she mumbled. "But I'd really like to stay with Star Media, if at all possible. Maybe you can find me something back in New York.''

"Oh, I can find you something. I just want you to hang in there and finish out the season. Staley said he'll immediately call a press conference if Rick wins the rookie title. That's when he'll announce his plans for next season, and I'll be right there with a contract ready for him to sign. So see me though this, okay?''

"Okay.'' She told herself she could stand it a while longer. She only hoped Wendy didn't show up at a speedway. Seeing her with Rick would be like pouring salt in a wound.

She continued on to the garage. Rick was nowhere around, but she finally found him at the RV. The black-and-white awning had been rolled out from the side, and he was sitting in a chair beneath having a soda with Mack.

She went to stand in front of Rick. "So what's wrong with your cell phone?''

He shrugged. "I guess I forgot to turn it on."

"Well, it would have saved me a trip all the way out here in this heat if you hadn't. I hate sidestepping tools and tires and oil spills in that nasty garage looking for you there. And I don't like having to walk all the way out here, either."

Rick and Mack looked at each other. It was the first time they had ever heard Liz complain about anything.

"So now that you are here what do you want?" Rick asked, a bit sharply because he was annoyed by her attitude.

"A reporter is waiting to interview you in the infield media center. I'd appreciate it if you'd get on over there."

"Sure. No problem."

"Want a soda?" Mack asked her.

"No, thanks. I've got a headache from the noise, so I'm out of here till race day. If anybody needs me, they can reach me on my cell." She shot a meaningful glance at Rick as she turned to leave. "I never turn mine off."

"What is it with her?" Mack said in bewilderment when she was out of hearing range. "I've never seen her like that."

"She's burned-out," Rick said. "I'm surprised she made it this long."

And he was sorry that she had, because if he could have gotten rid of her as he'd planned in the beginning, he wouldn't be sitting there with his heart hurting so badly.

Chapter Fifteen

Liz was a maelstrom of emotions as she waited at the terminal gate for her replacement to arrive on the morning flight from New York.

Jeff had first promised that Mike Bolton would join her in Arizona so she would have the last three races of the season to show him the ropes. But, as it turned out, Mike had some loose ends to tie up with his old account and had not been able to get away. As a result, he was flying in the day before the Atlanta race. After that, he was on his own, because once that checkered flag dropped Sunday, that was it. Liz had a late-afternoon flight out of there.

Her new assignment would take her to California. Jeff had given her quite a promotion. She would be heading up a new branch office opening in Los Angeles. It was a pie job, with a chance to move straight up the corporate ladder, stock options, and everything that went with success.

She knew she should be thrilled but could muster no enthusiasm. After all, she was leaving a job she truly liked...and a man she loved with all her heart. But it was—and had been from the start—a no-win situation. So it was time to move on, whether she wanted to or not.

In the past week, she had seen very little of Rick. Actually, she did not need him to get her job done, anyway. She had all the statistics on his season performance, knew all aspects of the points chase. She was able to keep the press releases going out in order to get as much exposure for him as possible. That was not difficult going into the last race since the biggie—the Grand National championship title—was all but a done deal. The driver leading by a huge margin only had to start the race and complete one lap. Not much news there, so writers were scrambling for something to write about and naturally turned to the rookie contest.

Rick's performance on the track once he got everything *dialed in*—racing terminology for everything working—he had done really well. But so had Jack Blevins, and he and Rick would start Sunday's race with Rick leading by only five points.

Besides a rookie's exploits on the track, points were also given by a vote of a special panel made up of NASCAR officials and others. Factors considered included relations with the public and the media. Liz had hoped Rick would come out ahead there, but the panel was almost equal in their balloting.

That morning she had invited the crew for breakfast at the hotel where they were staying. She was not surprised Rick did not show up. Mack said he had spent the night in the RV, which was parked at the track. He also remarked how Rick had been doing that a lot lately. Hearing that had cut Liz to the core as she thought of the stolen hours of passion they had shared in the RV...which he probably now shared with Wendy.

Liz had yet to see her. There had been several social functions where Rick might have brought a date, but always he showed up alone and left the same way. She supposed Wendy's schedule as a flight attendant and Rick's opposition to having women around him at the track explained her absence.

She had asked Mack if Rick was showing signs of last-race pressure. Mack's response was that he'd be surprised if he wasn't.

"He, along with a bunch of other drivers," he had emphasized. "The last race always brings out a bunch of potential sponsors. Everybody wants to do well."

He had added that she should not expect Rick to show for the big dinner she had arranged that night. Gary Staley and all the VIPs from Big Boy's were in town for a cocktail party and dinner dance. Mack also said he and the crew wouldn't be going, either. They wanted to get a good night's sleep and be ready for what was the most important race any of them had ever taken part in.

She had said she understood and was sure Mr. Staley and the others would, also.

Through the floor-to-ceiling glass, Liz saw the plane taxiing up to the gate.

She had never met Mike Bolton. He had been with the agency less than a year. Jeff had thought he would make a good replacement for her. Not only was he young and energetic, but Liz had things going so smoothly he could ease right into the position with little difficulty.

A few moments later passengers began filing through the door. She wondered how she would recognize Mike but needn't have worried. He was holding a homemade sign over his head that read Big Boy's Pizza, NASCAR 60.

Liz met him with outstretched hand. "That's a sure way to be identified, Mike, but it would have been nice to print our driver's name, too."

"Not necessarily." He was pumping her hand vigorously. "You haven't heard the news. Come on." He hoisted his garment bag over his shoulder.

Liz didn't like the sound of that. "Not till you tell me what's going on."

"I only found out this morning," he said as they walked

along. "According to Jeff, Gary Staley called him this morning and told him to leave the name blank on that new contract he's supposed to sign after the race tomorrow."

Liz stopped in her tracks to stare at him, hoping he didn't know what he was talking about. "That doesn't make sense."

"It does to everybody else."

Mike was grinning like a little boy proud to know something someone else didn't. Liz thought he looked younger than his twenty-eight years. He had wavy blond hair, blue eyes fringed by lashes too thick for a man, and a dimple in his cheek girls no doubt thought sexy. Jeff said he was single. Liz figured not for long.

"So?" she demanded almost waspishly. "Are you going to tell me or not?"

"Jeff said not to bother you with it, since you're off the account after tomorrow, anyway. He said you'd be upset, because you've really gotten to be good friends with the crew and all."

He took a few steps toward the escalator, but Liz did not budge.

"You're dying to tell me, and you know it. So out with it."

"Okay. Just don't let Jeff know I told you, okay?"

She nodded, apprehension growing.

"Staley said Big Boy's will double this year's sponsorship money for next season."

Liz felt a wave of relief. "That doesn't sound like anything to get upset about."

"You don't understand. He said the sponsorship will go with whichever driver wins the rookie title—Rick or Jack Blevins."

The wave puddled into despair. "I...I don't believe this."

"It has nothing to do with personalities. It's about which driver will get the most exposure by being champion, which is where advertising dollars pay off the most." He hoisted the garment bag from one shoulder to the other. "Can we go? This thing is heavy."

As was Liz's heart as she fell in step beside him.

When they were in her car, she switched on the ignition, then turned to look him straight in the eye and speak in the most serious voice she could muster. "I don't want you to say another word about this, Mike. To anybody. Understand?"

He blinked and shrugged. "Yeah. Sure. Why would I? Heck, you made me tell you."

"Nothing can be said, because I don't want Rick and Mack and the others to know. It would only make the pressure going into the race tomorrow that much worse. Understand? It has to be kept secret."

"Fine. But what if Mr. Staley tells somebody? Or some of the VIPs he's bringing in? I imagine it was a corporate decision and a lot of people know about it."

"Rumors always fly before the race of the season," she explained. "As long as no official announcement is made, it doesn't count. Besides, Rick and the crew aren't going to be at the party tonight, and I'll make sure Mr. Staley and the others only have pit passes for right before the race. He'd never say anything in all the excitement."

"Might work. Say, don't they have a lot of free food and stuff for us at the track? I'm starved." He settled back, no longer interested in discussing the sponsorship issue.

Liz wondered if it would have made any difference in her decision to ask for a transfer had she known of Mr. Staley's plans. After all, if Rick didn't win the championship she would have been working with Jack Blevins in the future. And Jack was a nice enough guy. She'd have had no problems there. But she knew it was important to distance herself from Rick, and the only way to do that was leave racing.

She drove straight from the airport to the speedway. Mike made friends wherever he went. He was a natural for public relations. When she took him to the infield media room for lunch, he blended right in with the hungry, thirsty, joke-swapping and clowning-around media and PR people. By the time they left an hour later, he knew everyone in the room by their first name, and they were all well aware of who he was.

Liz was annoyed, however, that Mike seemed far more interested in the perks associated with being involved with racing than anything else. He managed to collect several T-shirts, caps, coffee mugs—anything any sponsor was giving away to the media.

She was also not pleased that Mike made it a point to request hard-to-get credentials for the main press box, which was situated high above the grandstand. He said he'd been told that was where the best food was served, plus there was an open bar once the race was over.

No doubt noticing the disapproving way Liz was looking at him, Mike innocently asked, "Isn't that where you watch the race? Or do you come in here? Not that it isn't nice, but cold cuts and sliced tomatoes can't compete with a standing rib roast and hot vegetables. Don't you agree?"

"I've never thought about it," she said frostily. "I've always watched the race from the pits with the team."

"No kidding," he said, wide-eyed. "Out in the heat and dirt? Why? That's asking for misery."

Very carefully, Liz endeavored to explain how she felt it was important to be near the team in case she was needed. If something happened that caused the media to flock around, she wanted to be nearby to work her usual spin away from anything that might result in negative press.

"Oh, there'd be time for that later," Mike said airily. "Besides, you could have stayed in touch by radio and gotten there quick enough if need be. I can't imagine your opting to be in the pits when you can sit in air-conditioning."

Liz could not imagine Mike opting for anything that might get in the way of his personal comfort. But it would be up to Mack or Rick to complain should they not like how he was doing his job—*if,* that is, they wound up with Big Boy's as a sponsor in the future.

When she and Mike got to the team's assigned garage space, Liz was glad Rick was already in the car, buckling up and getting ready to go out for a practice session. She did not have to get close to him and could introduce him to Mike from a distance. Rick smiled, nodded, made welcoming noises, but it was obvious his mind was on the car and the final countdown to the rookie quest. He had no time for anything else.

Mack was equally preoccupied. He shook Mike's hand without looking at him.

After Rick slowly began driving toward the gate that would take him onto the track, the team followed behind to take up their position behind the pit wall.

Mike said, "Wow. I'm glad I don't have to hang around here during a race. They're not exactly a friendly bunch."

"Don't be silly," Liz said, sharper than intended. "They've got a lot on their minds."

"Yeah," he said, and laughed. "Like who's gonna sponsor them next year if Castles screws up tomorrow."

Liz exploded like a Fourth of July firecracker. "Screws up?" she echoed. "You've got a lot to learn, Mike, and first up on your list is realizing a driver screwing up—as you call it—isn't likely. He wouldn't be out there if he didn't know what he was doing. Racing isn't only a matter of skill when it comes to driving, it's attrition, car performance, fast pit stops. Many, many things. So if you think for one reason that Rick not winning the title happens because he, alone, screwed up, then you'd best worry about doing your homework instead of finding the freebies."

Mike's brows had crawled right up into his wavy blond hair. "I think somebody is definitely showing signs of burnout here. It's a good thing you're finishing up tomorrow, Liz."

"In more ways than one," she murmured under her breath.

Liz left the track early to get ready for the night's dinner party. It was obvious Mike didn't need her help, anyway. He would fit himself in where he wanted to be and didn't need her to pave the way. He knew where he was going, all right.

As she was walking toward the parking lot, she passed by the paddock area and the team's RV. Rick was just going in, and she would have sworn he saw her but did not turn to speak.

She had thought about not saying anything in the way of goodbye but decided there was no need for sentimentality. He had known for some time Atlanta would be her last race and hadn't bothered to say anything to her about it.

She wondered if Wendy was inside the RV waiting for him. Maybe he let her get that close since it was the last race.

Suddenly she yielded to impulse and swung around just as he was about to close the door behind him. "Hey, Rick. Wait a minute."

She wondered whether it was her imagination or did he really cringe when he heard her voice.

"Yeah, Liz, what is it?" He asked without turning around. "I'm in a hurry."

She drew a resigned breath and let it out quickly, as though unleashing all the nerve she had left in her body. "I was wondering if you'd like a pit pass for Wendy since tomorrow is the last race. I've got an extra."

"No thanks. She had a flight to Europe this weekend."

He closed the door.

Liz thought it strange Wendy hadn't arranged to be there on such an important occasion, but maybe she couldn't help it. Maybe Rick was so adamant about his feelings, that—

Liz gave herself another shake, harder this time. "Get over it, Mallory," she whispered vehemently, and quickened her pace.

Rick lifted the curtains inside the RV ever so slightly.

It was all he could do to keep from yanking the door open and chasing down the steps to run after her.

It was best she was leaving, because the past weeks had been hell, and he wasn't sure how much more he could stand.

He had heard about her new job. Mack said she was thrilled, because it was quite a promotion. Rick was happy for her, and, more than ever, he hoped he did well in the race for her sake. It would look good for her to have worked with a winning team.

As for himself, well, more and more lately he was asking himself if his career was all that should matter. After all, what joy was there in success, anyway, when he had no one to share it with?

Before he forced himself to walk away from Liz, there had been times he had thought maybe it might work between them. After all, she had her job in racing; he had his. But he could not be sure she could handle the pressures and, as time went on, became convinced she couldn't.

He watched as she got in her car and drove away.

Then he turned around and settled into the emptiness of the RV—the emptiness that was his life.

"Liz, you are stunning, as always," Gary Staley gushed as he squeezed her hands.

"And you're sweet, as always, to say so," she responded.

She was standing inside the hotel ballroom she had rented for the evening, greeting guests. She had chosen a pink satin gown with matching ribbons entwined in her sunny red hair. The effect was, she supposed, different, if not startling, but she had always enjoyed the colors together. She found them cheerful, and, oh, did she ever need cheering this night.

Mike was dutifully beside her as she introduced him to everyone as her replacement. Meeting Gary, Mike grabbed his hand and started pumping vigorously as he had Liz's in the airport. And, like Liz, Gary quickly eased himself from the overdone grip.

"I have really looked forward to meeting you, sir," Mike said. "It's an honor for me to be working this account. I just hope I can do half as good a job as Liz has, and—"

Gary interrupted, "Yes, she's a hard act to follow, that's for sure."

Liz froze as she looked beyond Gary to see Jack Blevins walking across the hotel lobby with his crew chief and their wives. "What is he doing here?" she demanded between gritted teeth.

Gary turned to see what she was talking about. "Who? Oh, it's Jack Blevins."

He had stopped to talk to someone, and Liz repeated, "I asked what he's doing here."

"I invited him," Gary responded with a frown. It was obvious he did not like how Liz was reacting. "Why? What's the problem?"

She drew him to one side, away from his wife, away from Mike, who was all ears trying to listen. "The problem is that I think you're being cruel, Mr. Staley. Once it gets out that Jack Blevins was here tonight, for what was supposed to be a party only for Big Boy's people and Rick and his team, rumors are going to be flying like dust all around that track tomorrow that you're going to replace Rick with Jack. Worse, Rick and the crew aren't here tonight. They wanted to get to bed early."

"Jack obviously didn't mind making an appearance," Gary said airily.

"You don't get it, do you?" she plunged on, not caring if he got mad.

"Maybe you don't get it, Liz…that it's my money, or Big Boy's, anyway, and we can change to another driver if we want to—which is exactly what I plan to do if Rick doesn't win the rookie title."

Liz was so mad she was shaking. "And *you* don't get it, Mr. Staley, that by not waiting till after that's decided before letting your plans be known that you've put a lot of unnecessary pressure on Rick and his team right before a race that was already stressful enough. I find that unacceptable, and, quite frankly, I'm very disappointed in you for doing such a thing."

"Well, now, just…just a minute."

Liz knew he was probably not used to having anyone question his actions.

"I'm sorry," she said crisply, not meaning it but knowing it was necessary to say. "I realize I'm out of line, that it's really none of my business, but I just felt the need to point out to you what you have done is wrong. And if you'll excuse me, I think it's best I let Mike take over here before it becomes obvious to others that I strongly disapprove."

He called after her, "Liz, wait, please…"

She kept on going but did have the aplomb to politely speak to Jack Blevins and those with him. It wasn't his fault. It was all due to Gary Staley's pomposity and thoughtlessness.

She went straight to her room and phoned Jeff to tell him what she had done. "If you want to fire me, go ahead. I just lost my temper."

"Fire you?" he hooted. "No way. I think you have every right to be mad. I told Gary this morning when he mentioned having Blevins invited that it wasn't the thing to do. It isn't fair to either driver to dangle a carrot in front of them this way."

"Well, it's done," Liz said miserably. "And I just hope now more than ever that Rick wins. And when he does, he'd better thumb his nose at Staley and his money for pulling a dumb stunt like this."

Jeff laughed. "I'm afraid there's no chance of that, not with Staley planning to double the money next season. So just forget it, Liz. Go back downstairs and mingle and smile and act like you don't care. Remember, after tomorrow, it's not your problem."

That was true, and even though she was in no mood to be gracious, it was childish of her to walk out.

She hurried back downstairs and, like Gary, pretended nothing had happened.

And all the while, she prayed that by some miracle Rick would not hear what was going on until after the race…and after he cinched the title.

Chapter Sixteen

Liz eased the rental car into the infield parking lot, sad to think it was actually her last day.

After meeting Mike and realizing the hands-off approach he was going to be taking on race day, and with the situation as it was with Big Boy's decision to go with the rookie winner, she was doubly glad she had opted to stay through the last event. The team would need a PR person around in the pits just in case. Should Rick not win the title, she intended to put a spin on his performance, in hopes of interesting a new sponsor for the team next season.

Her suitcases were in the trunk. She had shipped everything else out to California for storage until she could get there and find an apartment. She was, for all appearances, ready to go but wished once more it wasn't necessary.

If only she hadn't fallen in love she might have found a permanent niche in the racing world. She could even have left Star Media and gone with one of the big sponsors. It was without conceit that she acknowledged she had made a respected name for herself not only with the media but NASCAR and speedway officials, as well.

It was close to starting time. She had always made it a point to get to the track early on race day, but this was different. She dreaded being around the team for fear they had heard about what Gary Staley and Big Boy's had planned. She wanted no part of that.

She also wanted to avoid seeing Rick up close and personal, afraid to say goodbye for fear she would break down and cry. And wouldn't that make her look like a fool in front of everyone, especially Rick, and probably his girlfriend, if she showed up.

No, it was best she avoid the team as much as possible.

The pre-race festivities were almost over. Bands were playing, balloons had been dropped, and everyone was on their feet and cheering as the drivers were announced.

She heard Rick's name called, but only his first as the roar of the crowd drowned out the rest. He had grown in popularity through the year, and she liked to think she'd had something to do with that. After all, she had worked hard to put him in touch with his fans in dozens of ways. And though he grumbled about anything she planned, he was always good with his fans. And if he hadn't groused so much about having to do it, Liz would have thought he actually enjoyed it.

She was wearing comfort clothes, as she liked to think of her chinos, light sweater and sneakers. Her hair was pinned beneath her cap, which was embroidered across the front with Rick's name and car number. It was the last one she had and the only souvenir she was keeping. Everything else—the T-shirts and press kits and anything connected with the team—she had passed along to Mike.

She saw that the cars were already lined up on the track behind the start and finish line. Once introduced, the drivers would go and stand next to their cars while the national anthem was played. Then they would crawl in the window, settle in their seats, fasten their harnesses and wait, with pulses racing, for the ever-thrilling command to start the engines.

Mustering all her courage, Liz made her way through the infield crowd to the gate leading to the pit area. A guard checked her credentials and motioned her through.

The air was charged with excitement. She could feel it tingling through her bones. It was a familiar sensation, one she had come to look forward to and revel in.

The crew, she noted, was still hovering around Rick's car. He was starting in twentieth position. Jack Blevins was two spots ahead.

She started to continue on to the area where they would be set up for the pit stops Rick would make during the race, but then she made the mistake of glancing toward the car.

Rick was looking at her through the window netting.

He raised his gloved hand from the steering wheel in a sad little salute.

Liz bit her lip and quickly looked away, pretending not to have seen. Dear God, she silently, achingly cried, would it ever stop hurting? Would she ever be able to stop loving him?

She told herself the sooner she was gone, the better. She also swore to make it a point to neither read the sports section of the papers or watch ESPN. She did not want to hear Rick's name and be caught up once again in the anguish of it all.

And then it came, a booming voice over the loudspeakers that rang out and echoed throughout the multitudes: "Gentlemen. Start your engines."

The ensuing explosion was deafening.

Crew members ran from the track to their pit areas to make sure everything was ready for the frantic stops for fuel and tires. Each second would count, and everything and everyone had to be in position when the time came.

Even in his frenzy, Mack stopped what he was doing when he saw Liz. "We are sure going to miss you," he said, hugging her. "You just don't know how much me and the guys have come to love you, Liz."

Me and the guys. The words rolled around within her like a tennis ball, bouncing off each raw nerve. *Me and the guys.* If only that included Rick, as well, but in a different way.

"I love you, too," she said, eyes misting with tears. "And I know you're going to do well. I'll be thinking about you."

"Oh, we made sure of that," Mack said, grinning as he took a small box out of his pocket. "We all chipped in and got you this."

With shaking fingers and the rest of the team looking on, Liz opened it and gasped at the sight of the beautiful gold pendant. On one side was an etching of the car; the other inscribed with the date. "I...I don't know what to say," she whispered, overcome with emotion.

"Just say you won't forget us," Mack said gruffly, and the others chimed in.

She promised, all the while thinking she would never wear it. Instead, she would hide it away in her jewelry box to take out on the long, lonely nights sure to come. Then she would hold it in her hand and, for a little while, allow the beautiful memories to return and provoke with thoughts of what might have been.

"By the way," Mack said soberly. "We heard about what Big Boy's is planning."

"I'm so sorry," she quickly said. "I got so angry with Mr. Staley for letting word leak before the race. Did Rick hear about it, too?"

"Oh, yeah."

She sighed. "It's bad enough for him to consider he might not win the title without knowing he'll lose his sponsor if he doesn't."

Mack scratched his chin thoughtfully and gazed toward the track. The drivers were dutifully following the pace car for the warm-up laps. "I don't think that's bothering him, but something seems to be. He hasn't been himself lately. He acts like he's got a lot on his mind."

"Well, whatever it is, try to get him to take a vacation when this is over with, Mack. You too. You both need it."

"I told him we ought to take the RV and drive out West for a few weeks. Do some camping. A little fishing." His lips curved in a wry smile. "But after today there's a chance we might not have an RV to drive, right?"

"Think positively," she urged.

One of the crew called to him, and Mack turned away. Just then Mike walked up, looking very nice in a suit, white shirt and tie.

"How's this for the best-dressed PR rep around?" he said proudly.

Liz pointed out, "Isn't that going to be awfully hot? Once the cars get to racing the temperatures can really soar."

"Won't bother me." He winked. "I was able to get credentials for the press box, remember? I'm on my way to drive through the tunnel and get over there now."

Sarcastically Liz said, "Better hurry before the food gets picked over."

But he did not hear, because her voice was drowned by the sound of the cars revving up, ready to take the green flag for the first lap.

Liz could not bear being around the crew any longer, afraid her feelings were going to show. Sooner or later someone might suspect her melancholy was not entirely due to leaving her job. After all, she was the one who had requested to be moved to another account and had spent the last weeks griping over every little thing she could think of. Several times she had even waspishly said she couldn't wait to move on. So it looked strange for her to be standing around with tears in her eyes when it was supposed to be something she wanted.

She went to the infield media room where it was cool but soon left after facing a barrage of questions about Big Boy's decision to sponsor Jack Blevins if Rick didn't win the title. Ordinarily she would have put her spin on it, trying to emphasize it was purely a business decision and had nothing to do with how Big Boy's felt about Rick personally. But she could not muster the enthusiasm and retreated instead.

For a time, she sat in her car but could not hear what was going on out on the track. She had already given her headset to Mike and recalled he hadn't been wearing it. She wished she had asked to use it one more time.

She tried to get the race on the radio, but it was on the blink.

Then she heard the screams that go with a crash or spinout and knew she couldn't stand not knowing what was happening any longer. It was easy to hear over the loudspeakers between the turns, so she went to watch from between three and four.

Several cars had spun, and a caution flag was out, which meant the drivers were once again dutifully coasting behind the pace car. During the lull in action, she heard the positions called and thrilled to hear Rick was one place in front of Jack, but they were on the same lap. The pressure had to be enormous, especially with several hundred miles left to run.

The afternoon wore on. Liz was able to keep up with things and knew Rick and Jack were swapping positions. Each time they did, there was another exploding roar from the crowd. Gary Staley was certainly getting his money's worth when it came to attention this day. Every so often the track announcer would preface Rick's position by saying, "The Big Boy's Pizza number sixty."

With only fifty laps to go, Liz made a dash to the rest room. There had been a lengthy caution period the last time because an engine had blown. Cleanup crews had to get the oil off the track so other drivers wouldn't slide.

It was later than it was supposed to be at that point in the race. Liz planned to stay to the finish and would have just enough time to get to the airport and catch her flight. However, if there was another delay, she might have to forgo the ending and leave, lest she miss her plane.

Another caution flag was brought out when a car hit the wall. Liz gritted her teeth during the long moments of caution, constantly darting glances at the time. It was going to be close, but she wanted to stay, if at all possible. Rick was ahead of Jack by nearly a lap. If nothing happened, he was going to win the title.

Every time number sixty came out of turn four heading down the front straightaway, Liz's eyes would dart to the scoreboard.

Ten laps.

Then nine.

And then he was one lap ahead of Jack Blevins. Nothing could stop him from finishing, and Liz was jumping up and down and cheering.

Several times, she got too close to the retaining wall, and a security guard motioned her back. It was a dangerous place to be. If a car crashed and got airborne, it could very easily soar right over the wall.

Liz was happy for Rick, even if she wasn't going to be the one to hug him and shower his face with kisses when it was all over.

Then, like horror unfolding in maddeningly slow motion, the car directly in front of Rick suddenly spun out of control. Rick, trying to avoid a T-Bone crash, which could be deadly, took the high side of the track.

A scream locked in her throat as number sixty went end over end to land mere feet from the retaining wall in front of her, flames erupting from the rear.

She still did not scream.

Neither did she stand there, frozen in panic, unable to move.

Instead, she joined with the fans that had scaled the ten-foot chain link fence and rushed toward the flaming car.

She knew the safety crew was on the way, but there was not a second to spare.

The security guard went into a frenzy as he shouted at everyone to get back, stay away. But he was no match for the horde descending.

A man had reached the car and was trying frantically to get Rick out.

Liz saw Rick was unconscious and also that the man trying to help didn't know what he was doing.

"Can't get the harness off. Get me a knife," he shouted to no one in particular.

"Out of the way," Liz elbowed her way through the crowd. "It has a catch. I know where it is."

Smoke was billowing from the car. Coughing and gagging, people began to back away until Liz found herself standing alone. And, to her horror, the bravado she had so proudly mustered began to slip away as she stared at Rick. It was as though she had suddenly become encased in ice, frozen to the very core of her being, unable to move.

He was slumped back in the seat, head lolled to one side, mouth agape. He was not moving, and she could not tell whether he was breathing…could not tell if he was alive.

Someone frantically yelled, "Hey, lady, get away from there. It might blow."

The ominous warning had the effect of a blowtorch, quickly freeing her of the frozen prison. She came alive and reached to press her fingertips against the pulse in Rick's neck. She felt it beating and whispered thanks to God. There was no sign of blood, but he had flipped several times. Probably there were internal injuries, but there was no time to worry about that now.

Having watched him snap himself in and out so many times, she knew exactly how to pop the harness free.

"Help me get him out of here," she shouted, but it was with calm, not hysteria.

Right after Rick was lifted and quickly carried away from the car, the whole inside was engulfed with flames. A few more seconds, and it would have been too late.

"Hey, lady, you saved his life," somebody yelled.

"Sure, she did," someone answered. "I've seen her. She's with his crew."

Liz had no time to bask in the glow of praise, nor was she concerned with being thought a heroine. Her focus was on Rick, who still had not moved nor opened his eyes.

''I think he needs oxygen,'' she told the attendants when they leaped out of the ambulance. ''He might have gotten some smoke in his lungs.''

They took over and it was not long before they were loading him into the ambulance. Liz got in right beside him, not asking permission and with such a determined air no one dared say anything.

She stayed with him till he was taken into the infield infirmary, then waited with Mack and the rest of the crew.

''It looks bad,'' Mack said, tears leaving trails on his oil-streaked face like gullies in the rain. ''The car is totaled. He has to be hurt bad, Liz. Was he conscious at all?''

''No,'' she said, swallowing against the burning of her own tears she was fighting to hold back. ''But he's going to be all right, Mack. We have to believe that.''

Mike arrived, having had to wait till the race ended before being able to get across the track to the hospital. ''Is he going to be okay?''

''We don't know yet,'' Liz replied dully.

He dropped into a chair. ''Man, can you believe this? He was so close to winning the title and—''

''We aren't concerned about that, Mike,'' Liz snapped. ''That's not important now.''

Mike nodded glumly. ''Yeah, I guess not. Well, is there anything I can do?''

''Yes, you can go outside and tell the press we'll have a statement for them as soon as we know something.''

Just then a doctor walked in. He said his name was Dr. Sadler and that Rick was to be transported by helicopter to a trauma center in Atlanta.

Mack rushed at him. ''How bad is it, Doc? We've got to know.''

Dr. Sadler unpeeled Mack's fingers from the lapels of his white coat, gently explaining all he could say at that point was that Rick's vital signs were good. There was no sign of internal bleeding.

''I'm riding with him,'' Mack said.

Dr. Sadler shook his head. "You're too upset. That might be bad for him should he regain consciousness and see how you're reacting."

Liz agreed. "You stay here, Mack, and try to call his sister and let her know he's been hurt. By the time you drive to the hospital we should know something. I'll go with him if it's okay with the doctor."

Dr. Sadler said that would be fine. "You're calm enough you won't get in the way, and I've already heard how you were able to keep the crowd from panicking and coordinate the rescue. Good work."

Liz had not thought about it. She had just done it. And not just because she loved Rick. Something told her she would have been able to do the same thing for anyone else, and that made her proud.

She asked Mike to see that her rental car was returned to the motel and to take her carry-on luggage to Mack so he could bring it with him to the hospital.

"You may not make that plane," Mack pointed out.

Liz knew she wouldn't but didn't care. She had no intentions of going anywhere till she knew Rick was going to be okay. She also did not want him to be alone. If Wendy showed up at the hospital—which wasn't likely since Rick had said she was in Europe—she would leave. Otherwise, she wasn't going anywhere till his sister arrived.

It was several hours later when Mack got to the hospital. She was able to tell him there was still no word on Rick's condition. "They're doing all kinds of tests, and we should know something soon. Did you find his sister?"

"Yes. She's on her way. She'll be here early tomorrow. I'll stay with him till then. You've got a plane to catch."

"Not anymore. I've already missed my flight tonight, but I rebooked on one at eight-thirty tomorrow morning. I can stay till then."

"That will be a help. I need to get on the road with the

guys back to Charlotte, but I'll hang around till we know something.''

A doctor came into the waiting room and glanced at Liz expectantly. "Mrs. Castles?"

Don't I wish, Liz thought as she stood. "No. I'm his public relations representative—Liz Mallory. This is his crew chief, Mack Pressley.''

He shook their hands in turn. "I'm pleased to tell you Mr. Castles is a very lucky man. He has a mild concussion, a few broken ribs, and some cuts and bruises. He should be fine in a few days. I guess I don't have to tell you it could have been much, much worse." He shook his head in wonder. "These drivers have got to have nerves of steel. Makes me cringe just to watch them out there.''

He left them, and Mack looked at Liz with fondness and said, "You do, too.''

She laughed. "I do what?"

"You have nerves of steel. You were great." He gave her a hug and left.

A short while later, a nurse came to tell Liz that Rick had awakened but not for long. He was in a lot of pain with his broken ribs and had to be sedated. "He'll probably sleep through the night, so there's no reason for you to stay.''

Liz felt like saying oh, yes, there was, because she wanted to be with him every possible moment between now and the time she had to leave in the morning. Instead, she explained she would like to stay with him until she had to leave for her flight the next morning. "Hopefully, his sister will be here by then. I don't want him to be alone.''

"As you wish," the nurse said, and led the way to his room.

He was sleeping soundly. Liz drew up a chair to sit close by the bed.

Now and then she would tenderly brush away a tendril of hair from his forehead, or kiss a bruise on his cheek. And each time her flesh touched his she felt the familiar rush of longing...of love.

She did not sleep, not wanting to miss a single moment. After all, she would never see him, nor be with him again.

It was over.

No, she corrected herself.

It had never really begun.

For Rick, it had been nothing but meaningless pleasure. *She* was the one who had so stupidly fallen in love; therefore, she was the one who grieved over parting.

It was just after dawn when a nurse came to tell her that Rick's sister had phoned from the airport to say she had arrived and was on her way.

When the nurse left, Liz knew it was time to finally say goodbye. Trembling with love, she leaned to whisper in Rick's ear, "I love you, my darling. And I always will."

She kissed him on his lips, then ran from the room before she broke down completely.

Chapter Seventeen

Rick felt as if he had been hit on the head with a tire iron.

He moaned, stirred and tried to open his eyes, but the effort was too great. He ached all over, and it hurt to breathe.

Cool fingers touched his forehead, and a soft voice said, "It's okay, Rick. I'm here, and you're going to be all right. I've rung for the nurse."

"Liz..." His whisper was thin, hoarse, and a faint smile touched his lips.

She had said she loved him. He had felt the warmth of her breath as she had whispered the beautiful words in his ear. He had tried to respond, tried to tell her that he loved her, too, and somehow, some way, they would work things out.

But where was she?

And why was he trapped in a horrible black void, every muscle in his body sore and aching?

"Mr. Castles?"

A different voice, also a woman's.

"Mr. Castles, your sister says you're trying to wake up. Can you open your eyes for me?"

With great effort, he managed to blink and thought how even his eyelids were hurting.

Everything was blurred, then, slowly, images came into view—a woman wearing some kind of print jacket was standing over him, a stethoscope draped around her neck. She was holding his wrist while looking at her watch.

Movement on the other side of the bed caused his gaze to shift.

Was he seeing things?

He tried to lift his head from the pillow. "Marcie? What are you doing here?"

His sister leaned over to kiss his forehead. "Don't you remember what happened?"

"He may not," the nurse said. "He had a concussion. Sometimes there's memory loss, but it's usually short-term."

He was in a hospital. That much was becoming clear. And his sister was there, having traveled a long way. But where was Liz? He was sure she had been there...sure she had told him she loved him. But was it just a dream? He'd had a concussion, the nurse had said. A blow to his head. He couldn't think clearly. Not yet. But gradually the pieces of the puzzle began to fit.

A few laps to go. A car in front, spinning wildly. No choice to be made. He wasn't about to hit him head-on on the driver's side. A slower car was right beside him. He couldn't drift low. He had to take the suicide side...and that's when it happened.

He hit the wall too hard and the car had begun to flip, end over end. He winced to remember the jolting pains each time it hit the asphalt.

The smell of gas.

A flash of panic.

And then...nothing.

"I crashed," he said quietly, soberly.

Marcie said, "Yes, honey, but you're going to be okay."

"Where's Liz?"

Marcie looked to the nurse for explanation.

She shook her head. "I have no idea who he's talking about. When I came on duty a little while ago there was no one in here."

Rick was struggling to sit up. "She was here. I know she was. She talked to me."

The nurse gently pushed him back on the pillows. "Mr. Castles, you were probably dreaming. You've been heavily sedated, because you have some seriously broken ribs and a lot of bad bruises. The doctor wanted you to rest."

"No," Rick said firmly, stubbornly. "She was here. I know it." He looked to Marcie in desperation. "Call Mack. Get him on his cell phone. Ask him if Liz left—" It suddenly dawned he did not know what day it was. "How long have I been out?"

"Since yesterday," Marcie answered.

"Then ask Mack if Liz left yesterday after the race. Call him now, please."

"But what's his number?"

Rick was still light-headed and could not remember. He slammed his fists on the bed in frustration.

The nurse said she thought she'd seen some phone numbers for people to contact if need be on his chart. She left to go see.

"How do you feel now?" Marcie asked. "Are things getting clearer?"

"Yes, bit by bit." He tried to pull himself up again, but it hurt like hell. His hands slid down his sides to feel the bandages.

"I'm so sorry, Rick," Marcie said, close to tears. "But it could have been much worse."

He knew that, just as he knew, and appreciated, NASCAR's rigid safety features were probably the reason he was still alive.

Marcie talked on, but he wasn't listening, eyes riveted to the door.

Finally the nurse breezed back in. "I was right. A number is listed for a Mack Pressley."

She handed a slip of paper to Marcie, who promptly took her phone from her bag and dialed. When Mack answered, she said, "This is Marcie. Rick wants to talk to you," and gave him the phone.

Mack was relieved to hear Rick's voice. "Thank God, you're going to be okay. Listen, I've got some good news for you. You know you didn't win the championship, but—"

Rick cut him off. "I don't care about that. I don't care about anything but Liz, Mack. When did she leave?"

For a few seconds, Mack was too stunned to speak. Then, with a soft laugh, he said, "Man, oh, man. I never would have thought—"

"Just answer me, damn it."

"I don't know when she left. The last time I saw her, she was at the hospital with you. She was planning on staying till her flight this morning and was hoping Marcie would get there before she had to leave."

"Then I was right. She was here."

"Rick, she was more than just *there*. She happens to be the reason you aren't a crispy critter this morning, because she was the one to reach inside the car and unfasten your harness so they could get you out. The fuel bladder ruptured, and the car caught fire before the emergency crews could get there."

"I…I don't believe it," Rick said dizzily.

"Well, it's true. She was cool as a cucumber. Took right over. And she not only rode with you in the ambulance to the infield hospital but flew in the helicopter to the trauma center, as well.

"I hate to tell you this," he added sheepishly, "but I was the one who went all to pieces. That was a hell of a crash. Wait till you see it on the news. It's been on all morning."

Rick had something more important on his mind. "What time was her flight?"

"I think she said eight-thirty."

"Thanks." He heard Mack shouting for him not to hang up, but there was no time to spare.

He turned pleading eyes on Marcie. "Help me get up and out of here."

"Rick, you can't—"

The nurse joined in. "No, you can't leave. You have to wait for your doctor to make his rounds and discharge you, but he's probably going to want you to stay another day for observation."

"Well, I've got other plans." He beckoned to Marcie. "I swear, sis, if you don't help me get to that airport, I'll crawl if I have to."

"He means it," Marcie told the nurse, well aware of how her brother could be once his mind was made up.

The nurse turned toward the door. "I'm getting the doctor."

Marcie spotted a bag in the corner. Evidently someone in Rick's crew had thought to bring his things. She found a pair of slacks and a shirt and, against her better judgment, assisted him in dressing.

She was trying to help him stand when the doctor arrived. Irate, he demanded, "And just where do you think you're going?"

Rick's smile was a little stronger. It was amazing what vigor love could muster. "I'm going after a dream, Doc. With or without your permission."

Marcie tried to explain. "I think he wants to go to the airport to try and see some girl before her plane leaves."

The doctor gave a deep, exaggerated sigh. "Oh, all right. I can't stop him." He turned to the nurse. "Just make sure he signs the release forms so we won't be held responsible. Then get him a wheelchair and help him to a car."

"We have to get a cab," Marcie said. "I don't have a car."

"Let's do it," Rick said, spirits soaring as he tried not to think about how it hurt every time he drew a breath or moved a muscle.

Everything else in his life was on hold until he found Liz, because if it hadn't been a dream, if she did love him, then nothing was going to stand in the way of their being together.

Not even his career.

Because the crash had given him a wake-up call, making him realize that nothing was more important than loving someone…and being loved in return.

"Flight 270 to Los Angeles is now boarding," came the loudspeaker announcement. "First-class passengers may proceed."

Liz stared at her boarding pass. Row twenty-six. It would be a few moments yet, and she was in a hurry to run to her future…to run from her past.

A little boy of perhaps ten or eleven was seated across from her. She had noticed how he kept staring. She probably looked a sight in rumpled clothes she'd been wearing over twenty-four hours now.

He pointed at her cap. "That's a Rick Castles cap."

"Yes, it is," she replied somberly.

"He crashed yesterday. Right here in Atlanta."

Her stomach lurched as the image flashed in her mind. "Yes, I know."

"I saw it on TV last night. The car caught fire. But he's going to be all right."

"Yes, I know," Liz repeated, not wanting to talk about it, not wanting to talk at all.

The speaker boomed again. "Rows one through fifteen may now board."

Liz closed her eyes, hoping the boy would take the hint and leave her alone.

But he didn't and began talking about how Rick Castles was his favorite driver. "I'm sorry he didn't win the rookie championship, but Jack Blevins is a real nice guy."

"Yes," she murmured politely. "He is."

Then came the announcement Liz had been waiting for. "Rows sixteen through thirty may board."

She stood and began rolling her carry-on bag.

The boy fell in step behind her. "Hey, lady. Would you want to sell that cap? I can give you a couple of dollars."

She smiled, pleased as always to accommodate a true race fan. "I'll do better than that," she said. "Here." She took it off and placed in on his head. "It's yours."

"Gee, lady, thanks," he cried.

"That's real nice of you," a voice called loudly from across the room, "but you might want to hang on to that cap, because there aren't going to be any more."

Liz turned, swayed in wonder, and had to reach out and clasp the boy's shoulder to keep from falling.

Rick was coming toward her, as fast as his bandaged ribs would let him. A woman was beside him, helping him along.

"Hey, it's Rick Castles," the boy shouted. "Oh, man, will you autograph my cap?"

Someone produced a pen. Rick scrawled his name on the cap's bill, eyes on Liz all the while. "You can't go," he said. "Not till I know if I was just dreaming when I heard you say you loved me."

Liz was oblivious to those around staring and listening. "I...it was no dream," she stammered. "I did say it. I had no right. I mean, you have someone." She glanced at the woman with him. Was it Wendy?

Rick sensed what she was thinking. "This is my sister, Marcie. Marcie, meet Liz. I'm hoping I can talk her into being your new sister-in-law."

Marcie smiled and nodded.

Liz was too overwhelmed right then to do anything but murmur, "I don't understand."

Rick closed the gap between them and put his arms around her. "I lied to you. There never was a Wendy. There never was anybody else after I met you, Liz. Can you forgive me for being such a fool? I thought I couldn't give up my career for you, and I knew you couldn't deal with it, but it doesn't matter now. All I want is you."

Liz blinked in wonder. "Deal with it? But Rick, I've been dealing with it for nearly a year, and—"

"No, no, honey. I don't mean *things PR*. I'm talking about your being so miserable the past few weeks, how you couldn't stand being around racing anymore."

"But that was so you wouldn't know how it was killing me to leave it."

"And," he rushed on, "there was that incident in Talladega when you were about to come to blows with a girl for coming on to me so strong, and—"

"Wait a minute." Liz recalled the incident and quickly moved to set him straight. "That wasn't about you. I figure you can take care of yourself when it comes to female fans. The reason I got in her face was over a dog she'd left in her car as hot as it was, with the windows rolled up. If she hadn't left to take care of it, I probably would have gone nuts, because—"

"Because you're wonderful," he said with a laugh, then grimaced and bent slightly with pain from his bandaged ribs. "Sorry. It hurts to laugh. But you are wonderful, Liz, and I apologize for getting the wrong idea."

"What do you mean by that?"

"I thought you were like other women I've known who go to pieces over the least little thing. They can't handle the stress connected with racing. But believe me, Liz, if you were like that, it wouldn't matter, because I'm ready to give up my career for you. And I'd still feel the same even if I had won the title and kept the sponsorship. I love you, and I want to marry you."

"You…you're proposing?" she gasped as a spattering of applause broke out among those still waiting to board the flight to L.A.

"Yes," he said, lips trailing across her face. "I love you, Liz, and now that I know you love me, too, I want you to be my wife. I'll get a real job, and—"

"But you've got a job," she cried, eyes brimming with happy tears. "You're a race driver, Rick. That's all you've ever wanted to be, and that's fine with me. And the only pressure I've had was with *my* career. Not *yours*. I was so determined I wouldn't fail, and I was afraid to fall in love. But then it happened. When I saw it could never work because you didn't want me, I just pretended to be fed up with everything so you wouldn't guess the real reason I asked to be transferred.''

''And I was such a fool, Liz. Such a fool.''

Neither cared that others were listening, but the number became fewer and fewer as the trailing passengers boarded the plane.

''As long as you love me,'' Liz rushed on, ''there's nothing the two of us can't handle.''

Rick blinked against his own tears as he cajoled, ''Well, if you're sure you don't want me out of racing, maybe you can use your connections to get me a new sponsor.''

She grinned. ''What's the matter? Don't you like pizza, anymore?''

''I don't understand.''

She pulled from his embrace and took the morning paper from her bag, opening to the sports section so he could read the headlines.

''Castles Crashes But Keeps Big-buck Sponsor.''

Rick sucked in his breath and again winced with pain. ''Does this mean what I think it does?''

''It does.'' She wound her arms about his neck. ''Mr. Staley announced at the press conference last night that even though Jack Blevins won the championship, Big Boy's is staying with you. They said anybody who would do what you did to keep from T-boning a driver is the kind of hero they want to sponsor.''

''So that's what Mack was trying to tell me when I hung up,'' Rick said, remembering the excitement in Mack's voice.

Giving her a playful tap on her chin, Rick said, ''So now that you saved me, you've got to take care of me the rest of my life.''

"That wasn't heroics. I just happened to know how that harness worked when nobody else did." She wrinkled her nose impishly. "After all, I learned about it while I was trying to figure out how the potty worked that NASA was supposed to be so interested in."

"I refuse to laugh," he said, struggling not to, "and there's only one way to prevent it."

Their lips met in a kiss that threatened to never end, and it was only when someone called out that they drew apart.

It was the gate attendant. "Miss, if you don't board right now, you're going to miss your flight."

Liz was clinging to Rick, unable to take her eyes from his adoring face. "Maybe I will miss the plane...but not the chance for happiness with the man I love beyond belief."

Rick drew her closer, no longer caring about the discomfort of his injuries. "And he loves you just as much, Liz," he fervently vowed, "and always will."

Epilogue

Mack, standing next to Rick, gazed across the lake and infield to the packed grandstands and grinned to say, ''I thought she just wanted a small wedding with a few close friends.''

Rick, also sweeping the distant crowds, grinned right back. ''That's what we're having. A small wedding next to the infield lake with a few close friends.'' He nodded to acknowledge the rest of the pit crew, along with Jeff Strohm and Gary Staley, who were nearby.

''And what about a couple hundred race fans?''

''They'll be listening over the loudspeakers. But it's the reception that will test the fire code at the country club. We've invited all the drivers and crews, the media, and the track personnel. It's going to be something.''

''You just keep your mind on the race,'' Mack said, giving Rick a playful clip on the shoulder with his fist. ''That's some tux you're wearing, by the way,'' he added to tease.

Rick glanced over at Gary Staley with a nod of approval

for his new racing uniform with the Big Boy's logo. He would have worn a tux if Liz hadn't scheduled the wedding right before the start of the Daytona 500. As it was, there was no time to change. But she'd said that's how she wanted it—that since they met at the track, she wanted the wedding there. And that was fine with him. Heck, anything she wanted was okay, because he never knew he could love someone so much.

"I guess the bride will be wearing slacks and a blazer," Mack said. "Since she'll be going directly to the pits as soon as the race starts."

"Not this time," Rick said, beaming to see the white stretch limo coming off the fourth turn and heading down the backstretch.

It eased into the grassy area and stopped. The driver hurried to open the door, and Liz stepped out, dazzling in a white satin and lace wedding gown.

Tears came to Rick's eyes as he watched her coming toward him. She was carrying a bouquet of black and white carnations with checkered ribbon streamers. She had told him when they were making plans that since racing was a vital part of their life, so, too, would it be a part of their wedding. As for the gown, she had firmly asked where was it said that white was reserved for virgins? In her opinion, it meant first and lasting love…which was what she felt for Rick and swore she always would.

He held out his hands to her, and she clasped them as she stepped to his side. Leaning close so no one else would hear, he intimately whispered, "Thank you for coming into my life, Liz."

Liz's eyes also glimmered with happy tears. "And I thank you for making me a part of it. I love you so much, Rick Castles, and I always will."

He could not wait for the end of the ceremony to kiss her, and, drawing her into his arms, claimed her lips then and there. Only when Mack and the rest of the crew began whistling and teasing did he let her go and declared, "You made me realize there's only one race that truly meant anything, Liz—the race to the altar.''

''And here we are, my darling.'' She lovingly touched her fingertips to his cheek. ''And our own special checkered flag is about to wave.''

* * * * *

SILHOUETTE®
MAKES YOU
A STAR!

Look in the back pages of
all June Silhouette series books to find an
exciting new contest with fabulous prizes!
Available exclusively through Silhouette.

Don't miss it!

Silhouette®
Where love comes alive™

P.S. Watch for details on how you can meet
your favorite Silhouette author.

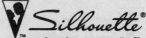